CHRISTINE RIMMER

came to her profession the long way around. Before settling down to write about the magic of romance, she'd been an actress, a salesclerk, a janitor, a model, a phone sales representative, a teacher, a waitress, a playwright and an office manager. Now that she's finally found work that suits her perfectly, she insists she never had a problem keeping a job—she was merely gaining "life experience" for her future as a novelist. Christine is grateful not only for the joy she finds in writing, but for what waits when the day's work is through: a man she loves, who loves her right back, and the privilege of watching their children grow and change day to day. She lives with her family in Oklahoma.

LEANNE BANKS,

a *USA TODAY* bestselling author of romance and 2002 winner of the prestigious Booksellers' Best Award, lives in her native Virginia with her husband, son and daughter. Recognized for both her sensual and humorous writing with two Career Achievement Awards from *Romantic Times,* Leanne likes creating a story with a few grins, a generous kick of sensuality and characters that hang around after the book is finished. Leanne believes romance readers are the best readers in the world because they understand that love is the greatest miracle of all. Contact Leanne online at leannebbb@aol.com or write to her at P.O. Box 1442, Midlothian, VA 23113. A SASE for a reply would be greatly appreciated.

Almost TO THE Altar

Christine Rimmer
Leanne Banks

Silhouette Books
Published by Silhouette Books
America's Publisher of Contemporary Romance

SILHOUETTE BOOKS

ISBN 0-373-23020-6

by Request

ALMOST TO THE ALTAR

Copyright © 2003 by Harlequin Books S.A.

The publisher acknowledges the copyright holders
of the individual works as follows:

COUNTERFEIT BRIDE
Copyright © 1993 by Christine Rimmer

MILLIONAIRE HUSBAND
Copyright © 2001 by Leanne Banks

This edition published by arrangement with Harlequin Books S.A.

® and TM are trademarks of Harlequin Books S.A., used under
license. Trademarks indicated with ® are registered in the United States
Patent and Trademark Office, the Canadian Trade Marks Office and in
other countries.

Visit Silhouette at www.eHarlequin.com

Printed in U.S.A.

CONTENTS

Dear Reader,

Eve Tanner is passionately in love with Jordan McSwain. He's burst into her life like a whirlwind and swept her right off her feet. Now their wedding is a few days away.

They're *almost to the altar,* and Eve is having second thoughts. She doesn't want to break it off with him— she just wants to slow things down a little. She's had one disastrous marriage and she's determined to never let anything like that happen again, not to her...and especially not to her two innocent children. But Jordan McSwain has his own demons. For him, it's all or nothing at all. Eve won't be rushed into their marriage—and Jordan will not be slowed down.

This impasse is the end for them as a couple— or it would be. If not for Jordan's loving grandmother and his big, rambunctious family. Eve and Jordan's "reunion" starts out as a loving deception. But in only a few short days—and magical nights—they discover new depths to their relationship and new hope for the future.

I do hope you find pleasure in the story of Jordan McSwain and his *Counterfeit Bride.*

As always, all my very best,

Christine Rimmer

COUNTERFEIT BRIDE
Christine Rimmer

For life's real heroes and heroines,
those who dare to love and to raise children.

One

"Jordan, I can't marry you now."

There. Eve had spoken the words. And as soon as they were out, all she wanted to do was call them back. But she couldn't. They were words that had to be said.

Jordan shook his head, blank disbelief on his face. "What did you say? I don't think I heard you right." His deep voice, a voice that had always warmed her with its teasing humor, held no laughter now.

Eve longed to turn away, to look out the window of the beach house at the peaceful sands, the gleaming sea, the sickle of moon. But she forced herself to keep facing him.

"I said I can't marry you now. I can't go through with it. Not Saturday as we've planned." She paused, groping for a way to explain to him why she was doing this.

Nothing came. And she knew why. Her own heart

was fighting her all the way. Eve Tanner was deeply in love with Jordan McSwain. But being in love wasn't enough. There was so much more to consider.

She held out her hands in a pleading gesture and added feebly, "It's all...happening too fast. I just have to slow things down a little."

There was an awful, gaping hole of silence. Then Jordan's stunned look faded. He smiled, a slow smile, one that managed to be both relieved and devastatingly sexy at the same time.

"Damn it, Eve. You scared me."

She swallowed. "Jordan, I—"

He put up a hand. "It's all right, honey." His dark eyes were as soft as velvet. From outside, faintly, Eve could hear the slow and rhythmic lapping of the waves. It suddenly occurred to her that the waves sounded like breathing, like long, voluptuous sighs. Jordan's voice soothed her. "I understand. You're nervous." He moved toward her.

She stepped back. "No, Jordan."

"It'll pass."

"No. It's more than that." She had to make herself speak firmly. It was a considerable effort when she yearned simply to agree with him, to sigh and sway against him. Then he would sweep her into his arms and carry her upstairs to his room, where the bed was wide and the white sheets inviting, where the long breaths of the sea could be heard just as well as they could from down here.

"Eve. Listen to me."

She drew herself up. "No, Jordan. *You* listen to *me*. It *is* more than nerves. Since we met, I haven't had a moment to think about where we're going. I feel like—"

He interrupted, relentlessly gentle, "Come on. What you've got is a case of prewedding jitters. And it's okay. You'll get over it. Everything will be fine."

He was, she could see now, choosing not to believe her.

And why should he believe you? a castigating inner voice accused. *You've shown no hesitation before. Since the night you met him, Jordan has planned every date, picked up every check, and orchestrated your every moment together. How in the world can you blame him for not believing that you've suddenly changed your mind about doing things his way?*

He pressed on. "Do you love me?"

Oh Lord, did she love him? Yes, with all her heart. She loved him to distraction.

It seemed as if she had loved him from the moment she first saw him, in the kitchen of this very house, exactly thirty-two days ago. She'd come to serve at a small dinner party, and ended up falling head over heels for the host.

He'd said, "*You're* from the Staffing Source?"

She'd laughed. "I *am* the Staffing Source. I'm the boss. Debbie called in sick at the last minute, and I couldn't find a replacement on such short notice."

He'd smiled, and to her it had seemed that the whole world lit up. "Good. Add a nice bonus for Debbie onto my bill, would you?"

"What for?"

"Having the good sense to get sick, so you and I could meet at last."

She'd blushed. "You're crazy."

"You're right. It's hit me like a bolt out of the blue, from the moment I stepped in here and saw you, arranging those mammoth shrimp on that bed of crushed ice. I'm crazy all right. Crazy for you. What are you doing tomorrow night?''

"Well, I—"

"Great. It's a date. Mark your calendar. For tomorrow—and the rest of your life. How are you on boats?''

"Boats?"

"Yeah. I thought we'd take the ferry, over to Catalina. They have this terrific little restaurant there, and—"

Oh, sweet heaven. How could she *not* love him? He had burst into her ordinary, well-ordered life with all the excitement and magic of a fireworks display, lighting up her nights and making every day a celebration.

Even her children adored him. From the moment he'd met them, he'd set out to woo them, right along with their mother. He planned one day trip after another—to the San Diego Zoo, to Knott's Berry Farm, to Disneyland.

And then there were the wonderful times right here in Seal Beach, where they all played in the sand until late afternoon and then came inside to bake a homemade pizza in the kitchen and watch a movie together on the VCR. Both Wesley and little Lisa looked at Jordan with wide eyes and expressions of musing wonder. They crowed with joy at the mere mention of his name.

"Are you going to answer my question?" He covered the short distance between them and tipped her chin up with a finger. Her whole body warmed at the slight touch. "Do you love me?"

"Yes." Infuriatingly, she felt tears welling in her eyes. She blinked them back. "I do love you."

"Then keep your promise and marry me. Saturday, as we agreed."

She shook her head. "Please, Jordan, try to understand."

"Understand what?"

"I…I need more time. We've barely known each other a month. And since then, I've felt like…a spinning top. I haven't had a spare second to pause and consider. It's been crazy and beautiful and fantastically romantic, but—"

"But what?"

"But I married Teddy the same way, after knowing him only a few weeks. I just can't let that happen again. This time I have two children to consider. It would be devastating for Wesley and Lisa if they had to live through another divorce."

"Divorce?" He made a scoffing noise in his throat. "There won't be a divorce. I come from a family where people marry for life. That's how this marriage will be."

"Oh, Jordan. Of course we think that now—"

He took her by the shoulders. "I don't *think* it. I know it. And I am not your ex-husband." There was a real edge in his voice now. And a tightness around his mouth.

She forced herself not to waver. "I know that."

"Then why are you comparing me to him?"

"Well, I…"

"You what?" His fingers were digging into her shoulders. She winced. He must have noticed her discomfort, because he released her.

She tried to explain. "I only meant that the…situation is too similar to be reassuring."

"In what way?" He didn't wait for an answer, but turned and began pacing the room, his body tight with a tension she'd never seen in him before. "Am I a self-absorbed stand-up comic? Do I seem like the kind of man who'd father two children and then decide that settling down wasn't for me after all? Do you think I'm going to be heading off for New York soon to pursue my show business career—and sending the divorce papers in the mail when I get the time?''

She put out a beseeching hand. ''Jordan, stop it. That's not what I meant.''

He paused in his angry pacing. ''Oh no?'' He turned on her, pinning her with a look. ''Then suppose you say what you meant.''

''I'm trying,'' she got out.

He glared at her, and then raked an exasperated hand back through his dark gold hair.

Watching him, seeing what she was doing to him, she longed to tell him to forget everything she'd just said, that he was absolutely right, she was being foolish. It was prewedding jitters, no more. They'd go on with the wedding as planned. He could go ahead and take care of everything—as he'd been doing since they'd met. She'd just give up her life and her future into his hands, and trust that everything would work out fine.

Oh, it was tempting. Because Jordan was everything a woman could ask for. He was a gorgeous and generous man who could send her pulse into overdrive with just a glance, one who wanted nothing but her happiness and the happiness of her children. And he had a big extended family up in Northern California, a family she was supposed to be meeting in a little more than a week. Eve had always longed for a big family.

It all seemed like a dream come true. It *was* a dream come true. But Eve Tanner had already learned the hard way that you had to be careful about dreams. They could slowly turn into nightmares before your very eyes.

Jordan closed the distance between them again,

though this time he didn't touch her. His gaze scanned her face. "I think you'd better talk, Eve. I think you'd better explain this."

"I told you—"

"Everything?"

"Well…"

"There is more, then?"

"Yes."

"Then talk."

"All right."

He waited.

She chose her words cautiously. "I feel like…one of your business ventures, Jordan. You've wined me and dined me and now you're ready to close the deal. And I'm just supposed to be swept off my feet and leave everything to you. Sign on the dotted line and become Mrs. Jordan McSwain. But I'm not a *deal*. I'm a flesh-and-blood woman. And I need more time."

"How much more time?"

She wasn't sure. "A few months. I don't know. Awhile longer, for us to get to know each other better. For us to become more *real* with each other."

His guarded expression became pained. "You're not making any sense at all. What do you mean, *real?*"

"I mean, it's like a fairy tale, or something. You're so bold and extravagant—"

"And that's bad?"

"No, of course not. I…"

"You what?"

"I feel like I can't keep up with you half the time. I feel like I don't really have anything to offer you that you don't already have."

"That's not true."

She put her hand on his chest, a gesture that was

meant to communicate her sincerity. But touching him right then did much more than that. It reminded them both of the elemental fires that burned between them.

His dark gaze kindled. ''I'll be the judge of what you have to offer me.'' He reached out and pulled her close.

With a soft expression of surprise and yearning, she found herself pressed against him. She knew she should push him away, go on trying to explain what he refused to understand. But the very feel of him was taking over: the solid strength of him, the delicious hardness of his chest against her soft breasts, the scent of him, which was clean and manly and hinted of sand and sea.

''I'm real,'' he said. ''And what we have is real, just as real as it gets.''

''Oh, Jordan…''

With a husky, hungry sound, his mouth covered hers.

Eve sighed. She sought valiantly to remember that she was trying to tell him—what? Lord, who could think? His lips brushed across hers and his arms held her close. Then his tongue began teasing at the little seam that was formed where her lips were pressed together.

''Let me in, honey.…'' He breathed the coaxing plea against her mouth.

With a soft moan she did as he bid, reluctantly parting her lips so his tongue could enter and begin its teasing torment. Within sinful seconds she was relaxing in complete surrender and her own tongue was sparring shamelessly with his.

Her hands grew eager; they roamed his broad back. And he pressed her closer, harder against him, so she could feel his desire, bold and extravagant as the man himself, through the fabric of his slacks.

And as he aroused her body he breathed his lover's demands against her heated skin. "Say you love me."

"I do. You know I do."

"Do what?"

"Jordan…"

"Say it."

"Oh, Jordan…"

"Come on. I want to hear it…."

"I love you, Jordan." His lips were on her throat. She moaned. "I do love you…."

"And you'll marry me. Saturday…"

"Jordan…"

"Say it."

"Jordan, I…"

"What?"

"I can't."

"You can."

"No, I…"

"Tell me. Tell me yes."

"Jordan…"

"Yes. Say it."

"Jordan…"

"Say it, honey. Say it now…." His lips were against her ear, taunting, teasing, pleasuring her. She felt her *yes* take form on her lips.

But somehow, her resolve rekindled. She managed a faint but clear, "No."

And with that word, the stunning, incredible kisses ended.

Jordan ended it, as Eve should have. He took her arms from around him, and gently pushed her away.

Then he turned from her, to study the waves beyond the window. She knew he was getting his body back under control, just as she herself was trying to do. Trying to stop thinking of what they could be doing, if she'd only gone ahead and let herself say *yes*. Trying to stop picturing the two of them, naked, joined at that vital place, moving together toward the ultimate ecstasy…

He spoke harshly, without turning. "What the hell kind of game are you playing here, Eve?"

Eve rubbed her temples, despising herself. Since this morning, when she'd looked in the mirror and known she had to slow things down before a disaster like her marriage to Teddy Tanner could happen again, she'd been scared to death about how she'd handle this.

And she could see now she'd been right to worry. She was blowing this. Royally. She'd stumbled over her own arguments as if she didn't believe them herself— and then melted right into his arms the moment he pulled her close.

She said with a weary sigh, "It's no game. I swear it."

"Then what the hell are you trying to prove?"

"Nothing. Only what I've already told you. Please won't you try to understand? I want us to be equal partners. And I don't feel that we are yet. With you I just seem to go along, to let you handle everything. I think that's dangerous for me, as a person."

He turned to look at her then. "That's insane. We're as equal as we need to be. And I adore you. I'll give you the world if you'll let me."

"That's just the point. I have to get what I want for myself. No one else can do it for me."

"Fine." He spoke with building impatience. "Get what you want for yourself. And marry me Saturday."

"Jordan. I can't marry you. Not right now."

They were right back where they started.

Except that now Jordan was really beginning to believe Eve meant what she kept saying. She actually intended to call off their wedding.

And nothing—not his quick wits, nor his charm, not his considerable powers of persuasion, nor even the way her body caught fire the moment he touched her, was going to change her mind.

He studied her, his gaze measuring her, where she stood by the coffee table in the middle of the room. He knew his gauging regard was unnerving to her. But right then, he didn't give a damn.

She had said she would marry him on the beach at sunset just nine days ago. All he had to do was turn and look out the window to see the spot where she'd told him yes.

And now she was standing there, looking so soft and unsure, her long, dark-honey hair alluringly tousled, her wide mouth slightly swollen from his kisses. And she was saying she was backing out on her promise. She wouldn't marry him after all.

From the first night he found her, in his own kitchen, he hadn't even considered the possibility that he could lose her. She was his from the moment she had blushed and told him he was crazy and he had answered that of course he was crazy, crazy for her.

But now he was finding out that the impossible *was* possible. She was saying no.

And, by God, what he felt for her now was a thing very close to hate. Because she had unmanned him. It took every ounce of willpower he possessed to keep from flinging himself at her feet and begging her not to leave him!

Why the hell hadn't he realized before that the hold she had on him was this strong? This was bad. This was damn agony.

And Jordan McSwain didn't need agony.

Jordan McSwain took life as it came. He'd never been the kind of man to get too invested in other people. He *liked* other people. But, except for the grandmother who had raised him from the age of seven, he'd always been smart enough never to let any one person become too important to him.

However, with Eve, he'd somehow forgotten his own rules. And now he was paying the price.

He spoke harshly then, in a voice very few had ever heard him use. "I've had enough of this, Eve. It's on or it's off. One way or the other. I'm not waiting around the rest of my life for you to decide whether you'll be my wife or not."

He watched her huge blue-green eyes widen even further at the finality of what he'd just said. He felt a perverse stab of satisfaction. There. He was through being tender and cajoling. Let her decide once and for all. "Make up your mind, Eve. And do it now. Yes or no?"

Eve, who sensed the sudden shift in him, but couldn't really understand what was happening, tried desperately to get him to back down a little. "Jordan, please. Let's avoid ultimatums. Can't we—"

"Are you marrying me Saturday?" His voice was as hard as his expression.

She looked at him, her eyes pleading. "Jordan, don't do this—"

"Yes or no?"

"If you'll just give me a little time. If I could just—"

"Yes or no."

"Jordan—"

He simply looked at her.

Eve made herself hold firm. "If you force my answer now, it has to be no."

For a moment there was silence.

Then he shrugged. "All right, then," he said quietly. "There's nothing more to say. The wedding is off. For good and all."

Eve stood there, hardly believing. She had wanted time. And he was giving her time. He was giving her forever. Without him.

"Jordan…"

His mouth tightened, as if he feared she might approach him, and do something inadmissable. Like *touch* him…

"Jordan, what is it? Don't close yourself off from me. Let's talk about it. Please—"

He made a short, chopping gesture with his hand, a gesture that said there would be no more discussion. And then he turned away.

Eve stared at his back, trying vainly to accept what was happening here. She had expected to have trouble convincing him. She had even realized he might become angry. But somehow, she had trusted that in the end she would make him understand. She had been sure that ultimately he would give her the time she needed to reassure herself that their dream-come-true was exactly what it appeared to be.

But that hadn't happened. Instead, she had lost him. *Lost him.* Oh God, how could this be?

Eve looked down at her hands. She saw that she was twisting her engagement diamond, back and forth, back and forth. She made herself stop.

Then slowly, like a woman moving under water, she removed the ring and laid it on the coffee table. "I'll just—" she had to clear her throat "—leave the ring here."

He gave no sign he heard her, but only went on staring past his shadowed reflection toward the beach and the smooth roll and retreat of the waves.

She whispered his name once more, in fading hope. He remained unmoving. She turned and went out the door.

Two

"Call him, I'm telling you. Trust me on this." Rosie Holland, Eve's best friend and housemate, stopped talking long enough to glance down at the chocolate-glazed donut she held in her hand. "God. I'm going on a diet, I swear. Tomorrow, without fail." Rosie bit into the donut.

Eve, grateful for the brief reprieve from Rosie's well-meaning advice, stared out the dining-area window at the backyard where her children were playing. She watched Wesley take a swat at a whiffle ball with a plastic bat. Not far away from him, Lisa was squatting on the grass, staring intently down at something on the ground between her plump baby legs. Overhead the autumn sky was cloudless. The sun shone down cheery and bright.

"Eve," Rosie grumbled, "did you hear a single word I said?"

Eve looked at her friend and forced a smile. "You're going on a diet. Tomorrow."

"Very funny." With a plump finger, Rosie blotted up donut crumbs. "I'll say it again, then. *Call the man.* Now." Rosie neatly licked the crumbs away.

Eve shook her head. "It won't do any good."

"You'll never know unless you try."

"You're wrong there, Rosie. I already know. He won't see me." Eve glanced out the window again. Now Wesley was climbing on a swing and Lisa was crawling along on all fours across the grass. They were both smiling. Looking at them, anyone would think all was right with the world, that today was no different than yesterday, that nothing in her life had changed.

"This is ridiculous," Rosie scolded. "You're being totally self-indulgent. Take it from me. The guy is out to lunch over you. He'll be ready to compromise now that he's had time to cool off."

Eve swallowed the lump in her throat that threatened to turn into tears. "You weren't there, Rosie. Something…happened, inside him. I can't explain it. But I *know* he meant what he said. He's through with me."

Rosie sat up straighter in her chair. "All right. Say your instincts are right on, and he *is* through with you. That doesn't mean *you* have to be through with *him,* does it?"

Eve pinched the bridge of her nose in a futile effort to massage her tiredness away. "Oh, Rosie…"

"Don't *oh, Rosie* me. I'm serious here. What's with you, giving up like this? Look around you." Rosie spread her arms wide. "You're not even thirty, and you're buying your own house. Your kids are happy and healthy. You run a business out of your home so you can be with them during the day. You've found yourself an able assistant with a positive attitude, *moi,* who can help you with the business or the kids, whichever is required. In short, you have created the ideal life for the contemporary single mom, with no support at all from your one and only gross error, Teddy Tanner, may he choke on his own stale one-liners—''

''Rosie, Teddy does send support checks, every once in a while....''

''Support checks are not the issue here, and neither is that skunk who deserted you three months before Lisa was born. What I'm trying to tell you is, *you are not a quitter.* So why the hell, when you've finally found the guy of the century, the perfect guy for you, are you willing just to roll over and play dead at the first sign of a problem between you?''

''Rosie, you don't understand—''

''Why? I ask you, why?''

''Rosie, you weren't there. You didn't see the way he—''

''You let him intimidate you.''

''I didn't let him. He did it all on his own.''

Rosie looked pained. ''This is the problem. You say he runs everything when you're together. You say you want to change that, to be more of an equal contributor to the relationship. And then you won't stand up and be equal when things get rough. You let him run you off. I think what's really going on here is you still don't believe you deserve a man like Jordan. You don't see yourself as his equal. And so the first time he gets mad at you, you turn and run.''

Eve felt a little uncomfortable at her friend's analysis. There was some truth in it, after all. She *didn't* feel like Jordan's equal. But the fact remained that she couldn't work on being his equal when Jordan flatly dismissed her and told her not to return.

"Rosie," Eve argued wearily, "you weren't there. He was much more than mad. He was…"

Right then, the telephone in the living room, which Eve used as her office, began ringing.

Eve's heart skipped a beat as hope bloomed inside her. Maybe it was Jordan….

But of course, it couldn't be. Jordan always called on her house line.

Then she remembered. Several days ago, Jordan had asked her to book Debbie Conley to serve a small dinner party he was giving tomorrow night. Until last night, she had been planning to be there too, to play hostess for him. Even though it was all arranged, maybe there was something they hadn't taken care of, some little detail that he'd forgotten to mention….

She jumped up. "Time to get to work."

Rosie gave her an ironic frown. "Right."

Eve headed for the living room at the front of the house.

Rosie, who knew very well that her advice was being filed under *ignore,* grunted and got up to pour herself one more cup of coffee. Then she trailed out into the sunshine to look at the bug Lisa had found and give Wesley a push on the swing.

In her office, Eve lifted the phone and tried to make her voice calm and professional, in spite of the fact that it might be Jordan calling. "Good morning. The Staffing Source. How may I help you?"

"Hello." The voice was female. "I'd like a quote, please. I'm giving a little Christmas party on the eighteenth of next month and…" The woman's voice droned on.

Eve sighed and felt her heart settle back into its normal rhythm. It wasn't Jordan, after all. She had been foolish to even let herself imagine it might be. "Just a moment," Eve told the voice. "I'll look that up for you." She brought up the figures on her computer, and tried not to think that the first day of the rest of her life without Jordan had begun.

"Jordan." Melba Blecker was beaming at him, the lines around her eyes etching more deeply as her smile claimed her whole face. "It's so good to be able to get together like this, to have a chance to really get to know each other." Melba tossed a quick glance at her husband, who was seated across the gleaming glass dinner table from her. "This is a big step for Mort and me."

"I understand, Mrs. Blecker."

The woman wiggled a finger at him. "Melba, Jordan. Melba."

He smiled, an unassuming smile. "All right. Melba. And I really do know what you're talking about. That's why I always like to have prospective clients over, to spend time together where every possible question you might have can be answered before any solid decisions are made."

"Such a lovely way to do business," Melba proclaimed, and then bent her head to concentrate on her Greek salad.

Jordan, who was not at the top of his form and knew it, was aware that he should be filling the silence with conversation that was witty as well as enlightening. His job, during evenings like this, was to show the prospective client a gracious and enjoyable time, while slipping in as many incentives to buy as possible.

Ordinarily he was damn good at his work. He was

always prepared, and he liked entertaining. Also, he'd always had sense enough only to sell things that were worth buying—like this, his most recent project, which was finding franchise investors for a successful chain of ice-cream parlors.

But tonight, his heart wasn't in it. He felt edgy and distracted. He was having trouble making himself care whether Melba and Mort, two perfectly nice folks, bought a Chilly Lilly's franchise or not.

From his seat at the head of the table, Jordan could see a corner of the kitchen counter. Debbie, whom Eve had sent over to serve this dinner, was doing an excellent job.

But every time he saw movement in there, he was reminded of what he'd sworn not to think about: that Eve should be here, too.

She was supposed to be sitting at the other end of the table, wearing that little black dress of hers, the one with the cutaway shoulders. When he'd asked her to wear that dress, he'd joked that if Mort and Melba Blecker were less than stimulating guests, all he would have to do was look down the table at Eve to get all the stimulation he could possibly need.

"—Don't you think so, Jordan?"

Jordan realized he had lost the thread of the conversation, something which had happened more than once in the forty-eight hours since Eve had walked out the door. He rushed to apologize. "Forgive me, Melba. Would you say that again?"

Melba, who really was a nice lady, gamely did as he requested. Jordan gave her a thoughtful answer. Then Mort had a few questions of his own. Debbie glided in to clear for the next course.

In spite of Jordan's lackluster performance, by the

end of the evening Mort and Melba were ready to buy. A Chilly Lilly's franchise, it turned out, was just the little business they'd been looking for, something they could do together, a real family business, their dream come true at last. They would call their bank tomorrow and then let him know when things were all set up to sign the papers.

He walked them to their car at a little before ten. Then he went back inside to find Debbie in his now-spotless kitchen, waiting patiently to learn if he preferred to be billed later—or to settle up right now.

He settled up, adding an enormous tip, one even larger than the huge tips he usually handed out. The efficient, unflappable Debbie actually gave a small gasp when she saw the amount—before she caught herself, smoothed out her features and thanked him politely.

He smiled to himself, the first spontaneous flash of humor he'd felt in two days, thinking that Debbie probably secretly thought he was crazy. A month ago he'd tipped her for getting sick. And now he'd paid her a gratuity almost equal to what the bill had been.

Of course, the big tip had nothing to do with Eve, nothing at all. He had done it because it amused him. He needed a little damn amusement. The fact that Eve would see it on the invoice, purse her wide mouth and call him extravagant under her breath had nothing to do with it at all.

By ten-thirty he was alone. He showered.

After that, he wandered into the bedroom, rubbing his hair with a towel. He reminded himself that he was going to have to call his grandmother and tell her the wedding was off, that he'd be coming alone to the big family reunion his great-aunt Dora was throwing over Thanksgiving weekend. Jordan dreaded making that call—which was the reason he hadn't quite brought himself to do it yet.

Naked, Jordan dropped to the edge of the bed and looked at the clock. It was nearly eleven, too late to bother Alma tonight, anyway. He'd deal with it tomorrow, somehow. But there was no point in worrying about it now.

Jordan glanced at the phone. Near it, he caught sight of the little velvet box which held Eve's engagement diamond and her wedding band. He had to remember to return the damn rings to the jeweler one of these days soon.

His eye was drawn back to the phone. He wondered…was Eve in bed yet?

Letting out an angry growl, he wadded up the towel and tossed it into a corner. He'd made the right decision, he knew it. He just had to stop thinking about her, that was all.

The more he considered it, the more positive he was that he wasn't a man cut out for marriage and a family after all. He'd been kidding himself, deluding himself.

Ask anyone he knew. They'd tell you about Jordan McSwain. Jordan McSwain loved two things equally: closing a deal and having a hell of a time. And after the deal was locked up, it was Jordan who always wanted to go out and party all night.

And it would be that way again, Jordan knew it. He'd get back his old enthusiasm for the game. He was thirty-five, a confirmed bachelor. And as soon as he got over Eve, he'd go back to being a good-time guy and loving it.

Damn straight he would.

Jordan looked out the window. From here, as from the living room right below, it was possible to see that place on the shore where he had proposed and Eve had said yes.

It had been windy that evening, and strands of her golden brown hair had blown across her face. He'd gently stroked them away.

"Marry me."

"Oh, Jordan..." Her lips had been slightly parted; her face was so tender, so vulnerable.

"Marry me, Eve."

"Yes, Jordan. Oh, yes..."

Alone in his bedroom, Jordan swore feelingly. He stalked to his dresser and got himself a pair of shorts. Roughly, he shoved his legs into them. Then he went out on the beach for a long, hard midnight run.

The next day, Jordan reminded himself more than once that he had to make that call to Alma. But somehow, the time just never seemed right.

The wedding gifts were also becoming a problem. They kept arriving, six of them that day, by UPS and parcel post. Jordan was beginning to feel as if his house was a post office. His grandmother had three sisters and one brother, and all of their children and their children's children seemed to think they had to send a present now that Jordan was finally tying the knot. He was stacking the damn things in a spare room, and they were really piling up. He didn't look forward to the task of returning them all.

More important now, though, was to call Alma. He really meant to do it that day. But somehow, before he knew it, it was eleven at night again—much too late to call an ailing eighty-eight-year-old woman and tell her that her dearest wish wasn't going to be granted after all.

He would do it tomorrow, he promised himself. Tomorrow, without fail.

Tomorrow was Saturday, the day he and Eve and the kids had been scheduled to fly to Tahoe, the day he was supposed to have been married in a wedding chapel in South Shore.

All that day he continued to postpone the phone call. But by seven in the evening, he knew he was going to have to get it over with. It would be the best time—if, for this news, there was such a thing—to call her. She'd be in her room at the board-and-care, reading or watching television before bed.

Jordan called from the phone in his bedroom, standing by the side of the bed, too nervous to sit down. He punched up her number from the phone's memory and waited bleakly for her voice on the other end of the line.

The velvet box with Eve's rings in it was still there on the dresser. He absentmindedly picked it up and turned it in his hand as he listened to the phone ring.

"Hello? This is Alma McSwain."

Jordan's heart turned over with love and longing at the sound of his grandmother's voice. There was an obvious quaver in it now. But it was still the voice of his childhood, the voice that had ordered him to clean his room and praised him when he got an *A* in Algebra. It was the voice that had soothed his hurts and explained the facts of life when his grandfather was too embarrassed to do it.

"Grandma, it's me."

He could hear her smile. "Jordan. What a lovely surprise."

"How are you feeling? How's that hip?" A few months before, she had fallen and broken it. In fact, it was her health problems that had kept her from planning to be at the wedding.

"Better every day, though I'm still on the walker."

"And your heart?" She suffered from congestive heart failure, a condition where the heart slowed dangerously, sometimes all the way to a stop.

"Jordan, we can talk about my health any time. But now there's something much more exciting to discuss. Oh, I'm so pleased you called. Tell me, how did it go?"

"Excuse me?"

"Oh, Jordan. The wedding. How was it? Were you nervous? And Eve, how is she holding up as the new Mrs. McSwain?"

"Well, that's what I..." His damn throat closed up then, and he had to suck in a breath before he could go on.

"Jordan? Are you calling from your hotel? I think we have a bad connection."

"Well, I...that is, uh, no..."

She was starting to worry, he could hear it in the quality of the silence before she said, "Are you all right, dear?"

"Yes. Yes, Grandma. I'm just fine."

"Eve, then? The children?"

"They're fine."

"Well, that's a relief. You had me worried there for a moment. I swear, I didn't know what was going on." He realized she'd found her own reasons for the strange way he was acting when she challenged cagily, "Jordan McSwain, tell the truth. You are feeling emotional, aren't you?"

He was glad she couldn't see his ironic smile. "Yeah, Grandma. I guess you could say that. I guess I am."

"Well, that's perfectly natural, given the circumstances."

"Yeah, I suppose so."

"Everything went just fine, then?"

He said, "Yes, fine," without really letting himself realize what that would imply.

"Congratulations." She said the word softly, the quaver all the more evident right then. He knew she was getting misty-eyed.

"Thank you," he heard himself reply.

"Perhaps," she suggested, "you could put Eve on the line just for a minute, so I can tell her how happy I am for you. And then I'll let you go."

The time had come, he knew it. He should open his mouth and say it: *Eve isn't here. I'm not married after all. I'm not in a hotel in Tahoe, I'm at home. The whole thing's been called off…*

But Alma sounded so pleased. How the hell could he do this? It was going to break her heart.

He lied, "She's…giving Lisa a bath."

"Oh, of course." Alma gave a little chuckle. "At my age, it's so easy to forget the constant demands of little ones. You'll give her my love? And tell her I can't wait to meet her face-to-face on Wednesday."

"I…yes. Yes, Grandma. I'll do that."

"Good. Dora's just brimming with plans. She's saving you and Eve the nicest guest room, the one with the private bath. And she's been insisting that I go ahead and stay over for the entire Thanksgiving weekend. And I am feeling so well, I think I just may do that. It would be a chance for me to really get to know Eve and those two little children."

"Yes. Good. But Grandma—I really do have to go now."

"Oh, just listen to me rambling on. Of course I know you can't stay on the phone all night."

"Yes. I…we'll see you Wednesday, then?"

There was a little silence; he thought again that she was sensing something not precisely right about all this. But then she answered, "Yes. Wednesday. I love you, Jordan. I'll see you all then."

He heard the click and the dial tone before he said, "I love you, too, Grandma." After that, very carefully, he hung up the phone.

He sank slowly to the edge of the bed, hardly believing what he'd just done. He'd blatantly lied, made things worse than before.

What the hell was wrong with him? He had never been the kind of man who couldn't bring himself to do what had to be done.

He'd just have to tell her Wednesday, that was all. But he winced at the thought of it. And he couldn't help but wonder how the hell he was going to tell the truth to her face when he couldn't bring himself to do it over the relative safety of the phone.

When he told her, he would be taking back the only gift she'd ever wanted from him. For years, she'd longed to see her only grandchild happily married and settled down. And she was just so damn frail these days. To face cold facts, there weren't too many years left for Alma. Nowadays, with most of his business in the southern half of the state, Jordan saw her only once or twice a year. And lately, every time he saw her, he was tormented by the thought that this could be the last time.

He realized he was still holding the little velvet box. With his thumb, he flipped back the lid. The diamond winked coldly at him.

He snapped the box shut and stuck it in his pocket.

He'd take it out to his car and lock it in the glove compartment. That way, he wouldn't have to look at it. The next time he was out near the jeweler's he could just drop in and get rid of it.

He glanced at his watch: seven-thirty. The long, lonely night stretched out before him.

And Jordan realized he was sick and tired of sitting at home. He knew a great restaurant up in Malibu where he could always get a table on a moment's notice. He'd go there for a leisurely and excellent dinner. And after that, who knew? An Irish pub he liked in Hollywood, maybe, where the bartender knew how to listen and when to talk. Or even one or two of the bars on Melrose, where the clientele were a show in themselves.

Hell, it didn't matter where he went, really. The point was to get out and start learning to have a good time again, to forget Eve Tanner and stop acting like a lovesick fool.

He grabbed a light jacket and headed for the door.

The maître d' at the Malibu restaurant was delighted to see him. Jordan slipped the man a little something extra and waited in the bar for his table.

As he waited, a beautiful black-haired woman smiled at him, gesturing to the bartender to put his drink on her tab. Her come-hither midnight eyes told him that the seat next to her could be his.

He instructed the bartender to put her next drink on his tab, and he stayed in his seat. He stared at the angelfish that floated in the fish tank behind the bar, trying not to think of tawny hair, of blue-green eyes....

At last his table was ready. He ate dinner slowly, telling himself he was really enjoying this, that he was savoring the excellence of the food and the hushed attentiveness of the service.

Afterward, he drove east on Santa Monica Boulevard. He stopped in briefly at a Century City club he knew, but was soon behind the wheel again. He went on, into Hollywood, dropping in at that Irish pub, where a different bartender was on duty—one who talked too much and asked too many questions.

By midnight, he was trying valiantly not to admit how completely futile this whole episode was. He'd run into more than one acquaintance. He'd been invited to two private parties.

And he was bored stiff—when he wasn't morosely contemplating how he was going to bring himself to tell his grandmother that he was still a single man.

He decided to go on home. But somehow, his car had ideas of its own. It got off the freeway in Lakewood, a nice middle-class community several miles north of Seal Beach. Lakewood just happened to be where Eve lived.

At 1:00 a.m., he found himself pulling up in front of her house. With a half-formed, totally crazy idea in his head, he got out of the car and strode up her trim front walk.

Three

Rosie answered his knock. "Oh. It's you." She squinted at him around the door, looking vaguely disapproving and still half-asleep.

"Hello, Rosie." Jordan actually felt himself smile. He'd always liked Rosie—both her bluntness, and her big heart. "Is Eve home?"

"Yep."

"I'd like to talk to her."

Rosie looked at him sideways for a moment, then grunted. "Just a minute. I'll—"

But then from behind her, he heard Eve's voice. "What is it, Rosie?"

And then she was peering over Rosie's shoulder, clutching the facings of a modest robe. Her hair was rumpled, her face soft and sleepily vulnerable. She blinked owlishly at the sight of him. "Oh!" she said on an indrawn breath.

Jordan's hands, which were stuck in his pockets, clenched into fists. It was an act of will for him to stay right where he was. What every fiber of his being shouted for him to do was to reach out, to push the door—and Rosie—aside. He wanted to pull Eve against him, to lift her chin up and then cover her lips with his own. He wanted to demonstrate for good and all that she was his and his alone.

The urge was primitive, he knew it. And totally uncalled for. She wasn't his; she'd made her choice about that. Still, the fact that she'd cancelled their wedding didn't make his urge to reach for her any less real.

He looked into Eve's wide, apprehensive eyes. "I know it's late. But I want to ask you a favor."

"Oh," she said again. Then, "Yes. Of course. What?"

Between them, Rosie groaned. "Maybe you should ask him in, Eve."

"Oh. Oh, yes." Eve started to smile, but then seemed to decide against it. "Come in."

"Thanks."

Rosie and Eve both moved back. Jordan stepped over the threshold into the small foyer. Then the three of them stood there, Eve and Jordan staring longingly at each other, Rosie glancing back and forth between them.

Finally, Rosie wryly suggested, "How about if you two go into the family room to talk, and I'll just head on back to bed?"

Never taking her eyes off Jordan, Eve murmured, "Yes, good idea. Good night then, Rosie...."

"Yeah," Jordan concurred. "Good night, Rosie."

Rosie trundled off to bed, though neither Eve nor Jordan really noticed she had left.

Eve, who was still having trouble believing Jordan

was actually here, cleared her throat. "Um. Well. Let's go into the other room, all right?"

"Yes. Fine."

Somehow, she managed to drag her gaze away from him long enough to turn and lead the way through the dining area and down the two steps to the family room. There, she switched on a lamp and indicated the couch.

"Please. Sit down." She knew she sounded absurdly formal, but she was powerless to change her tone.

"Thank you." He sat where she'd told him to. She perched on the arm of an easy chair across the coffee table from him. He glanced around the room for a moment, as if he'd never been there before. Then he asked with studied politeness, "How are Wesley and Lisa?"

"Fine. They're just fine."

"Good. I'm glad to hear that."

Lord, Eve thought, they sounded as if they hardly knew each other, like two people with no real common ground, stiff and formal, parceling out each weary cliché.

Her stomach knotted with anxiety. She didn't know what else to do, so she heard herself continuing in the same superficial vein. "Can I...get you something? I don't know, some coffee? A beer?"

"No. No, thanks."

"You're sure? It's really no trouble."

"I'm sure."

"Well." She arranged her robe over her knees. "All right then..."

The pleasantries, too quickly, had run out. For agonizing moments neither of them seemed to know what else to say.

Eve found herself wishing with a heated, hopeless fervor that she could simply launch herself across the distance between them. She longed to throw herself into his arms and promise him anything, if only he would kiss her and hold her and whisper those tender words of love that he had once lavished on her with such passionate generosity.

But in the long silence after the pleasantries had all been said, she could see that his expression was changing—and not for the better. The anxious, almost hopeful look he'd worn at the door was hardening, as if he were arming himself emotionally against her. His gaze cooled, became distant and measuring.

She knew then that whatever had brought him here in the middle of the night would be less than what she had dreamed of; he would *not* be asking her to give what was between them one more chance.

She thought, painfully, that launching herself into his arms right now would be a mistake. She'd never reach him. She'd drop into the chasm between them, never to be heard from again.

At last he spoke. "I called Alma last night to tell her what was going on."

Eve nodded, feeling worse by the minute, thinking about how much he loved his grandmother and how hard it must have been for him to tell her the wedding was off.

He went on, his voice flat and matter-of-fact. "I couldn't do it."

Eve, who was looking down at her lap, glanced up sharply and met his eyes again. "What do you mean?"

"Just what I said." His flat tone had turned suddenly impatient. "She started congratulating us, and I didn't have the heart to tell her there hadn't been a wedding. She's very old—"

"I know, but—"

He cut back in without even acknowledging her interruption. "And she isn't well. She's barely ambulatory again after the fall she took a couple of months ago. And you know about her heart."

"Yes, but Jordan—"

"Will you please let me finish?"

"Sorry. Certainly. Go on."

He was quiet for a moment, as if seeking just the right words. "What we had—" he gestured, indicating the two of them "—you and me, the kids. It's what she's always wanted for me, a wife and a family."

"I understand."

"Do you?" His look was aloof. To Eve, it insinuated his doubt that a woman like Eve, a woman who took her promises so lightly, could ever understand what his faithful, beloved grandmother might feel.

"Yes," Eve said firmly, knowing a flare of irritation. "I do understand. And I *am* sorry, Jordan. However, I still—"

He stood up, a sudden, pouncing movement that made her lose her train of thought and flinch on the arm of her chair. "How sorry?" he demanded.

She recoiled. "Jordan, I—"

He loomed over her. "Just answer the question. How sorry? Sorry enough to help me out?"

She made herself sit up tall and carefully folded her hands in her lap. Then she asked, with much more self-possession than she felt, "What are you getting at?"

"Answer my question. Will you help me out?"

"If I can, certainly. But what do you want me to do?"

He looked at her, not answering, his gaze boring into her. She stared right back, keeping her hands still, her back straight and proud. For an eternity, their glances held—and in the darkness of his eyes, she saw clearly the desire he was holding so carefully in check.

His gaze shifted down to her mouth. For a moment it hovered there. And then it began roving. He looked at her neck, and lower at the little V of skin where her robe closed over the swell of her breasts.

Eve felt a hot flush begin, up her neck and over her cheekbones. She was suddenly achingly aware of her nipples beneath the robe, of the rub of the fabric against them.

She thought of one tiny incident, one brief and erotic event that had taken place in this very room, late at night, not two weeks ago.

They'd been sitting on the couch, talking about— music, she thought it was. She wasn't sure, really. And what they'd been saying scarcely mattered anyway. What had mattered was that she had been leaning back against him and, very lightly, he had been rubbing her breast as they talked, so that the nipple grew hard and aching against his palm.

Now, she could feel his gaze on her breasts, just as his hand had been that other night. She knew, with a heated blooming in her belly, that if she looked down at her breasts now, she would see her nipples, like two hard little buttons, clearly outlined beneath her robe.

Jordan swore under his breath. Then he spun on his heel and paced to the other side of the room.

Eve, embarrassed and aroused, drew in a shaky breath and crossed her hands over herself in a protective gesture. She let the unsteady breath out slowly and told herself that she had to keep at bay thoughts of all they'd once shared. Such thoughts would only cloud the issues right now, make things more painful and confusing than they already were.

Having put a safe distance between them, Jordan glared at her balefully for a moment and then accused, "You should see all the gifts I've been getting from my family. It'll end up being a major project just to ship them back where they came from."

Eve felt her frustration with him building. This was getting nowhere. It was the middle of the night. What did he want from her? "Do you want me to call them, is that it? Do you want me to call your grandmother and explain what's happened?"

"No, Eve." He sounded grim. "That's not what I want."

"Then what? Tell me. What?"

"I want you to go home to Malachite Junction with me—you and Wesley and Lisa. I want you to be my bride. For five days, Wednesday through Sunday."

Eve stared at him, refusing to believe for a moment. Then she gave a groan of pure amazement. "What? You can't be serious."

"I'm dead serious."

"Pretend we're married. For the reunion?"

He nodded.

Numbly, she shook her head. Really, he couldn't mean this. "That's crazy. We can't—"

He waved her objections away, as if what he suggested were actually possible, as if it were the only reasonable solution to the problem of dealing with Alma. "Yes, we can. I rarely see them anyway. And my grandmother is failing. Why shouldn't she get her dearest wish for me before she dies?"

"B—but, Jordan," Eve sputtered, "we can't do that. It's wrong."

"What do you mean, wrong? It hurts no one. If anything, it'll make a lot of people happy—much happier than telling the truth and casting a shadow on the whole damned reunion.''

"But it's a lie.''

"A lie in a good cause. And eventually, after Alma's gone, when I have to tell them all the truth, at least it won't be during the biggest get-together my family's had in twenty years.''

"But what about Wesley and Lisa?''

He was ready for that. He pointed out, ''Wesley is just four, and Lisa's not even two. They won't know what's going on. They'll have a great time. My family will fall all over them, and there'll be other kids their age to play with.''

Eve stared at him, her heart breaking. How could she lie about a thing like this? How could she pretend she and Jordan had bound their lives together when, as soon as they returned home, they'd go back to being what they were right now: split up, finished, through?

Uncomfortable with her anguished silence, Jordan prompted, ''It will work, Eve. I know it will.''

Eve wanted to cry. How could he ask this of her? It was too painful, too cruel.

Very softly, in a torn voice, she dared to ask the question that was in her heart. ''And what about…you and me?''

He just looked at her, his face expressionless. ''There is no you and me. You've already decided that.''

"But I—''

He stopped her with a wave of his hand. ''Look. I've done some thinking since the other night. And I've realized that you made the right decision. I'm not good husband material. And though I'm crazy about the kids, I'll never be the kind of guy who can handle the tough stuff when it comes along.''

"The tough stuff?" she murmured dully.

"Yeah. All the problems that come up in a family. Between husband and wife. And with the kids, as they grow up."

She leaned toward him on the arm of the chair. "But how can you know that?" A pleading note crept into her voice. "You haven't given yourself a chance."

"I know myself."

"No—"

"Yes."

"You…you're not giving yourself the credit you deserve. And besides, you've got it all turned around, you know you have. Calling it off between us wasn't my decision. I wanted us to work things out, Jordan. I did. But you—you laid down an ultimatum. I swear to you, Jordan. All I wanted was…" She realized from the pained look on his face how frantic she must sound. She forced her voice to even out. "…a little time. And that's still all I want. If you would only—"

But Jordan had had enough. "Let it be, Eve. Whoever made the decision, it *is* made. And it's the right one, I'm sure of it."

"But—"

"I mean it. It's over."

Eve stared at him, biting her lip to keep from bursting into futile tears. Rosie had accused her of not working hard enough to get through to him. Well, she'd just taken a big stab at getting through. And look how far it had gotten her.

Eve tried to get her feelings under control before she said anything more. She cast about for a new way to approach this thing, a means through which she might batter down the seemingly impenetrable barrier he'd thrown up against her.

As she tried to figure out what to say next, she did her best to control the expression on her face. Still, she knew Jordan saw the shadow of hurt in her eyes—not to mention the moisture from the tears she was barely managing to hold back.

Suddenly he threw up his hands. "Damn it, never mind. You're right."

She gaped at him. "What? Right about what?"

"This was an insane idea." He turned, tossing the words over his shoulder. "It's a rotten thing to ask of you. I'm sorry I woke you. Go back to bed." He was headed for the door.

"Wait!" She stood up.

He stopped halfway through the dining area. He turned his head to look back at her. Right then, she could have sworn she saw a flicker of hope in his eyes. For a second, she was sure that, deep in his heart, he wanted her to stop him.

"What?" he said gruffly.

Rosie's advice echoed in her head. *You let him intimidate you. You let him run you off. You won't stand up and be his equal when things get rough...*

But if he wouldn't even talk to her...

Well, then, she needed more time with him. And time was something she wasn't going to get.

Unless...

Unless she accepted his proposition, took up his challenge and met him on the only grounds he was willing to offer her now. Unless she agreed to be his bride for five days...

"Well?" he demanded. He had turned fully back to face her.

Why not? Eve thought with frantic optimism. *Why not*

take the only opening he'll give me and do what I can with it? Who knows what can happen in five days?

Maybe five days together, even under false pretenses, would give them a chance to start over. Maybe, given some time in close proximity to each other, she could convince him not only to give the two of them another chance, but also to take things more slowly and sensibly than before.

Besides, getting to know a man's family was also a way to get to know the man. And that was what she'd really been after—to know him better—four days ago when she asked for more time.

He'd waited long enough for her to say something. With a shrug, he turned for the door again.

She spoke at last. "I'll do it."

He spun, pinned her with his dark gaze. "What?"

She swallowed and continued, "I said, I'll do it."

Now he was the one to look nonplussed. "You mean this?"

"Yes."

His expression grew suspicious. "Why now, when you wouldn't a moment ago?"

She considered telling the truth—*Because I love you, and this is the only chance you'll give me to show you how much*—and had to reject it. Right now, the way he turned and bolted whenever she tried to speak honestly to him, the truth might send him running off so fast she'd never catch up.

She lied. "I...I've decided you were right. It's the least I can do, after waiting to call it off until everything was already arranged."

He still looked wary. "I don't know. The more I think about it myself, the more I'm not so sure. It would be a lie, as you said. And how do I know you won't back out on *this* agreement like you did on the last promise you made me?''

The words cut deep, but she answered them evenly. ''This was your brilliant idea, remember? And I won't back out. But if you don't believe me, well, you're probably better off to stop this before it starts.''

He looked at her, gauging, deciding. Then he said, ''All right.''

She didn't realize she'd been holding her breath until right then. She made herself breathe again.

He went on, ''We're agreed, then. From Wednesday till Sunday, we're a pair of blissful newlyweds.''

''Yes. We're agreed.''

He reached into a pocket. ''Catch.''

On reflex, her hand went up and snared the little velvet box as it flew through the air. She looked down at it mutely for a moment, then flipped the top to find what she already knew was inside: her engagement diamond and her wedding band.

Her heart felt as if a cruel hand was squeezing it. She exerted all her will not to think of that night on the beach, when he'd tenderly slipped the diamond on her finger, and then turned her hand over to lay a burning kiss in the heart of her palm.

She couldn't help but wonder how all that beauty and magic had come to this: a fake marriage to ease an old lady's mind, her rings tossed at her from ten feet away, like an afterthought, as if they were little more than a necessary prop in some tawdry play.

Eve felt the tears trying to come again. She pushed them back. The past was done, gone. If there was to be another chance for her and Jordan, she had to create it out of the time he'd allowed her as his counterfeit bride.

Eve schooled her features. When she looked up, she

had only a gentle smile for the man across the room.
"Thanks."

He said nothing for a minute, but went on staring at
her distantly. She allowed herself to wonder if, just possibly, he could be fighting the memories of that night
on the beach, too.

She hoped so. In her campaign to get him to open his
heart, the memories of all they'd shared would be her
ally—as long as *he* was the one lost in them.

Very deliberately, while he was watching her, she
took the rings from their velvet bed and slipped them
in place on her finger.

"There," she said quite cheerfully. She stuck the box
in a pocket of her robe and stretched out her hand to
admire the gleaming engagement stone. "It is beautiful,
Jordan. And I've missed the feel of it…" She glanced
up and shrugged. "Oh, well." She let her hand drop
and focused on him again, waiting patiently for whatever else he had to say.

Jordan seemed, at first, to have nothing to say. He
went on watching her, his dark eyes hooded. Then, almost defensively, he launched into the arrangements.

"I'll call my travel agent in the morning. I imagine
we'll fly into Tahoe and rent a car from there. I'll try
to book us out of Orange County, or maybe even Bur-
bank. Anything but LAX, if I can manage it. We should
leave sometime Wednesday, so have everything ready.
Rosie can handle things for you here?"

"Yes, it was what we originally planned. I'm sure
she won't mind."

"Good. I'll call you to let you know the details as
soon as I have them all worked out."

"That will be fine."

"All right. Good night, then." He was headed for the door once more.

Eve remembered her new resolve, to make the most of the only opportunity he'd given her. She thought that this time around, she'd like to start things off differently from before. She'd like to make a little gesture of her own, instead of letting him control it all.

"Jordan." She spoke to his retreating back.

He turned, looking vaguely irritated. "What?"

"Will you wait here just a moment? I have something for you."

"What?" He looked at her sideways, mistrustful and eager to be gone.

"Please," she said, "it will only be a minute."

"All right. Fine."

She allowed herself a tiny smile. "Thank you."

Her room was down the hall opposite the entry foyer. She had to walk past him to get there. She felt his impatience with waiting, with not being firmly in control, as she brushed past him, just as she felt his brooding gaze on her back when she turned into the hall.

She found what she was looking for quickly. It was right where she'd left it, in her top bureau drawer, stuck in the back corner between a stack of silk bikinis and a net sachet scented with her own perfume. She grabbed the small box, removed what was inside and put the box back where she'd found it. Then she slid the drawer shut and hurried back to Jordan's side.

Meanwhile, Jordan waited where she'd left him. She would have been shamelessly gratified to know he was feeling just what she hoped he'd feel: edgy and curious—and vaguely off-balance.

What the hell was she up to? he wondered. They'd made their agreement, now he wanted to get going.

But then he realized he'd have his answer soon enough, because she swiftly reappeared, just as promised. She had the strangest little smile on her face as she marched right up to him.

"Hold out your hand, please."

God, he could smell her. That smell like roses and morning mist that had driven him to distraction since the first night they met.

She laughed softly. "No. Your left hand."

He felt like a fool, looking down, seeing he'd stuck out his right hand when she'd told him to, like some trained puppy eager for the chance to shake.

"What the hell is this?"

"Come on, Jordan. Humor me. Please?"

Not knowing what else to do, more off balance by the moment, he gave her the hand she'd requested. She took it in her smaller, softer one.

"This won't hurt a bit," she teased.

He stared down at the crown of her head as she slipped a ring on the third finger of his hand.

"There," she said chirpily. Then, before he could react, she turned his hand over and put her soft lips in his palm.

He felt that she burned him, branded him, with that single little breath of a kiss. He couldn't move. Beneath his slacks, as if he were some randy kid who got aroused at the brush of a female against him, his manhood stirred.

She looked up, turquoise eyes alight. "It matches mine. I was going to surprise you, on our wedding day."

He knew he should jerk his hand away. This wasn't part of the agreement they had made, not at all. When they got to his hometown, they'd be putting on a new-lywed act. But right now, there was no one but the two of them, no one to pretend for, no excuse for her to touch him with her soft lips, or for him to go on letting her hold his hand.

He managed, "It's not necessary."

"Oh, but I think it'll make a nice touch, don't you?"

"Touch?"

"Yes. I'll tell your family how I went to the jeweler's and ordered it specially made so it would match mine, and in a rush too, so it would be ready in time for our trip to Tahoe."

Something inside him tightened. "Did you...really do that?"

"Yes."

"You should have returned it." His voice was ridiculously husky.

"I think it's good I didn't. It will come in handy now."

Just what was she getting at? And what the hell was she up to? She was acting so damn *cheerful* all of a sudden, when before she'd looked so torn and confused. He wasn't sure he liked this.

But then he decided that asking probing questions would only bring him trouble. What the hell did it matter that she'd bought him a ring? All that, all they'd promised each other, the rings and the commitments and the life they might have shared, was gone, erased—a possible future that would never come to be.

So what if his whole body shouted at him to pull her against him, to slide his fingers under that robe and touch the sweet, soft secrets there? He was a grown man, damn it, old enough to control his own lust.

They had an agreement. That was all. In little more than a week, it would all be over.

Carefully, he pulled his hand free. She let it go without resistance, as if to show him that the length of time she had been touching him had as much to do with him as with her.

His voice thick with the desire he was determined to deny, he said, "I suppose it won't hurt to wear it, for the weekend."

"Good." She was still smiling, that soft, Mona Lisa kind of smile.

"I'll call you by Monday evening at the latest with all the details," he said.

"Okay."

He turned quickly, then, and left.

Four

"When are we getting there?" Wesley complained from the back seat. "I hate sitting in this car."

Jordan glanced over his shoulder and replied patiently, "Not long now, Wes. Ten or twenty minutes at the most."

"Are you sure? Because I'm getting hungry. And I'm tired."

Jordan opened his mouth to answer. Eve touched his arm. He stiffened a little, but accepted her unspoken message and let her deal with the recalcitrant Wesley.

Eve twisted in her seat to look at her son. "If you're tired, take a nap."

Wesley stuck out his lower lip. "But *he* said ten minutes. How long is ten minutes?"

Eve shot the boy an I-mean-business look. "Stop it, Wesley. I don't want to hear any more."

He did what she expected him to do: stuck his lip out farther and turned his head away.

Eve sighed. Since Jordan had arrived at her house to pick them up, Wesley had been acting as if the word "brat" had been coined with him in mind. Complaining about the relatively short drive from the airport in Tahoe to Jordan's hometown was just more of the same.

And now he was sulking.

Briefly studying her son's mulish pose, Eve considered ordering him to change his attitude. But then she reconsidered. A wise parent learned early to pick and choose the time for all-out confrontation, and Eve didn't think right now was that time. She wasn't sure exactly what was going on with her son. At this point, she was simply hoping that whatever it was would simply pass.

At least while he was sulking he was quiet. Why not enjoy it while it lasted? Eve had enough to think about, between wondering what could be going on behind Jordan's dark eyes and anticipating the coming meeting with his family.

With a tiny shiver at the thought of the weekend ahead, Eve turned forward in her seat again and stared out the windshield at the twisting highway, the blue lake and the tall trees. It was nearing five, and darkness wasn't far off. In the distance, whenever gaps in the trees allowed, she could see high, craggy peaks dusted with white from a recent storm.

Eve tried simply to enjoy the scenery, and not to dwell on any doubts. She put from her mind Wesley's behavior—as well as the astringent remarks Rosie had made when informed that her best friend was off to fake being married for five days.

From her car seat behind Jordan, Lisa suddenly crowed "Twuck!" as they passed a big logging rig. Eve turned toward the sound in time to see Jordan's slight grin. Their glances connected—and Jordan actually gave her a little conspiratorial wink. Eve grinned back, feeling as if the whole darkening world were suddenly bathed in a warm glow.

Since the night she'd agreed to play his wife for the reunion, he'd called only once to tell her when he'd be picking them up. During that brief conversation, he'd been reserved and businesslike. She'd spent the intervening days alternately longing for him and wondering if she was crazy to have agreed to live a lie for five days.

But from the time he'd pulled up in front of her house this afternoon, he'd treated her with warm cordiality. Such treatment was a far cry from the passionate affection he used to bestow on her. Still, it was better than nothing. She was beginning to think he'd decided to make the best of a difficult situation. And for that, she was cheered and grateful.

"Here we are," Jordan said.

They were turning off the highway, passing a sign that read:

MALACHITE JUNCTION, CALIFORNIA
Pop. 2,408
A friendly place to live!
Enjoy your stay with us!

"Are we getting there yet?" Wesley whined from his seat behind Jordan.

Jordan and Eve exchanged a look before Eve answered, "Yes." Her tone clearly communicated that her son would do himself a big favor by saying nothing more.

Blessedly, Wesley got the message. At least, he kept his mouth shut as Jordan drove them through a small downtown area, where the buildings were either aged brick or weathered clapboard and the street lamps were black wrought iron, the old Victorian kind. Soon enough, they left the stores and shops behind and entered a residential section. The houses there were big and old and set back from the streets behind gently sloping lawns.

In minutes, Jordan was turning onto a street called Autumn Lane. Then he was pulling up to the curb in front of a huge, white-accented yellow Victorian. A massive chestnut tree dominated the front lawn. The wide driveway, which curved to the street from the side of the house, was already packed with cars parked nose to tail.

Eve realized her heart had picked up a faster rhythm. "Is this it? Your great-aunt Dora's house?"

"None other." He cast her a warm smile which seemed, marvelously, to carry reassurance in it; it wished her good luck. Her heart now knocking crazily, Eve smiled back.

"Look out. Here they come," he warned, still grinning, gesturing toward the house. Jordan was already unbuckling his seat belt and shoving open his door. "The best thing we can do right now is to get out of the car, so they can hug us without having to drag us out first."

In the back seat, Wesley, for once today, was following Jordan's lead and eagerly pushing his own door wide.

Eve glanced back at the door of the house, and saw what Jordan meant. He had explained earlier that, between the six families who still lived in the Junction and all the others who'd decided to attend, there would be well over forty people coming to the reunion. Judging by the crowd piling out onto the wide porch, everybody else was already here.

Eve snapped off her own seat belt and swung open her door. The crisp fall air brought up the goose bumps on her skin. In spite of her many apprehensions, she smiled to herself, thinking that Southern California was a lot of miles away.

Jordan was already at Lisa's door, pulling her from the safety seat. Wesley stood on the curb, staring at all the people descending on them as if he were witnessing the first friendly visit of the little green men from outer space. For the moment, all his surliness was forgotten.

"Wow. Awesome," he was murmuring. "That's a lot of family."

"Jordan, at last!" a heavyset, gray-haired woman, who led the pack, was calling.

Jordan turned with Lisa in his arms. "Aunt Dora!"

And then they were surrounded. Dora's meaty arms enfolded Jordan and Lisa. Eve heard her daughter laughing. An old man grabbed her hand and asked, with great intensity, "Did you have a good trip? Enjoy your stay at South Shore?"

"Oh, yes. It was fine. Just fine..."

The old man went on, "I'm Ernest, Alma's *little* brother. It's easy to remember us. Alma, Blanche, Camilla, Dora and Ernest. Our mother started with *A* and went on until she was through having children. Very simple, eh?"

Eve chuckled. "Thank you. I'm sure that will help me remember you all...."

An attractive woman with slanted green eyes and a gleaming cap of short brown hair explained, "I'm

Nancy, Matt's wife. And this is Phyllis, our youngest.''
Nancy turned her smile on the toddler in her arms. Little
Phyllis gave a cheerful ''Goo.''

''She's adorable,'' Eve managed, before someone
else lunged forward and bussed her on the cheek.

''I'm Lori, and here's my husband, Russ.''

Nancy touched Eve's arm. ''Look. Your Wesley and
my Kendrick have already met.''

Eve shot a quick glance in the direction Nancy
pointed and saw that her son was standing nose to nose
with a dark-haired boy who appeared to be near his own
age.

And then they were all introducing themselves at
once:

''I'm Dove, Camilla's granddaughter...''

''I'm Dean, and this is Aggie, my wife.''

''Evelyn, Alicia's daughter...''

''Jim Davis, Denise's husband...''

By then, Eve decided it was futile to try to keep track
of them all. She gave up on matching faces with names,
and simply smiled and repeated ''Hello'' over and over
and waited for this boisterous crew to finish welcoming
her to their family.

As the group quieted a little, she heard Jordan ask
after Alma.

Dora answered, ''She's here, but we thought it would
be easier on her if she waited for you inside.''

''Oh, really?'' Jordan was looking past them all, toward the house. Eve followed the direction of his gaze.

A silver-haired woman in a high-necked blue dress
stood on the porch, her body stooped painfully over a
metal walker. She was smiling.

''Grandma!'' Jordan called.

The woman on the porch lifted a hand and gave a jaunty wave.

Dora, who had somehow laid claim to Lisa and was holding Eve's daughter against her big bosom, grumbled, "I told her not to come out here. My land, she doesn't even have her sweater on. She'll catch her death."

Another of Alma's sisters, the second one, Blanche, advised, "Oh, give it up, Dory. You know how stubborn she can be."

"She's got to be careful. You know the doctor said…"

But Eve didn't really hear the rest, because Jordan reached through the press of people surrounding her and snared her hand.

"Come on, honey. Meet my grandma."

Eve gasped at the warmth of his touch—and the sweet intimacy of the endearment. She hadn't realized how much she'd missed the possessive, offhand way he used to call her honey, until right now, when he was calling her honey again.

For the briefest of seconds their gazes locked. She caught his infinitesimal shrug and read it instantly. It said, *As long as we're playing this, let's play it right.*

Eve thought, *That's just fine with me,* and gave him a thousand-watt smile.

He pulled her up against his side. Lord, it felt wonderful. She pushed the thought that he was only holding her close for Alma's sake out of her mind and concentrated on the fact that at least he was doing it.

She swayed against him, snuggling her head into his shoulder. And then, together, they elbowed their way through his milling family toward the front porch where the old woman waited to meet her grandson's new wife.

Their arms around each other, she and Jordan mounted the wide brick steps. When they reached the top he took his arm from around her so he could embrace the old woman who waited there.

"Grandma." Jordan's voice was low, full of frank affection. "It's good to see you." Careful of her balance on the walker, he gave his grandmother an awkward hug and kiss.

"Yes, Jordan," the old woman answered in a voice unsteady with both age and restrained emotion. "It's good. Very good." And then she was turning her dark eyes—Jordan's eyes—on Eve.

Her smile was so kind, so full of wisdom and warmth. "Hello, Eve McSwain."

Jordan's grandmother craned toward her. Eve found herself reaching out for an awkward embrace of her own.

Moments later, Eve stood just inside the front door and watched her suitcases disappear up the stairs, carried by a dark-haired man who she thought was Dora's grandson and another man whose identity she couldn't even faintly recall. Then, somewhat wide-eyed, she remained for a moment in the entrance hall, admiring the medallion on the high ceiling, the butter yellow walls and the expansive, airy feel of the place.

"I like a bright house." Dora seemed to appear out of nowhere at her elbow. "I knocked out a few walls several years ago, to open things up."

Eve grinned at the thought of that—take-charge Dora looked the type to knock out walls all on her own if the occasion demanded it.

Dora started up the stairs. "Follow me, I'll show you where I've put you." Eve looked around and realized everyone else, including Jordan and her children, seemed to be headed the other way. "Oh, don't worry about the children." Dora waved a dismissing hand. "Carla and Nancy will see to them."

Eve tried to recall who Carla and Nancy were as Dora, forging upward, was still talking. "...And I'm sure Jordan can survive without you for five minutes, even if you *are* newlyweds." Dora glanced back to where Eve stood, uncertain, with one hand on the newel post. "Come along, dear," she urged. Shaking herself into action, Eve began climbing the stairs to join Dora at the top.

"I've put you in the gray room," Dora said, once Eve had caught up with her. "It has its own bath. I was once newly married myself. I know how much privacy can mean when everything is new between you." Dora gestured Eve ahead of her. "This way."

Eve went first, across the landing and down a short hall into a room with dove gray walls and a big window overlooking the front lawn. Their suitcases were lined up neatly on the rug.

"I hope you and Jordan will be comfortable here. Ah. I see my grandsons have already brought up your luggage as I asked them to." Dora, standing behind Eve at the entrance to the hall, peered into the bathroom. "Good," she declared. "Those boys are on the ball. They even put your vanity case in the bathroom. There are spare blankets in the closet, in case you need them and..."

Eve hardly heard her. She was looking at the double bed, the only bed in the room.

Lord, she and Jordan hadn't even discussed what they'd do about sleeping arrangements. But had she stopped to consider, she would have realized that as blissful newlyweds, they would have no choice but to share the same room. That was what newlyweds generally did: sleep together.

Eve swallowed, remembering the magic she and Jordan had once known, recalling the feel of his hands on her body, the touch of his lips against hers. Would they find that magic again, here, posing as a married couple in this lovely gray room that looked out on the spreading chestnut tree, the sloping lawn and the quiet residential street?

And even more than the erotic enchantment they had shared before, would they come to know each other better? Would they find understanding and learn to share the secrets of their hearts?

Let it be so, Eve silently prayed. *Oh, let it be so...*

"Eve, dear?" Dora was looking at her with a perplexed frown. "Is this room all right?"

Eve blinked and reminded herself to quit daydreaming and stay alert, or sharp-eyed Dora would discern that all wasn't as it should have been between Jordan and his new bride.

"Perfect." Eve rushed into the breach. "It's just perfect. We'll be very comfortable, I'm sure."

Dora's frown disappeared. "Good, then. The children's room is right across the hall. If you'll show me which suitcases are theirs, we can take them over right now."

"These two." Eve picked up the children's bags, one in each hand. Dora grabbed the bag of diapers, which Lisa still wore to bed. "Lead the way."

Dora turned, full of bustle and purpose, and showed Eve to a smaller room papered in tiny roses, with a window overlooking the backyard and a pair of single beds. Eve set down her children's suitcases on the tasseled rug and declared the room perfect for the kids.

After that, Dora led the way down the back stairs, to a beautiful gazebo-shaped room that jutted out from the kitchen, a room furnished with chairs and couches along the walls and a big table in the center. The large room was filled with Jordan's family, standing, sitting, milling around.

"This is the sunroom," Dora explained.

In the kitchen area, Niles, Dora's husband, was supervising Carla and Nancy in the preparation of dinner. Eve could smell the savory aroma of roast beef. Judging by the expert way Dora's husband was peeling potatoes, she thought the coming meal would be a good one.

Dora caught the direction of Eve's glance. "He always was better in the kitchen than me," Dora explained rather proudly. "So Niles is the cook in our house. But I think I will go see if I can lend a hand." Dora began making her way through the press of family to her husband's side.

Eve found herself on her own. She looked around for her children and saw Lisa right away. She was sitting in Alma's lap, in an easy chair against one of the many windows that framed the round room.

Alma caught Eve's eye and smiled. "Wesley's gone out in the backyard with Kendrick and Lori's boy, Billy. Is that all right?" She had to raise her voice to be heard above the drone of conversation in the room.

"Yes. Yes, that's fine." Eve watched her daughter cuddle her curly head against Alma's shoulder and gaze up at Jordan's grandmother with frank devotion in her wide blue eyes.

"Gammy," Lisa cooed.

"You are my precious, precious girl," Alma said

softly into Lisa's upturned face. Though she spoke too low to be heard above the noise in the room, Eve read the words on her lips.

Eve stared. Though Lisa was an open, friendly toddler, Eve had never seen her take to anyone this fast. Why, they'd been in the house for less than half an hour!

A new apprehension crept into Eve's heart. She had readily accepted Jordan's statement that her children were too young to be much affected by the masquerade they planned. But already her son was acting up. And now Lisa appeared to be calling Alma Grandma, when it was distinctly possible that the child would never see the woman again once this weekend drew to a close.

"Doesn't that just bring a tear to your eye?"

Eve turned and forced a smile for Camilla, Alma's third sister. "You mean Alma and my daughter?"

"Yes. Alma has been on pins and needles, waiting for you all to arrive. And really, it *is* her dream come true, you know. She and her husband, Jordan—your Jordan was named after his grandfather, did you know that?"

"Yes," Eve said, nodding. "I think Jordan mentioned that."

"Well, Alma and her Jordan had only one boy, Zachary, though all Alma ever wanted was a houseful of children. But it just wasn't meant to be for her. And then Zachary only had one child, your Jordan. So naturally when your Jordan grew up, we all kept waiting for him to find a lovely woman like you and settle down, to give Alma a few of the great-grandchildren she's always longed for. But the years have gone by, and—how old is Jordan now, anyway?"

"I'm thirty-five, Aunt Camilla."

Eve caught her breath at the sound of his voice. He was standing right behind her. She had to quell a soft gasp as he put his hands on her waist and pulled her back against his body. She trembled a little, at the closeness of him after all these barren days. And then she forced her body to relax, to lean into the firm strength of his as a loving bride would be expected to do.

He chuckled, the sound a warm vibration against Eve's back. Then he teased his great-aunt, "Aunt Camilla, are you telling tales about me?"

Camilla let out a giggle that was downright girlish. "Not at all, Jordan. I was merely explaining to Eve how much your marriage—not to mention those beautiful children—means to my sister."

"Eve already knows." Eve felt his hands tighten on her waist. "Don't you, honey?" His voice betrayed nothing. It sounded warm and teasing as before. But the tension in his touch reminded her that their "marriage" was because—and only because—of what his having a wife and children meant to Alma.

As she was sure he intended, Eve felt a momentary urge to back away from the challenge his covert dig implied. She almost cast her eyes shyly down and made a soft, modest sound of assent.

But then she reminded herself that this was her weekend to prove to herself that she could stand equal with him. Part of being equal was showing she could give back any challenge he cared to toss her way. So instead of looking down, Eve tipped her head back enough to catch his eye. She gave him a slow smile, one that matched his own.

"Yes, darling," she said sweetly, "I do. And I think it's wonderful that what we've found together makes your grandmother happy, too."

Jordan went on smiling, but something flared in his eyes. Eve wasn't sure whether it was rancor or desire—and right then, she didn't much care which it was. The point was that he'd tossed her an underhanded message, and she had shot a message of her own right back at him.

Eve, reckless with her own daring, put her hands on his hands. She stood on tiptoe and canted her head back to brush a quick kiss against his square jaw. The heat in his eyes increased. He made a low noise in his throat and pulled her closer, back against his hard strength.

"Ah, you newlyweds." Great-Aunt Camilla gave a voluptuous little sigh. "I remember the time. I do remember the time...."

Five

In the succeeding half hour, most of the family went their separate ways. Tomorrow night, Thanksgiving, the entire crowd would be sharing dinner at Dora's. But tonight they broke up into more manageable groups.

After everyone else left, the big house actually seemed relatively quiet with *only* twelve people in it. They shared a meal in the sunroom at the breakfast table, which easily seated the entire group.

After dinner, Alma sat at the table with the four children who were staying at Dora's—Wesley, Kendrick, Lisa and baby Phyllis—and created a series of miniature roads and houses using dominoes as blocks. Eventually both Kendrick and Wesley produced matchbox-size vehicles they had brought with them from home. Then they drove the cars on the domino roads and parked them in the domino garages.

Eve sat in a big chair by one of the windows, watching, thinking of the care and attention Alma showered on the little ones. Alma was the kind of elderly woman—doting, humorous and wise—that children almost invariably respond to. Watching Wesley and Lisa around her, Eve couldn't help thinking that there was no one quite like Alma in their young lives.

Which was not to say that they didn't have a grandmother; they did. Though both of Teddy Tanner's parents were dead, and Eve's father had passed away just before Wesley was born, Eve's mother, Faye Brant, was still very much alive.

Faye was an art dealer in Palm Springs, a very busy and successful woman. She was also attentive and loving toward her daughter's children. Faye did her best to make it to Eve's house each Christmas; she kept her engagement calendar carefully marked so she'd remember to send gifts for the children's birthdays. Yet she had never been a woman to sit down with a group of children and make up a game using only a bunch of chipped dominoes and a healthy dose of imagination.

"You're very quiet."

Eve looked up and smiled at Jordan. "Just thinking."

He casually rested a hand on the back of her chair. "About what?"

"About Alma, and how good she is with kids."

Jordan nodded, and then both of them turned their attention to the old woman and the children. For several minutes, they were quiet together, just watching the others. Eve found it a companionable silence and was content.

Jordan swore under his breath. "One damn bed." Eve looked at him across the bed in question. "What did you expect? We're supposed to be newlyweds, remember?"

"I didn't expect anything. I didn't think about it."

Eve made a little noise in her throat.

Jordan glared at her. "What is that supposed to mean?"

"Nothing. I cleared my throat is all."

"You don't believe I didn't think about it?"

"Jordan, it doesn't matter if you thought of it or not."

"It doesn't?" His expression said he wondered what trick she had up her sleeve.

"No."

"Why not?"

"Because, if we plan to go through with this scheme of yours, the result is the same. We'll be expected to sleep together, and if we don't, we're going to cause suspicion."

Slowly, he nodded. "All right. Good point."

"Well, thank you."

"I just want you to know I didn't plan for us to be stuck in the same bed."

Eve gave him a noncommittal smile. "I never thought you did." She was fibbing. She *did* think he'd planned it this way—but only subconsciously.

"Well, good."

They were silent, looking at each other over the barrier of the bed.

Then he said, "Were you always this... levelheaded?"

"I like to think so. Why?"

"Well, before, while we were together, you seemed...a little shy, I guess. Not quite so cool and collected."

Eve's smile warmed. "Well, Jordan, it's hard to be

cool and collected when you're being swept off your feet.''

He seemed to be lost in his own thoughts for a moment. ''I did sweep you off your feet, didn't I?''

''Um-hm.''

''And we had a hell of a time.''

''Yes.'' She sighed a little, remembering. ''We did. An absolutely incredible time.'' The only light in the room came from the small candelabra fixture by the door, which Jordan had flicked on when they entered. To Eve, the world seemed softly shadowed, like Jordan's eyes.

She could feel the rhythm of her own heart speeding up a little, quickening like her senses at the thought of the beauty the two of them had once shared.

The beauty they could share again, if only…

Abruptly, he was turning away. ''Go ahead. Use the bathroom first.''

''Jordan, I—''

He paced to the pair of chairs by the window. ''I'll sleep on these.''

Still half-lost in forbidden reflections, Eve tried to get her bearings. She glanced at the chairs in question. One was a straight chair with a padded seat, the other a wooden rocker. ''Don't be silly,'' she told him. ''You won't sleep a wink on those chairs.''

''I'll be fine.'' He started arranging the chairs. ''If it's too uncomfortable, I'll stretch out on the rug.''

She marched over to him and grabbed the straight chair he was moving to use as a footrest. ''Come on, Jordan.'' He gave her an infinitely patient look and then just waited, keeping a firm grip on his half of the chair. She blundered on, ''We can share the bed without… anything happening. We are two grown adults.''

He made a disbelieving sound. "Right. Two grown adults who've never been able to keep their hands off each other."

"That was before. Things are different now. You've said so yourself."

"Not different enough," he muttered darkly. "Now let go of this chair."

"No. You let go. And come to bed."

They glared at each other.

Eve knew she was being ridiculous, but she just wasn't going to give up on this. Maybe it was because of the way he'd always taken charge of everything during those magical weeks of their courtship. Maybe, the way things were now, she'd grown plain contrary for the sake of contrariness. She wasn't sure why. She just knew that tonight they'd share the darn bed even if she had to tie him up to make him lie down beside her.

She pressed on, "Aunt Dora said there were spare blankets in the closet. One of us can use them on top of the covers. And I have a flannel nightgown that goes up to here and down to there."

She failed to mention that she'd also brought that black lace negligee he used to love. She was saving that. Just in case a miracle happened and they managed to iron out their differences in the next four precious days.

She granted him a mature, no-nonsense look. "Honestly, Jordan. This doesn't have to be a big issue, unless we make it one."

He glared at her some more. "Damn it, Eve."

"Come on." She lifted her brows at him. "Get a decent night's sleep—you'll be glad you did."

"This is ridiculous."

"My sentiments exactly."

At last he let go of the chair. Without a word, he

strode to the closet, shoved the door back, and pulled down two spare blankets. He tossed the blankets onto the bed. "I'll use the bathroom first. I won't be long."

"Take your time," she sang out sweetly as he closed the door between them.

Twenty minutes later, they were lying side by side in the darkness. Eve lay staring up at the ceiling, listening to Jordan's breathing, which was too uneven to indicate any level of relaxation.

"Jordan?"

"What?"

"I...like your family."

For a moment, he said nothing. Then, "All of them?"

She could hear the humor in his voice. She wanted to turn toward it, toward him, to feel the warmth and strength of him, to cuddle up close and have him wrap his arms around her.

But she knew that he would not be embracing her tonight. To him, they had an agreement. And he was holding on tight to the belief that their agreement was all they had.

She wondered what had happened to him in his life, what it was that had made him turn from her so completely when she had asked him for more time. She wanted to talk about it, but she sensed that if she did, he would only tell her there was nothing, and remind her again that what had been between them was no more.

"Eve?"

"Hm?"

"I thought you'd gone to sleep on me."

"No." She smiled into the darkness. "I'm still with you. And I did hear what you asked."

"So?"

"The answer is yes. I like all of your family—or at least what I've seen of them so far. Even the ones I just said hi to seemed like nice people."

"I don't know." His voice was teasing. "You looked pretty damned dazed when they all came running down the steps to meet you."

"I guess I was. But I survived it."

There was a pause. Eve lay there, grinning at the ceiling, congratulating herself that she'd gotten him into this bed, and that they were talking—somewhat superficially, it was true, but talking nonetheless.

Eve shifted a little, feeling awkward, trying to respect his side of the bed. She slid her arms out from under the covers and rested them on top of the blankets. Then she lay very still, feeling suddenly absurd, like some latter-day Sleeping Beauty with a case of insomnia. A Sleeping Beauty whose prince wouldn't be kissing her anyway, even if she did manage to drop off to dreamland.

"Alma likes you." Jordan's voice cut through the silly images in her mind. "Even more than I thought she would. And did you notice the way she and Lisa took to each other?"

"Yes." Seeing a good opening, Eve decided to express her concern about Lisa to him. "It worried me, a little."

"Why?"

"Well, she's already calling Alma Grandma. I'd hate to see her get too attached, given the circumstances."

The silence from his side of the bed was heavy. But then he said, "I really don't think Lisa will be hurt by this. She's so young, after all. And this will only be for a few days."

"Yes, I'm sure you're right," Eve replied after a moment's consideration. Then, since he seemed reasonably receptive, she went on, "Wesley's the one who really worries me."

His reply surprised her. "Yeah. He's been acting up all day—at least when it comes to anything to do with me."

She felt relief. He'd noticed it, too. "Yes. Exactly."

Jordan grunted. "To tell you the truth, I keep hoping it's just a phase with him, that he'll get over it."

"Me, too. But then I wonder..."

"What? Say it."

"Well, when we were going to get married, I never really sat down and explained it to him. Everything happened so fast with us. I kept meaning to have a nice talk with him. But I guess I kept putting it off because..."

"Of your own doubts?" His voice seemed neutral.

She made herself answer truthfully. "Yes. Because of my doubts. And, after we...broke up, well, it just seemed easier not to go into it. He *is* only four."

"Did he ask about me?"

"Not really. He'd say things for the first few days like, 'When Jordan comes,' or 'When I see Jordan.' I was feeling pretty bad myself. So I put off explaining what had happened, just like I put off telling him about our marriage. And then, you came and asked me to play 'newlyweds' with you for the weekend, so I..."

"You put it off again." Now his tone was beginning to sound accusing.

"Jordan." She made her voice firm. "Whether you like it or not, this has to do with you, too."

For a moment he didn't answer. Then he admitted, "You're right. I'm sorry. What do you want to do?"

"I'm not sure yet. He didn't start acting up until to-day—when he saw you again. I wonder if he hasn't got you a little confused with his dad somehow, though Teddy never spent much time with Wes anyway, and he left for good when Wes was only two. I've kind of told myself that Wes doesn't have much memory of Teddy. But I've begun to think that he does have a sense that he's been abandoned by his father. And—"

Impatient, Jordan cut in. "What you're saying is that I'm abandoning him, too."

"No, I'm—"

"What, then?"

"I'm saying that might be how he sees what's happened."

Jordan's arm, resting between them, accidentally brushed hers. He quickly pulled away. She could feel the tension in him. "Okay. But you still haven't told me what you want to do about it."

She answered evenly, "Wait. See if he keeps it up."

"And if he does?"

"Then we'll have to take some kind of action. But right now, if you want to maintain the fiction that we're married..."

"We have to keep a four-year-old boy in a state of unhappy confusion." He sounded disgusted, and she knew it was more with himself than anyone else. Then he said, his tone flat, "Do you want to call the whole thing off?"

She shook her head at the ceiling. "If Wesley is acting this way because he feels you're abandoning him, then calling it off isn't going to save him any pain."

"You mean I'll still be abandoning him, either way."

"Jordan, I—"

"Just say it. Tell the truth."

She sighed, longing to inform him that he wouldn't be abandoning her son; by the time this weekend ended, they'd be together again. But if she said that, he'd only tell her once more that it was over between them. And she just didn't feel like hearing that again.

So she conceded, "Yes, if we call it off now because we think he's feeling abandoned, and it turns out it's true, then he will still have to deal with the pain of losing you. So we might as well see if we can get through the weekend. We'll keep a close eye on him. Right now, he's just being periodically bratty, and it seems to center around you. But once or twice before, I've seen him act this way, and it turned out he was coming down with something. Who knows what it is at this point? It's really too soon to tell. So let's wait and see."

"You're sure?" He sounded doubtful.

"I'm sure."

He said nothing more after that. Eve lay still for a few moments, then rolled away onto her side and closed her eyes.

Jordan must have felt her settling in to sleep, because he murmured softly, "Good night…Eve."

"Good night, Jordan." A little smile curved her lips. She had heard the hesitation in his voice. He had almost called her "honey," before he stopped himself. Eve tucked her legs up close to her body and rested her cheek on her hand. She felt better, she realized, now that they'd talked a little. She yawned, and it occurred to her that she was more tired than she'd realized…

Jordan, beside her, was not so fortunate. He stared up at the shadows on the molded ceiling and thought about that old line concerning tangled webs. He kept seeing

Wesley's accusing little face, hearing the hurt and hostility in his voice.

Damn. He had been so sure that this well-intentioned deception wouldn't really hurt anyone. He had arrogantly told himself that no one would suffer.

But now it was beginning to look as if he might have created significantly more problems than he'd solved. Lisa *was* growing very attached to Alma. And there really was something going on with Wes.

Well, he told himself, for right now Eve's plan was probably the best one. They'd wait. And see how things developed.

Jordan cradled his hands behind his head and closed his eyes, knowing he was a long way from sleep—unlike the captivating and infuriating woman beside him, who seemed to have dropped off as if she hadn't a care in the world.

She was a puzzle, and more so all the time.

Strange, but it seemed as if today he was seeing a whole new side of her. An opinionated, feisty side. When he'd delivered that dig in front of Aunt Camilla, she'd pounced right back at him. And then she'd been so matter-of-fact about their sharing a room, not to mention damned determined that he'd get half of the bed. Hell, she'd held on to that chair as if she'd break it in two rather than let him try to sleep on it.

And it had been good, lying beside her after they'd turned out the light, talking about the day, about his family and her kids. Back when they were lovers, they never really had time for companionable chats; then, a bed had one obvious and all too pleasurable purpose.

Jordan rolled over toward her. She was breathing evenly, turned away from him, curled up on her side.

Even through the wall of blankets that separated them, he could feel her body heat. And her softness.

He wondered—if he gathered her against him, would she nestle her round bottom into the cradle of his hips, would she sigh and snuggle up and...?

Jordan swore softly and turned onto his other side. Then he pressed his eyes closed and grimly waited for sleep.

Six

Great-Uncle Ernest was there, waiting to take everyone out to breakfast when Eve and Jordan and the kids went downstairs the next morning. They all piled into three cars and drove to a local restaurant, where several family members from the other houses joined them. They were twenty-three for breakfast and they took over the restaurant's back room.

Eve found herself sitting next to Louise Blair, who was the "baby" of Great-Aunt Blanche's family. Louise, Eve quickly learned, had married a lawyer, Kevin Blair. They owned a large house "right here in the Junction," had two teenage children, whom Louise pointed out across the room, and were absolutely thrilled that footloose Jordan had finally found Eve—not to mention two terrific little ones like Lisa and Wesley.

Louise leaned close to Eve. "So tell me. Is the silver salver too ornate?"

"Excuse me?"

Louise, whose dark brows already met over her nose, scrunched them up even more. "The salver I sent. In the mail."

Down the table, Wesley and Kendrick were using straws to blow bubbles in their milk. Eve was wondering if she should tell them to stop before they got too rambunctious and knocked over a glass.

But then Jordan, who was closer to them, instructed Wesley to put the straw aside. There was a quick exchange of challenging looks between the boy and the man. And then the boy gave up, sulkily lowering his eyes and taking the straw from his glass. Kendrick, who'd received a similar order from his mother, followed suit.

Louise was still talking. "It's an heirloom, you know. It belonged to Grandma Mary. She was Alma's—and my own mother's—mother."

Eve said, "I'm sorry, I wasn't paying attention. The salver?"

"Yes. The silver salver I sent you in the mail. For a wedding present."

Eve put it all together then. Jordan had mentioned to her that a lot of gifts had arrived at his beach house. "Oh. Yes. The salver." With a sinking feeling, she realized that many of the people here this weekend must have taken the time to choose and mail her a wedding gift. She had no idea what any of those gifts might be.

And what in the world was she going to do about them when she got home? Send everyone a thank-you letter?

Yes, she staunchly decided. That would be exactly what she would do. Because by then, she and Jordan would be back together again. She knew they would. She was sure of it.

She gave Louise an abashed smile. "Oh, Louise, things have been so absolutely crazy, what with planning the wedding and arranging everything so we could come here, that I've been putting all the gifts aside, to open all at once when we get home."

Louise's scrunched-up brows relaxed into a straight line again. "So you haven't even seen the salver yet?"

"No. I'm afraid not."

"Well, I want you to know, if it isn't what you want—"

Eve rushed to reassure her. "I'm sure I'll love it. And of course, there'll be the sentimental value, since I'll know it once belonged to Alma's mother."

"Well." Louise looked thoroughly pleased with herself. "That was my thought, of course."

"And you were right."

Louise gave a modest titter. "Now, show me that ring." Eve obligingly stuck out her hand. Louise took it and oohed and ahhed over the diamond for a while. When she gave Eve her hand back she whispered in her ear, "I must say, I never thought it would really happen."

Eve pulled back. "Excuse me?"

"I said I never thought it would happen, that Jordan would actually marry. I mean, well, you know how he is."

Eve leaned toward Louise again. Anything she could learn was worth probing for. "No, tell me. How *is* Jordan?"

"Well, you know. He never lets anyone get too close. He's everyone's good buddy, but that's as far as it goes."

Eve wanted to hear more, but she was afraid Jordan might interrupt if he heard he was the subject of their conversation. She glanced quickly around the noisy room, and saw that Wesley was eating his toast in a reasonably civilized manner, that Lisa was sitting in Dora's lap and that Jordan was talking football with one of Dora's grandsons, Mark.

Eve suggested, "How about a visit to the ladies' lounge? I'll bet it's a little quieter in there."

Louise nodded, her expression knowing. "And more private, too." She got up and went out.

Eve stood up to follow her, pausing where Dora sat holding Lisa. "Would you keep an eye on both Wesley and Lisa for a few minutes, Dora? I want to visit the ladies' room."

"Certainly I will."

Lisa was reaching for the sugar shaker. Dora pushed it toward the center of the table, and gave Lisa a big kiss on her plump cheek. Lisa giggled. "No. No kisses. No, no…" She wriggled in Dora's lap, delighted by the attention she was pretending to resist.

Smiling, Eve turned to leave the room. But when she brushed by Jordan, he reached out and snared her hand. "What's going on?"

She looked down at him, feeling that familiar shiver of heat and longing, poignantly aware of his hand enclosing hers. "Nothing. Just answering nature's call."

He chuckled. "You and Cousin Louise?"

"Oh. Is Louise going, too?"

"You're a lousy conspirator, honey."

"Excuse me?"

"You'll be sorry."

"And why is that?"

He tugged on her hand, so that she would lean closer.

Then he whispered in her ear, "Once Louise finds an audience, she won't let it go. She'll follow you around all weekend."

Eve answered, only slightly self-righteously, "I think Cousin Louise is perfectly nice—and I'm sure I don't know what you're talking about."

"Liar."

He was looking up at her in teasing challenge. If only she could see into his mind. This deception of theirs could be so confusing. Right now it would be easy to forget that they weren't just what they pretended to be, teasing newlyweds, passionately in love.

He still held her hand. She wished he'd never let go.

But he did. "Better hurry. Louise will wonder where you've gone."

She gave him her sweetest smile. "What are you talking about?"

He only grinned and went back to his conversation with Mark.

Louise was waiting in the lounge. "I was beginning to wonder."

"I'm sorry, Louise. Jordan was—"

Louise didn't need to hear more. "Don't even say it. Kevin was like that at first, too."

"Like what?"

"Oh, you know. He hated for me to be out of his sight. But they get over it. Believe me." Louise gave a heartfelt sigh. "Now, I have to insist that Kevin take me out to dinner once or twice a month, just so we can sit across a table from each other with no distractions and try to keep track of each other, touch base with each other, you know? Of course, Kevin often complains that it's impossible to lose track of me, since I'm always talking. You just follow the sound of my voice. He thinks that's funny. I suppose he means it affectionately, but nonetheless, I—''

''Um, Louise. About Jordan...''

Louise blinked, and then looked at Eve sideways. ''Oh. Right. I more or less forgot. We were talking about Jordan.''

''Yes.'' Eve smiled unassumingly.

''Er, where were we?''

''Well, you said that he's everybody's good buddy, but that no one can really get close to him. I was wondering how he got to be that way.''

Willing, it appeared, to change topics on demand as long as she could continue holding forth, Louise lowered her voice to a confidential pitch once more. ''What causes anybody to be that way? His childhood.''

''How so?''

''Well, his father, Zachary, virtually deserted him when his mother died. And before that, it was his mother, Willa, who was never really there in any way that mattered.''

''Did Jordan's mother and father get along with each other?''

Louise considered. ''What can I say? Zachary was fifteen years older than me, after all. So this is all secondhand. The story in the family was that they had 'problems,' though I never learned specifically what. I was nine when Zachary and Willa got married, and it seemed to me he was wild for her. I remember at their wedding—talk about a man who didn't want his bride out of his sight! But she never seemed as in love with him as he was with her.

''Willa wasn't the type of person to feel a passionate emotion like love, if you ask me. She always seemed to me to be one of those people who kind of wander through life, wondering how they got there. She was withdrawn and delicate, the type of person who should probably never have children because, God knows, it takes stamina and fortitude to raise a child. But anyway, Willa did have Jordan—and then it turned out she had diabetes. After that, she was too busy being sick to have much time for motherhood. And then when she died, Zachary just dropped the poor kid in Alma's lap and took off. Went to work back east, can you believe it? Thank God for Alma, or Jordan wouldn't have had a prayer for any kind of a childhood, I'll tell you."

"I see," Eve said, since she felt she ought to say something. She had known, of course, that Jordan's mother had died when he was seven, and that his grandmother had raised him. But Jordan had never said much about his parents, she realized now. And he'd said nothing at all about how he felt when it came to them.

Louise was really rolling now. "Anyway, Jordan's always been outgoing and friendly. But no one gets too close. That's why I...well, forgive me, but I'm sure it won't hurt to say this now. When I heard Jordan was finally planning to marry someone, I told my husband, Kevin, that I'd bet Grandma Mary's Spode china—she had a setting for twenty-four, can you believe it?—that *something* would come up to keep the marriage from happening, because Jordan, though we all love him dearly, was just not the marrying kind. But then, here you are with Jordan's ring on your finger, and you and Jordan are obviously about as married as two people can get."

"Yes." Eve forced a chuckle. "Here we are, as married as two people can get."

Louise shot Eve a look. "You okay?"

"Yes. Fine. Why?"

"Well, you kind of look…"

Eve schooled her expression into one of polite interest. "I look what?"

Louise shrugged. "I don't know. You just looked strange for a minute, that's all."

Eve glanced up at the glaring overhead lights. "Maybe it's the light in here."

Louise looked up, too. "Yes. You're right. That must be it."

Eve quickly suggested it was time they rejoin the others.

Louise, Eve learned as the day went on, was a font of information about Jordan's family. In fact, the only difficulty with Louise—as Jordan had warned—was in trying to get her to stop talking. She told Eve she was just thrilled to have someone new to tell all the family stories to.

Eve heard about how Mary Jurgenson and Stanley Swenson, a seafaring man, had met and married. She heard about Stanley and Mary's five offspring: Alma, Blanche, Camilla, Dora and Ernest, and the mates each had found. She learned how many children each of Alma's siblings had produced—and how many children those children had had.

She heard more than she ever wanted to hear about Louise and Kevin's relationship, as well as Louise's ongoing conflicts with her mother, Blanche.

"I am telling you," Louise fumed, "my mother has absolutely no sense of heritage, of posterity." It was shortly after noon, when preparations for the big feast were in full swing and they were standing in Niles's kitchen cutting up raw vegetables for a crudité tray. Cutting the vegetables and arranging them on the tray was a chore Eve had volunteered to do. Louise, fearful of losing her new audience, had jumped right up to help.

"Honestly, she's my own mother and I love her." Louise hacked a hapless cucumber into slices. "But right after Father died, she decided to just off-load all of her precious family heirlooms." Louise looked up from the cucumber and darted a glance around the room, presumably so she could cut herself short should the subject of her tirade—in this case her own mother—appear. Assured that Blanche was nowhere near, she forged on. "I'm telling you, if I hadn't gotten there in time, I swear she would have sold the Swenson silver—the everyday set, of course. Alma got the company silver—in a *garage* sale. I promise you, I had to take everything, the antique furniture, the trunks of handmade blankets. You name it. Or she would have just sold it away. Now she lives in a condo over on Spring Street. She says she loves it. And she seems perfectly happy, but I tell you honestly that I cannot see how she could be happy without all of her beautiful things around her...." Louise grabbed up a bunch of broccoli and began dismembering it into florets, never pausing in her harangue except for an occasional necessary breath.

More than once, Eve managed to escape the endless monologue. She'd excuse herself for this or that reason, and heave a sigh of relief as she went off to put Lisa down for a nap, or bandage a scrape on Wesley's elbow, which he'd acquired playing something called "slide and crash" on the hardwood floor upstairs in the big den where Matt and Nancy's family were staying.

Jordan, who seemed to become more and more involved in playing their "newlywed" game as the day progressed, began ambushing Eve in the hall or elsewhere whenever she managed to get away from Louise.

Then he'd teasingly demand to know what Louise had said since Eve's last escape. Once, he even stole a swift, brushing kiss—for the benefit of the family, of course, who were in and out of any room they found themselves in.

Eve played right along with him, even naughtily encouraging him. It was so lovely to be having *fun* with him again, though she was sure he was telling himself that it was all part of the act.

But Eve didn't mind. For now, whatever excuse he had to give himself in order to let down his guard was okay with her. And his kisses, however fleeting, were something she would never refuse.

In the afternoon, less than an hour before the big feast, when almost every room of the old house was full to bursting with the descendants of Mary and Stanley Swenson, Eve left Louise with the excuse that she needed to "freshen up" for dinner. She checked on her children, found they were both doing fine, and then went on up to the gray room and closed the door behind her.

With a hefty sigh, she fell across the bed and groaned at the ceiling in relief. Then she went to the bathroom to get her overnight case. She brought it back out to the bedroom and sat at the little vanity bureau between the bathroom and the closet. She'd just picked up her hairbrush when there was a tap on the door.

She sent a brief prayer to heaven that it would not be Louise. "Yes?"

"It's me."

Eve was looking at herself in the mirror right then. She almost laughed at her own expression—which went from dread to eager anticipation as soon as she heard the deep male voice. "It's open."

Jordan came in and idly pushed the door shut behind

him. Then he lounged against the wall to the left of where she sat. She could see him in the mirror, studying her with the characteristic look she loved: a corner of his mouth raised, a brow lifted, too.

"Admit it, you thought you'd escaped," he accused.

"I admit nothing." Eve began brushing her hair with long, even strokes. In the mirror, she watched him watching her.

He folded his arms, and the muscles of his shoulders became more clearly defined beneath his sweater. Eve felt a warmth in her midsection, an intensification of the longing that was always with her since she'd first met this man.

"Your hair's so damned beautiful," he said quietly. "Brown and gold. Like honey...."

Eve went on pulling the brush through the long strands, feeling both utterly brazen and discreetly restrained. She said nothing in response to his low-voiced compliment. She sensed, from the concentrated way he watched her slow strokes with the brush, that he was hardly aware he'd spoken aloud.

Their eyes met in the mirror. He blinked, as if coming back to himself.

His voice was teasing when he spoke again. "What deep secrets has Cousin Louise shared with you since the last time you got away from her?"

Eve set down the brush and smoothed her hair back over her shoulders. Then she adjusted the posts of her earrings. "Let me see. Camilla's oldest son, Rick, married a woman who actually calls herself Seafoam and has since the sixties, when she and Rick met at an acid-rock concert in Golden Gate Park. Everyone knows, of course, that Seafoam has a perfectly good real name, which is Ardelle Lee. And that's not all. Not only does the woman call herself Seafoam, she had the nerve to name her three children Dove, Freedom and Pagan, which any sane adult should know is a rotten thing to do to a helpless child."

His dark eyes alight, Jordan shook his head. "It's a crying shame."

"Isn't it? And did you know that our own Carla is truly someone to be admired?" She spoke of Dora's daughter, Matt's mother, who was staying in the small bedroom at the top of the stairs. "She went back to school ten years ago, after her husband died. And now she's a practicing P.A. Do you know what a P.A. is?" She didn't give him a chance to answer. "A physician's assistant. The next thing to a doctor. She works in a clinic in Austin—Texas?"

He acknowledged dryly, "I know where Austin is."

Casually, Eve took the cap off a lipstick and studied the color. She dared to add, "Louise also mentioned this morning in the ladies' room that your mother never paid any attention to you, and your father deserted you when your mother died."

There was a silence, during which Eve feared she'd gone too far. She knew his childhood was something she must someday get him to really talk about. But maybe now was too soon—and her brash words would only serve to destroy the budding camaraderie between them.

But she was wrong. He only shrugged. "That's Louise's opinion. And I suppose it's more or less true."

Eve capped the unused lipstick and spoke to his reflection in the mirror. "But Jordan, that must have been horrible for you."

He seemed totally unconcerned. "I got by. And I had

more than a lot of kids have. I had Alma, and my grand-father.''

"But you must have felt—"

"I felt bad." His eyes in the mirror didn't waver. "And I got over it. End of story."

"But I would think that you—"

"What?" He looked at her, his expression vaguely interested but in no way involved. Whatever she thought she might say died on her lips.

She chose another lipstick—a gloss this time—and uncapped it, thinking that his total lack of resistance, his utterly neutral response when she tried to get him to talk about his parents, was a better way to get her to change the subject than becoming defensive or angry would have been. Just as being outgoing and charming was probably a good way to disguise a fear of letting any-body really get too close....

Eve rolled up the gloss and studied the almost col-orless stick. But her mind wasn't really on lip gloss.

Okay, Jordan, she thought, *have it your way. I'll drop the subject of your parents. For now. But I'm not through with them, my darling. Not by a long shot.*

Eve looked up at the mirror and began applying the gloss. Jordan watched her primp for a moment more. Then he lazily made a circuit of the room. He wandered over to look out the window, paused to study a picture on the wall and then eventually approached her chair.

While he roamed the room, Eve moved the little tray that fit in the top of the case and straightened things underneath. Then, as he came near, she realized he might see the dispenser that contained her birth control pills—the pills she'd never stopped taking, though ac-cording to Jordan, the two of them were finished for good.

Swiftly, she slid the tray back in place so the dispenser disappeared from view. She made a great show of tidying the small items in the tray as he stood, silent, at her elbow.

Eve was acutely aware of him, of the way he had circled her, and then idly closed in. She looked up at him.

For a moment, she thought he was going to say something tender and direct, something honest about the two of them—or his childhood hurts. Or even about the birth control pills, which he just might have glimpsed. But when he spoke, it was in the bantering tones of a few moments before.

"So who got Great-Grandpa Stanley's sea chest, that's what I've always wanted to know."

Disappointment washed over her. But what else could she do? She went on playing the game. "I've been sworn to secrecy on that."

"Louise didn't mean you couldn't tell me. Wives in the family tell their husbands everything."

"But I'm not really your wife, am I?"

It was a dangerous point to make, and she knew it. He might just agree with her, and leave the room.

But he didn't. His eyelids dropped a little, and she saw that he was looking at her mouth. She was suddenly acutely aware of the moist feel of the lip gloss she'd so studiously applied.

He answered, "For the next few days—and the purposes of this absurd conversation—you *are* my wife."

Something curled and tightened in her midsection. To have him claim her as his, however temporarily, excited her. "I am?"

He didn't hesitate. "You are."

She closed the lid of her vanity case. "Whatever. It

still doesn't seen right, not when I promised Louise I wouldn't tell.'' She stood up, grabbed the handle of the case and started to move toward the bathroom.

He reached out. ''Don't go. Not yet.''

She froze. Lord, his touch was magic. Her whole body felt warm, when all he touched was her wrist. ''Why not?''

He seemed, temporarily, to have no answer to give. She swallowed, looking at his lips, thinking of the way they felt when they covered her own.

He found his voice again, a husky voice. ''Tell me. Come on.'' He loosened his hold on her wrist and began lightly stroking the back of her hand.

She drew in a shaky, longing breath that had nothing to do with the silly banter over the sea chest and everything to do with the way he kept touching her hand, so lightly and so thoroughly. ''Oh, all right. Try not to be too shocked.''

''I can take it.''

''Louise had to rescue it, can you believe it? And from her own mother, too.''

''It's appalling.'' He pretended to look stunned, but at the same time his stroking hand had moved up her arm, and was rubbing the kitten-soft sleeve of her white cashmere sweater, creating little crackles of static electricity. ''I never knew.''

''Yes. It's impossible, but true. Great-Aunt Blanche was actually going to sell that trunk.''

''I have no words to express my shock.'' His voice was hushed as his hand traveled upward, stroking cashmere, until he clasped her shoulder.

Eve could no longer pretend she was going to turn and put her vanity case in the bathroom. She deposited it back on the bureau instead.

Then she laid her hand on his chest, right over his heart. It was beating deep and fast. "You must promise never to reveal this horrible truth to a single soul."

He captured her hand. His fingers felt so warm, so right around hers. "I promise."

She dared to suggest in a breathless whisper, "Shall we kiss on it?"

He froze. She knew he was thinking that if he kissed her now, he couldn't tell himself it was for anyone's benefit but his own. They were alone in their room. The door to the hall was shut.

He muttered low and intensely, "What do you think you're doing?"

There was no retreating now. And maybe it was just as well. She tossed the challenge right back at him. "What are *you* doing, following me up here, closing the door? Playing this game when there's no one to see?"

He answered, looking both incredibly sexy and completely bewildered, "I don't know...."

She was bolder. "I do."

"What?" His voice was a growl. "What do you know?"

"That you like it. You like playing this game. You don't want to stop, even when we're alone."

"Is that so?" He had both her shoulders now, and he pulled her up against his chest. She went, sighing, utterly willing and not caring if he knew it.

"It's all right." She looked up at him, pleading with her eyes. "I feel the same. I don't want you to stop. Not ever."

"You don't?"

"No, I don't. Because I..." She drew in a breath. "I love you, Jordan."

His lips thinned. "Shut up, Eve."

She went on, shameless, past pretending, "I love you. That hasn't changed. I think you know that."

"I said, shut up."

"We can work out our problems. If you'll only give us a—"

He shut her up himself then, using the most expedient method available. He brought his mouth down on hers.

The world stopped on its axis, then went on spinning once more.

Reckless, triumphant, Eve pressed herself against him, sliding her arms up to encircle his neck and sighing in fervent submission. Oh, how long had it been—days and days, a lifetime?—since the last time his mouth took hers in this absolutely devouring, carnal way?

She had missed him so.

And she was absolutely determined to make up for all the kisses they hadn't shared since that night at his beach house when he sent her away. She clutched his big shoulders and tipped her head back, so he could have all of her mouth, so her body would curve up and into his.

He groaned, deep in his throat, and his hands moved down her back to cup her soft bottom, to aid her in her fevered attempt to meld their two separate bodies into one. His mouth tormented hers, and she revelled in that torment, sparring eagerly with his questing tongue, transported at the taste of him once more.

At last...

"This is crazy," he muttered, as he kissed a hungry trail down her throat, to the V neck of her fluffy sweater.

"Yes, crazy," she heard herself sighing. "Completely insane." She held his head at the swell of her breasts and she felt his lips there, his warm breath against her skin.

"I shouldn't be doing this...."

She held him tighter. "Yes, yes, you should."

But he lifted his head. She gave a little cry of protest. And then his arms were clasping her waist, and he was walking her to the bed they'd shared so chastely only the night before. He guided her down onto it.

It was utterly brazen of her, how eagerly she went, stretching out on her back, reaching out her slender arms, longing for him.

He came down to her, very close, his body a hard brand all along the side of hers. Lazily he propped himself up on an elbow and looked at her through heavy-lidded eyes.

"This is exactly what I *wasn't* going to do...."

"But it's what you want to do."

"Damn you, honey. Ever since you dumped me, you do nothing but argue with everything I say."

He'd called her honey when no one but the two of them could hear! Her heart soared. She answered pertly, "You don't want some meek little yes-person, anyway."

"I don't?"

"Absolutely not—and I didn't dump you."

"Right. And the sun comes up in the west."

"Please, let's not argue. Let's keep kissing instead."

"And besides arguing all the time, you're also damned...outrageous, lately."

"Let's stop talking altogether. Let's kiss some more."

"We have to go down soon."

She sighed. "Soon. But not right this second."

He shook his head. But he didn't try to get up.

She could see the traces of her lip gloss on his mouth, a colorless shine that excited her all the more as she remembered how he'd watched her apply it, as she thought that now he had kissed it away.

She reached up to touch him. He blinked, somewhat wary. "What?"

"Nothing. My lip gloss." Slowly, tenderly, she rubbed her fingers over his lips, wiping them clean of the moist, shiny stuff. Lightly, when she would have withdrawn, he kissed those fingers, and went on kissing them, nibbling them, looking into her eyes.

Her slim skirt had hitched up above her knees. He put his hand on one. She felt the warmth of that clasp, the strength, through the thin barrier of her panty hose. She gasped a little, and he went on kissing her fingers as his hand smoothly slid up her thigh and back down. Slowly, he stroked her, one thigh and then the other, long, slow caresses that made her aware of the building heat at her feminine heart. Then his hand was gently smoothing her skirt down and after that, trailing up, over her hips to her waist, across the fluffy softness of her sweater to her breasts.

Gently he cupped them, molding them. And she lifted herself toward his pleasuring touch, writhing a little, softly moaning. Her arm was suddenly too luxuriously weak to support her hand, which fell away from his caressing mouth.

And that was just fine, because his mouth was then free to come down on hers. He kissed her again, a long, drugging kiss. His hand found its way beneath her sweater and bra to her bare skin. He gently worked the bra and sweater up, out of his way, until she was bare for him. He lowered his head, his mouth closed on her breast, kissing, nuzzling, making her crazy with longing....

And then, with a low groan, he pulled back. She gazed up at him, too dazed with pleasure to understand.

His face was flushed, his eyes burned. She could feel his arousal, hard and ready, against her hip. And then he swore forcefully, and pushed himself off the bed.

Seven

"Jordan, please! Don't turn away...."

Jordan could hear the lost confusion in her voice, a confusion that echoed his own. He froze, though he knew he should do exactly what she begged him *not* to do: he should turn away, not look at her—deny her wounded sea-green eyes, the entrancing blush of color across her cheekbones, the tangled glory of her hair, the full, pale breasts, revealed to him because he'd bared them, not thinking and not caring where exactly they were going with this.

She kept looking at him, desire and entreaty in her eyes. "Jordan, I..."

Inside his slacks, he ached with the need for her. He was ten kinds of idiot, to tease himself—and her—the way he just had.

He thought of the two of them last night, sharing the bed without sharing their bodies. And he knew with absolute certainty that tonight he would either have to sleep on the rug or make love with her. And right now, looking at her, there was no doubt which it would be.

He'd been a fool to think he could forget her. He knew that now. And he also saw that he'd brought her here to play at being his bride for more than just his grandmother's sake.

He drew in one long, slow breath and then let it out. She continued to stare up at him as if mesmerized— slightly wounded, stunned by his sudden withdrawal.

He made himself speak gently, though what he longed to do was much more primitive. "I went farther than I should have. We have to get ready and go downstairs. Dora will be expecting everyone at the table soon."

She nodded, like someone coming out of a daze. "Oh. Yes. Of course. I didn't think…"

Cautiously, so as not to startle her any more than she already had been, he reached out a hand. Trusting as a child, she took it. He pulled her up. Then, with slow care, he helped her adjust her bra, pull down her sweater and smooth out her clothes.

"Thank you," she said in a small voice. Then she just stood there.

He wanted nothing so much as to reach for her all over again, to fall with her across the now-rumpled bed. And to finish what they'd started.

"Look." His voice was harsher than he meant it to be. "I'll be right back."

She nodded. "All right. Of course." He could feel her staring after him, as he closed the bathroom door between them.

He went directly to the sink and splashed cold water

on his face, avoiding his eyes in the mirror. He combed his hair and straightened his clothes.

All that accomplished, he went back to the bedroom where Eve now sat at the little mirrored dresser, combing the tangles from her hair. He watched her, longing to take the brush from her and comb the silken strands himself, to run his fingers through them, feel them stroke his skin....

He made himself look away. "Look. I'll go on down, okay?"

She finished brushing. "Wait. I'll come, too." She quickly got out that tube of lip gloss and reapplied what their kisses had erased.

She smiled at him in the mirror. "All ready." She stood up, snapped the case closed and carried it back to the bathroom.

When she returned, she held out her hand. "Let's go."

He took her hand. They went down the back stairs together.

"Okay, Jordan," Cousin Louise announced. "It's your turn."

The big feast was over. It was past nine at night, and the smaller children were in bed. The older members of the family were packed into Dora's big living room, overflowing into the foyer and halfway into the sunroom as well. They were taking turns swapping family stories.

Jordan, lounging against a wall near Alma's easy chair with one arm wrapped around Eve, looked up. "My turn for what?"

"To tell all."

"All of what?"

"All about you and Eve. Since none of us got to be

there, we want the whole story. Top to bottom. Start to finish. Every last intimate detail—of how you met and married your beautiful bride.''

Eve felt Jordan stiffen, but when he replied, his tone was light and unconcerned. ''There's too much to tell. I wouldn't know where to start.''

Louise was not to be put off. ''Fine. Then just give us the best part. Tell us about your wedding in Tahoe.''

''Well, I...'' He seemed to run out of words.

Everyone was watching him expectantly, probably thinking that, like many men, he was reluctant to describe such a significant and sentimental event. Only he and Eve knew that his reluctance actually stemmed from an unwillingness to invent an involved lie about a wedding that had never taken place.

From her chair, the usually quiet Alma spoke up, ''Perhaps some other time...''

Eve glanced at the old woman and saw the anxious expression that fleetingly crossed her worn, kind face. Eve wondered, then, if Alma might suspect the truth about Jordan and his ''bride.''

No. It couldn't be. Eve quickly rejected such a sobering notion. If Alma knew the truth, there was absolutely no reason she wouldn't have said something by now.

Louise, as usual, refused to be quelled. ''Come on, Jordan. Just a few of the spicier details...''

''Oh, give it up, Louise.'' The suggestion came from Blanche, who was standing well behind her daughter, near the door to the study.

Louise turned to her mother. ''No. I want to hear about it.''

''I'm sure you do, dear. But that doesn't mean Jordan has to tell you.''

Louise sniffed. "Thank you for your input, Mother. But it wouldn't hurt you to consider that there are still a few of us left in this family who care about precious moments—not to mention precious things."

"Oh, for heaven's sake." Blanche cast an exasperated glance heavenward. "Are you still holding all that old junk against me?"

"Junk?" Louise was a portrait of affronted pride. The rest of the family exchanged uneasy glances. Reunions did have their drawbacks; they presented the ideal opportunity for family members in conflict to air their grievances. "Junk?" Louise repeated, as if she hadn't said it clearly enough the first time. "You call Grandma Mary's silver, junk? I don't believe you, Mother. I honestly do not believe—"

Blanche only shook her head, refusing to be quelled by her overbearing youngest child. "What are you griping about? You got it all, didn't you? So enjoy it, and quit complaining."

"Well!" Louise huffed. "I never—"

Kevin, beside Louise, patted her hand and quietly suggested that maybe she ought to take this subject up with her mother some other time.

"Oh, all right. Fine," Louise grudgingly conceded. She pasted on a noble, too-bright smile—and turned it on Jordan again. "But I still want to hear about the wedding, Jordan. Really. I insist."

All around the room, the family members stirred in their seats. Eve knew what a lot of them were thinking—that since Louise was so relentless, things would go much more smoothly if Jordan would only give in.

For an uncomfortable moment, no one spoke. Then Nancy, by the fireplace, gently suggested, "Yes, Jordan. Please tell us."

Great-Aunt Camilla, on the couch, put in, "Yes. It must have been terribly romantic, like eloping. We'd all like to hear…"

And then came the chorus of voices, old and young, male and female, all urging Jordan to tell the tale of his marriage to Eve.

Eve could feel the tension in him and understood his resistance. The lie they were living was one thing. But to have to embellish it for everyone would be worse. He balked at the prospect of doing it, though he must know that if they wanted to maintain their pose, it was probably unavoidable now.

Eve knew what had to be done. She looked up at him adoringly and gave him her most devoted, indulgent smile. "Let me tell it, darling."

Around the room, there was a murmur of assent—not to mention relief.

"Yes, of course. Eve will tell it.…"

"Tell us, Eve.…"

"We can't wait to hear…"

She felt his big body relax. He returned her smile and squeezed her shoulder gently. "Yeah. All right. You tell them, honey. Tell them all about it."

Jordan swung the door of their bedroom closed and leaned against it, not even bothering to flip on the light. He faced her in the moonlight that glimmered in the window through the branches of the chestnut tree. "So I was so emotional, I could hardly manage to say *I do*, huh?"

"Actually, I thought that was a very nice touch." Eve removed her earrings and set them on the mirrored dresser. "All the women loved it."

"I am not the kind of man to get emotional over two simple words."

"Right. That's why it was so moving that you did."

"Wait a minute, here. We're alone now. Let's keep fact and fiction separate."

Eve dropped to the little chair at the dresser. "Okay, let's." She grinned pertly up at him. "Did I do a terrific job of describing a wedding that never happened, or what?"

"You did." He was quiet for a moment, watching her. "And thank you."

"You're welcome."

Eve smiled to herself, basking in his appreciation and feeling pretty satisfied with the way it had gone. In fact, looking back on it, it seemed to Eve that she had woven the tale so effectively that now she almost felt as if it really had occurred.

She'd let her imagination take the lead, and been surprised herself at how believable it had all sounded. She'd invented a mix-up of their suitcases at the airport, given the "minister" at their wedding chapel a plump, sighing wife in a lavender dress, and even explained how Wesley had mistaken the sunken tub in their hotel suite for a swimming pool. Once she really got going, Jordan had joined right in with her, adding more details to the story, laughing with her and the others, as if it all really were true....

By the door, Jordan was still watching her. He spoke softly, "You were incredible tonight. My beautiful, incomparable counterfeit bride."

For some reason, when he said that, she found she wanted to cry. She felt her smile turning tremulous. So she stood up. "Well." Her voice sounded brittle, falsely bright. "I'll use the bathroom first, okay?"

He looked away, like a man who's seen something he shouldn't have and wants it clear that he intends to pretend he saw nothing. "No problem. Go ahead." He crossed to his suitcase which lay open on a low dresser near the bed.

Eve went quickly into the bathroom and closed the door between them. Once alone, she turned on the light. The room bounced into brightness, garish and blinding after the soft dimness of the other room.

Swiftly, blinking against the glare, she slipped out of her clothes, put on the high-necked flannel gown that hung on the back of the door, and efficiently cleaned her face and brushed her teeth. She was careful *not* to think. Because she had no idea what was going to happen between them tonight in the double bed beyond the door.

If those searing moments they'd shared this afternoon meant anything, they'd be lovers again come morning. But before they made love again, she hoped for a better understanding between them. They still had yet to really talk.

She fervently hoped that when she went back out to him, they could sit down together and clear up their misunderstandings. That they could agree to work together, to make a life together—in time. And that he would share with her something of his own doubts and fears.

Eve's hand trembled a little when she reached for the door handle.

"Jordan?" Behind her, the bathroom light streamed into the moonlit bedroom.

"Yeah?" Jordan turned at the sound of her voice. He'd taken off his sweater. His bare chest, lightly dusted with gold hair, seemed to glow in the dimness.

"Your turn."

"Thanks." He came toward her. His steps were silent. She glanced down and saw that he'd already taken off his shoes and socks. Then he was closing the bathroom door, cutting off the bright light and casting the room into darkness once more.

Eve stared at the gleaming rim of light around the door, feeling strange—disappointed, and yet anticipating what would happen when he emerged again. Then she bestirred herself and bustled around for a few moments hanging up her clothes, which she'd carried with her from the bathroom.

After that, not knowing what else to do, she went and sat on the end of the bed, folding her hands in her lap and looking out at the full moon beyond the window. It seemed to peek at her through the chestnut tree as it hovered, soon to drop, on the rim of the nearby mountains.

After forever—and way before she was ready—he came out again. He was still wearing his slacks. She wondered if he was as nervous about what to do next as she was. He paused in the floodlit doorway. And then he turned off the light.

They existed in moonlight once more. Her eyes, again, had to adjust. Thus she felt, more than saw, his approach.

He came across the floor and stood before her. She watched him take form as her eyes grew accustomed to the limited light. She looked up at him, longing and hesitant.

"What now, Eve?"

She hitched in a breath. "Oh, Jordan, I..."

"You what?"

"I...guess I hoped we might talk."

"About what?"

"Well..."

"Yeah?"

"I hoped we could...talk about you and me. About us. Okay?"

He didn't say anything. And she found herself tongue-tied, waiting for an acknowledgment from him that he was willing to talk before she said more.

She wished she could think of something dazzling and insightful to say. But all of her wit, so sparkling downstairs as she invented the wedding that never happened, seemed to have deserted her now, when she needed it most.

She gazed up at him, half-dreading that he'd repeat what he'd told her that night when they agreed on this crazy deception: *There is* no *us.*

But apparently, he'd given up that lie at least. Because when he spoke, his voice was gentle. "All right. What about us?"

She knew massive relief, but still had no idea what to say. She stammered, "Well, I...I guess, I'm hoping that maybe you've changed your mind. That we can try again to make it work."

He seemed to be studying her. "What does that mean, 'try again'?"

"Well, it means stay together, keep working on it...."

He made a low, disgusted sound in his throat. "That's vague as hell. And I'm not sure I'm up to trying anything, anyway. Ever try to walk across the room?"

"Well, I..."

"My point is, you either do a thing or you don't. *Trying's* one of those excuses people give you when they don't really want to commit themselves."

Eve looked down at her clasped hands and knew he

was right. If she wanted Jordan McSwain, she was going to have to go after him—without reservation. *She* was going to have to take the chance, agree to stop hedging her bets and go all the way with him. Commit her heart and her life to him; tell him she wanted to be his wife.

She thought of Teddy Tanner, of the way he'd swept into her life and then breezed out again, leaving her responsible for two innocent children. Was there any chance that Jordan would do the same thing to her—and to Wesley and Lisa?

No. Over the last two days she'd learned that much about him at least. Whatever secrets he still held in his heart, she knew he was a man who stood by his commitments. She had only to witness him with Alma to see that. If she agreed to marry him—*and* if he would have her now—he would always be there, at least physically, for her and her children.

And that had to be enough for now, she understood. Those nebulous things she longed for—his absolute trust, the tender knowledge of his deepest fears—she would have to earn over the coming years, as they faced the challenges of life and surmounted them together.

"Well?"

She realized she'd been silent too long. She looked up into his shadowed face once more. "I..."

"Come on, Eve. Say what you want to say."

She straightened her shoulders. "You're right." Her voice was firm.

"About what?"

"About trying. It's not enough."

"So what does that mean?"

"Well, it means—"

"Yeah?"

She looked right into his eyes. "It means I want to marry you, Jordan. *Really* marry you. Right now—or whenever you say."

Eight

Jordan looked down at her, at her lovely shadowed face and her hopeful expression. He felt a hot surge of triumph; she'd agreed to marry him—now, as soon as he wanted.

But then the triumph faded. She'd said that before, and then she'd backed out. The pain had been bad.

He had to remember the pain.

"Jordan?" Her voice showed her anxiousness.

He felt angry, suddenly—at her, at the whole damn situation. "You said you'd marry me once before. And then you changed your mind."

She put out her soft hands to him, pleading. "I was afraid."

"And you're not afraid now?"

"Well, yes. I am. But I won't change my mind. This time you didn't steamroll me. I've had time to think, and this is my own decision."

He found it difficult to look at her. Because when he looked at her, he only wanted to put his hands on her. To gather up the hem of that so-proper nightgown and lift it up, over her slender legs, the sweet flare of her hips...

He turned away and stared blindly out at the shadow of the chestnut tree over the fat, complacent moon.

"Jordan. Please talk to me."

Having collected himself somewhat, he faced her again. "Not right now. Let's give it a rest for the night."

She was standing up now and she put out her hands again. "But I was hoping we could—"

"Listen." He forced a reasonable tone. "A hell of a lot has happened in the past two days. Let's get through this weekend. Then we'll see, okay?"

She stared at him. He could see the damn tears she was holding back, making her eyes glitter like wet jewels. She dropped her hands. "And then we'll see what?"

He shook his head. "Let's just wait. You think about this. Be sure."

"I *am* sure."

"Fine. Then it won't hurt to wait."

She was quiet. And then she gave in. "All right," she said softly. "We'll settle all of this, for good. As soon as we get home on Sunday."

"Fine." He looked at her, and saw the waiting bed behind her. There was no damn way he could lie beside her tonight without doing what his body kept demanding he do. And he knew if he made love with her, he'd have to admit his total powerlessness when it came to her. He'd be begging her to marry him before the night was through.

Since she had betrayed him once, something in him held out against such total capitulation.

"Look," he went on then, "I'm going back downstairs for a while." He found some socks and his shoes, then went to his suitcase again and put his sweater back on.

She watched him, her big eyes sad and baffled. She didn't rouse herself until he was striding to the door. "Jordan, I—"

"Don't wait up, okay?" He was gone before she could say anything more.

"Mommy! Mommy, can we come in?"

Eve groaned and opened her eyes. Her back ached dully and her neck was stiff. She looked at the smooth, still-made bed a few feet away.

"Mommy!"

Eve sat up in the rocking chair where she'd fallen asleep waiting for Jordan. She rubbed the back of her neck as her mind slowly registered that one, it was morning; two, Jordan had never returned to their room last night; and three...

"Mommy!"

"Mommy!"

Her children were pounding on the door.

She stood up, feeling much older than her twenty-seven years, and slowly hobbled across the room. "What is going on here?" She asked the question as she pulled the door open.

Two pairs of wide eyes looked up at her.

"Mommy, you were sleeping forever," Wesley said.

"Mommy!" Lisa held out her arms to be lifted up.

Eve scooped up the warm bundle that was her daughter and kissed her soundly on the cheek. Next, she bent and gave Wesley a hug, one he pretended merely to tolerate. Then she moved back into the room, carrying Lisa, herding her son.

She pointed out the obvious. "You two are already dressed."

"I could dress myself," Wesley informed his mother. "You know that."

"I know. And you did a great job, too." She noted that he must have chosen his own outfit, since his socks were red, his sweater yellow and his parachute pants purple and green. Usually they chose his clothing together before bed, which saved morning conflicts. But last night he'd fallen asleep on a chair and been carried up to bed; she'd forgotten all about his wardrobe. His blinding attire this morning was the result. "Very…eye-catching."

"Yeah. I know." His smile was modesty personified. "Auntie Dora helped Lisa. Gramma Alma and Auntie Dora said to let you sleep."

Setting Lisa on the floor, Eve turned to squint at her little travel clock on the stand by the bed. Ye gods, it was nearly 11:00.

Wesley prattled on. "But you slept and slept. And Kendrick's mom taked him and baby Phyllis over to somebody's house. Me and Leese were the only kids left, and we got tired of you sleeping so long. So Auntie Dora said to stop driving her crazy and go wake you up. So we did." Wesley looked his mother up and down. "You look pretty wrinkled, Mom. And you better get dressed now. It's *practally* lunchtime."

"Practically."

"Yeah. That's what I said."

Eve's mind was on Jordan. "Um, sweetheart…have you seen Jordan this morning?"

Eve almost regretted her question. Her son got that

recalcitrant expression she'd seen much too often the last couple of days. But he did answer, grudgingly. "Yeah."

"Is he downstairs?"

"He was. He leaved."

"When?"

Suddenly, Wesley was wandering away, up to the head of the bed, where he fiddled with the things on the small stand there.

Eve put aside her worries about Jordan, about why he'd avoided their room all night and now appeared to have left the house without saying a word to her. Instead, she studied her son, who was finding her travel clock of great interest.

She asked softly, "Wes?" He didn't turn. It was as if he knew by her tone that she was going to say something he didn't want to hear. She said it anyway. "Do you have some…problem with Jordan?" He went on fiddling with the clock. "Wes. Please turn around and look at me."

Still holding the clock, he reluctantly did as he was told. "Huh?"

"I asked you a question. Please answer me."

"What question?"

"I asked if you had some kind of problem with Jordan."

"Problem?" It was the four-year-old equivalent of a stonewall.

Eve kept trying. "Yes. Problem. Is there something wrong between you and Jordan?"

Wesley's glance darted away, down to the clock that filled his small hands. "Uh-uh."

"Are you sure? You act as if you're mad at him."

The clock had a leather case that doubled as a stand.

Instead of answering his mother, Wesley began flipping the clock down and shutting the case, and then unfolding it once more.

Lisa, meanwhile, had trotted over to the rocking chair, climbed up on it, and was enthusiastically pitching back and forth. "Oo-wee! Fast, fast!" She punctuated her galloping rocking with gleeful giggles.

Eve marched to her daughter, stopped the chair from moving and commanded, "Slow down, or no more rocking. Understand?"

Lisa nodded. "Slow down. Okay." Quite decorously, she began rocking once more.

Eve turned back to her son, who was still flipping the travel clock open and shut. She went to him and took the clock from his hands. He looked up at her. "Mom…" The word was exasperation personified.

"Why don't you want to talk to me about Jordan?" She kept her voice kind and curious.

He shrugged. "I don't know."

Eve wanted to groan out loud. On this issue at least, getting through to her son was almost as hard as getting through to the man she was trying to talk to him about. She forced herself to persevere. "Well, since you don't know, then let me tell you that I've noticed that when Jordan tells you to do things, you make angry faces at him and sometimes even tell him no. Why do you do that?"

He looked at her as if she were speaking a foreign language, his face scrunched up and puzzled. "*Why*?"

"Wesley, we don't seem to be getting anywhere. Would you like it better if I had Jordan talk to you about this himself?"

He shrugged again. "He won't."

"He won't talk to you? Is that what you're saying?"

"I don't know. Can I see that clock some more? Please?"

Eve sighed. "No. You leave it alone now." She set it back on the bed stand, and decided to concede the field on the topic of Jordan and Wesley's relationship for now. "Look, sweetheart. I'm going to take a quick shower."

Eve wondered if she imagined the shadow of relief in her son's eyes before he asked, "Can we wait here for you? In your room?"

"If you'll keep an eye on your sister—and leave my clock alone."

"Okay, Mom." He nodded, his expression so sweet and guileless that she wanted to grab him and kiss him and whisper her fierce mother-love against the downy skin of his cheek. She wanted to swear to him that Jordan would not desert him as his father had done.

But, given the circumstances, how could a responsible mother make her child such a promise? Things were still up in the air between herself and Jordan. She couldn't honestly say she was positive they would work out their difficulties.

And, reconsidering, she had to admit that such a promise wasn't hers to make anyway; it was Jordan's.

Great-Uncle Niles was at his usual post in the kitchen, slicing leftover turkey for sandwiches, when Eve and the kids came downstairs. Alma and Dora sat at the big breakfast table in the adjoining sunroom. Lisa made a beeline for Alma. Eve stared after her son for a moment as he wandered over to where the dominoes had been set out semipermanently on a low table. He began arranging them into roads and buildings.

Eve realized that everyone seemed to be very quiet. Was there an anxious quality to the silence?

She gave a nervous little laugh. "Guess I overslept."

"Nonsense." Dora was suddenly all bustle. "It's impossible to oversleep when you're on your honeymoon. You sit right down here. Niles, pour this girl a hot cup of coffee."

Eve felt more apprehensive by the second. Dora was acting downright fluttery. "I can get it—"

"No, no." Dora patted the back of the chair she'd just pulled out. "You sit down. Niles has already got it." Dora took the cup from her husband. "Thanks, dear." Dora waited until Eve seated herself, and then set the full cup in front of her. "Now. What will it be? Breakfast or lunch?"

"Lunch will be fine. One of those sandwiches you're making, Uncle Niles, if that's okay."

"Coming right up."

Eve sipped her coffee as both Dora and Alma smiled at her affectionately—and a little bit uneasily, she thought. Smiling back at them, Eve became more and more certain they all knew that Jordan's bride had spent last night alone.

A blush of embarrassment colored her cheeks. She ordered it away. "Good coffee."

"Niles just made a new pot."

Eve looked around. "Wesley told me that half the household has taken off."

Dora launched into an explanation. "Yes, that's right. Denise—my second-to-youngest daughter—is doing a family genealogy, and she wanted Carla to have a look at it. And then Nancy decided to go along for the visit and took Kendrick and Phyllis with her."

"And Matt and Jordan?" Eve tried to keep her voice

light—and to ignore the swift glance that shot between Alma and Dora.

Great-Uncle Niles answered, "It's a big day for college football. And Reggie, Jr., Blanche's oldest, has a giant-screen T.V."

"Oh." Eve forced an airy laugh. "Football. I should have known."

"Jordan told me to be sure to let you know he'd be back by four or so," Alma said.

"He did?" Eve knew her voice sounded ridiculously hopeful.

"Yes." Alma, who was at some pains to keep the squirming Lisa from falling off her lap, managed to give Eve an encouraging smile.

Eve made herself smile back. Whatever was going on with Jordan couldn't be *that* bad, could it? At least he'd thought to leave a message for her. But then she realized the message was probably just a part of the act, for the family's sake.

Great-Uncle Niles set a fat sandwich before her. "It is white meat you like best, right?"

Eve made herself smile. "Yes. Thanks. This looks great."

Louise stopped by around one.

"Hello, everyone. I'm just here to say hi. Can't stay but a minute. I've got to get home and get going on the chicken divan for tonight. And naturally, the kids have a mountain of clothes that need washing. I hear the guys are all over at Reggie's. Kevin's there, too. He'll show up around six and want to know where dinner is. That's what it all comes down to in the end. Laundry and football and chicken divan… You're very quiet, Eve. Is everything okay?"

"Yes, just fine."

"Oh. I get it. You're mooning around because Jordan's off with the guys."

"I'm not mooning, Louise."

"Now, now. No need to get snappish.... Everything is all right between you two, isn't it? Do I detect signs that the newlyweds are having a spat?"

"Of course not."

Louise waggled a finger and spoke in a cheerful singsong, "You sound defensive...."

They were sitting at the breakfast table. Eve wondered what dear Louise would do if she leaped across it and choked her until she shut up.

But then Dora, who was playing dominoes with Wesley, suggested levelly, "Louise, you really mustn't be so jealous of Jordan and Eve's happiness. It doesn't become you at all."

Louise's face turned red. "Jealous? I am not jealous...."

Dora smiled. "Well, good. I'm glad to hear it."

From the kitchen, Niles asked, "Louise, are you the one who puts chestnuts in your chicken divan?"

Louise sighed and looked martyred. "No. That's Mother. I swear, she's always adding something to a recipe that's perfectly good on its own. But then, you know how Mother is...." And she was off and babbling on her second-favorite subject next to how little her husband appreciated her now they'd been married for twenty years.

Eve smiled and nodded, and wished she could jump up and hug Niles and Dora, who had come to her aid without hesitation when nosy Louise got too close to the truth.

Louise left at a little after three, just as Nancy, Carla,

Kendrick and baby Phyllis returned. Carla then announced she'd like to take Kendrick and Wesley to a place called Fun Circus, a sort of glorified pizza parlor that provided all kinds of games and entertainment.

Eve, fighting a growing despondency, decided to go along and take Lisa. And then Nancy said she'd come too, and bring Phyllis. They all climbed into Dora's station wagon and headed for the other side of town.

Fun Circus was loud and crowded, which was just fine with Eve. All the noise and confusion kept her from obsessing on Jordan and what he might be doing now. She had her hands full watching Lisa and keeping track of Wesley.

Around five, Nancy suggested that perhaps it would be best to go ahead and feed the kids before heading back. Eve, resolutely not thinking of Jordan and whether or not he might be at Dora's by now, agreed it was a wise idea.

It was near eight before they returned to the house on Autumn Lane. Both Nancy and Eve headed straight up the stairs with the four drowsy children in tow. Eve tucked Wesley and Lisa into bed, kissed them, and stood for a moment in the doorway after she'd turned out the light. She smiled. They were both already asleep.

She backed from the room, carefully pulling the door closed—and ran into Jordan.

"Whoa." He chuckled softly in her ear. The sound warmed her right down to her toes. He caught her against him, and she felt him all along her body, big and solid and strong.

But then she remembered how unhappy she was with him. She whirled and pushed him away. "Shh. They're asleep."

"Sorry." At least he had the grace to look abashed. "I came up to say good-night to them."

"Well, you're too late."

"I can see that. You're angry."

"Angry? Why in the world should I be angry?" She looked him up and down. He seemed relaxed and in a good humor. To see him now, you'd think last night had never happened. "Did you have a nice afternoon?" The question dripped sarcasm.

He grinned. "Nothing like a day with the guys. A few beers, a good game or two on the tube, and a man feels he can face anything—even a hostile wife...." His eyes teased.

She hissed at him, "Oh, stop it. There's nobody here right now but the two of us, so you can drop the act."

Right then Kendrick came out of the big main bathroom. He plodded past them, not even looking their way, going to his trundle bed in the den off the small hall where they stood. "Let's go to our room." Eve slid around him. She didn't look back to see if he followed. As far as she was concerned, he'd better follow.

Apparently he realized there was no escaping her now. He slipped into the room behind her, flicked on the light and pushed the door closed.

She faced him. "You took off today without even telling me you were leaving."

"I left a message with Alma."

"For Alma's sake, not for mine."

"Oh, come on, Eve." He folded his arms across his chest. "If you were so eager to see me, why weren't you here when I got back?"

"Sooner or later, even a *bride* gets fed up with waiting around."

He looked away, then into her eyes again. "Okay,

then," he reasoned, "I left without letting you know, and you were gone when I came back. We're even."

She threw up her hands. "Oh. Right. Even."

"What does that mean? You don't think we're even?"

"What about the little matter of where you slept last night?"

"What about it? I stretched out on the couch in the living room, and I guess I must have dropped off."

"You expect me to believe that?"

"Believe it or not, that's what happened."

"You're saying you fully intended to come back here?"

"I'm saying that I fell asleep on the couch and didn't wake up until morning."

She wanted to grab him and shake him. But she knew it was unlikely to do any good. She went on to the next issue. "I've been getting sympathetic looks all day. Do Alma and Dora know you slept on the couch?"

He shrugged. "I woke up at a little past seven to find Great-Uncle Niles standing over me, looking anxious and holding out a cup of coffee, so I'd venture to say that, yes, they know."

She glared at him. "For a man who went to a world of trouble to make his family think he's a blissful new-lywed, you seem awfully unconcerned about everyone finding out you spent the night on the couch."

He thought about that for a moment, then said, rationalizing, "Newlyweds sometimes quarrel. I don't think it has to be any big deal."

"Oh, you don't, do you?"

"Settle down, honey."

His use of the endearment made her want to scream. "Look. We're alone now. Don't call me 'honey.' I don't want you to use that term in private until we've worked this whole mess out.''

An infuriating smile played around the corners of his mouth. ''Okay, honey.''

She glared at him some more, feeling powerless to really get through to him. While she was glaring, she noticed for the first time that he was wearing different clothes than the ones he'd left their room in the night before. And that, strangely, made her angrier than ever.

She pointed toward his slacks and chocolate brown sweater. ''You changed clothes,'' she accused.

''Is there some law against that?''

''Of course not. But I'd like to know, did you sneak in here while I was sleeping and shower and shave? Did you?''

''No. I came up when I got home from Reggie's. Why? Does it matter?''

She said nothing for a moment. Then she sank onto the bed, realizing her hostility was getting her nowhere, and finding that she now felt foolish and deflated. ''No. I guess it doesn't. I guess it doesn't matter in the least.'' Eve looked down at her hands and then back up at him. ''Can we stop this…bickering, please?''

Her dejection seemed to reach him where her belligerence hadn't. His gaze was level, if somewhat wary. ''Fine.''

''Can we talk honestly?''

''Fair enough.''

''Will you please tell me why you didn't come back last night?''

He spoke evenly. ''Because I needed time to think. Alone.''

''About what?''

''About whether or not we should just call off this

whole crazy mess, tell everyone the truth and be through with it.''

''And?''

He rubbed his eyes, looking suddenly tired. ''And then I thought of my grandmother, holding Lisa on her lap yesterday and singing a song she used to sing to me years ago. And I knew I'd go through with this no matter what. We've made that woman happy, Eve. I just want to let her have that, okay?''

She swallowed. ''But if we're going to get married anyway…''

He glanced away. ''Look. Just leave it alone, okay? We agreed. No deep, meaningful talks until after this…charade is through.''

''But—''

''Let it go.'' His voice was flat.

She wanted to strangle him—for cutting her out, for closing off his heart and mind to her. He'd gone off by himself and armed himself emotionally against her. Now he was back, all charm and male grace, and she was bound by the agreement they'd made to just pretend for two more days—and nights, heaven help her—that everything was fine.

''Come on,'' he coaxed. ''Let's go back downstairs. Great-Uncle Niles is trying to get a canasta game together.'' He held out his hand.

She took it, feeling his fingers close around hers and reminding herself that they had come a long way, really. She was through hesitating; if he'd give her the chance, she was ready to bind her life to his right this moment. And if he hadn't actually said he would give her the chance, at least he was no longer insisting they were through.

Things could be worse.

He pulled on her hand, urging her to go with him. She went, focusing on the positive, determined to ignore the growing anxiety in her heart.

Nine

They played canasta until midnight. And then they climbed the stairs together to share the double bed as they had the first night: side by side, but a thousand miles apart. For Eve, it was a mostly sleepless night.

In the morning, they were elaborately courteous and careful with each other when it came to taking turns at the bathroom for showers. Then, all through the day, Jordan was scrupulously tender and affectionate in front of his family.

He was also kind and reasonable when they were alone. But Eve could feel his emotional distance from her, like a cold draft in an otherwise sunlit room. Eve found herself grimly plodding through the hours, putting on a bright face, doing her best to hide the anxious, unsatisfied emotions that churned inside.

Louise dropped in around one as she had the day before and talked nonstop for an hour. Eve listened and tried to look relaxed and happy. She worried the whole time that Louise would ask her what was wrong. But Jordan was there, so it worked out well enough. He knew the threat his snoopy cousin posed to their deception. He hovered near Eve through Louise's entire visit, so adoring and attentive that Louise was green with envy by the time she left.

It was nearly dinnertime when Nancy unveiled her big surprise.

"Get dressed up, you two. Matt and I are taking you to Stateline tonight. It's our wedding present to you. A night on the town."

Eve, feeling guilty at the idea of accepting yet another undeserved wedding present, tried to demur. "Oh, Nancy. What a thoughtful idea. But Wesley and Lisa—"

Carla jumped right in. "I'm the baby-sitter, and Mother will help."

Dora nodded. "That's right."

"And I'll be here, too," Alma said. "So will Niles. I'm sure between us, we can handle four little ones until bedtime."

They were all in the sunroom, and Eve was sitting in one of the chairs by the windows with the local newspaper spread across her lap. Eve glanced from one to the other of them. They all looked determined.

She couldn't help but wonder if they'd cooked this up together, a family scheme to get the newlyweds out of the house for a little carefree time together. The idea that they might have done such a thing touched her. It showed that they accepted and approved of her, that they wanted to help in any little way they could to make the "marriage" succeed.

Eve felt a funny pressure in her throat as she realized

how easy it had been to come to care for them—and how hard it would be for her now, never to see them again. Somehow, in just a few short days of pretending they were her family, they'd *become* her family. Now, if things didn't work out between her and Jordan, she'd be doubly bereft. She'd lose him and she'd lose this family, who'd treated her with esteem and affection right from the first.

Eve realized they were all staring at her, waiting for her to agree. She swallowed the lump in her throat and looked at Jordan.

He shrugged. "Guess there's not much we can do, honey. They're going to force us to have a good time." His voice vibrated with warmth and humor. Was she the only one who saw the remoteness in his eyes?

"That's right." Nancy marched over, whipped the newspaper away and pulled Eve out of the chair. "Now get going and get glamorous. We leave in one hour."

In spite of everything, Eve felt anticipation growing as she got out the dress she'd never really thought she'd have a chance to wear this weekend: the black cocktail dress with the cutaway shoulders that Jordan had lavishly admired the last time she wore it.

The more she thought about going out, the more appeal the idea had. A night on the town wouldn't solve anything, of course. But at least it would be a diversion. They would no doubt return very late, which meant less time to lie together—yet so far apart—in the double bed.

Yes, Eve thought, a night out would be a welcome distraction. It wouldn't solve anything. But, except for Nancy and Matt, they would be among strangers. It would be a relief not to have to guard her every word for a change, not to have to be constantly wary that loving eyes might see too much.

Humming a little under her breath, Eve showered and put on the satin and lace underthings that went with the black dress. Then she pulled on her robe and sat at the mirrored dresser in the bedroom to do her makeup.

"Eve?" Jordan called to her from the other side of the door.

"It's open."

He came in and stood behind her in the mirror, somehow managing to make eye contact without really looking at her. "Are you finished in the bathroom?"

"Yes. Go ahead."

He went to the closet and pulled out a garment bag and dress shoes. Then he found underwear and socks in his suitcase and disappeared into the other room. Eve finished her makeup, brushed her hair and put on the diamond earrings that had once been her grandmother's. She was just trying to zip herself into the black dress when Jordan came out of the bathroom.

He stood there for a moment, looking at her. And she looked back at him, thinking her heart would break. He was so handsome, all dressed up in a loosely tailored evening jacket and satin-striped tux-style trousers.

There was something about Jordan when he got dressed up; he managed to look ready for the most formal event, and yet loose and casual at the same time. She knew there would be people in the casinos dressed in everything from jeans and cowboy boots to evening wear. And she knew that, whatever the attire, Jordan would fit right in. She'd always loved that about him, that though glamour and excitement seemed to emanate from him, his smile was a real smile, and his laughter deep and true.

Jordan, for his part, could hardly take his eyes off of Eve. The black dress clung to her curves, emphasizing the slimness of her waist and the tempting fullness of her breasts. Her lips were soft, her aquamarine eyes sparkling with expectation. She possessed a special allure, the allure of woman ready and willing to have a great time.

As he stared at her, it struck him anew how much he'd always loved to take her out. Of the thousand and one ways she had captivated him, perhaps the most enchanting was the way she approached a night out—as an adventure. She threw herself into it, enjoying everything—the sights, the sounds, the jostle of people around her. From their first date, the ferry ride to that restaurant on Catalina Island, he'd been bewitched by the way Eve Tanner had fun.

Jordan himself was famous as a good-time type of guy. But, over the years, with him hardly knowing when it happened, it had all begun to seem a little frantic and hard-edged, the laughter of the women he dated a little too brittle, the city lights at night garish rather than dazzling.

And then there was Eve. And it was all new again. Her laughter was real laughter, and the city lights dazzled again when he saw them reflected in her eyes.

"Jordan?" she asked, from across the room.

He cleared his throat, but still his voice was gruff. "I knew you'd wear that dress. You were supposed to wear it the night I had dinner for Mort and Melba Blecker. Remember?"

She nodded. She was thinking that the night in question hadn't been that long ago. She had sat at home that night, longing for a word from him, wishing she was at his side.

"How did it go with the Bleckers, anyway?" She made her tone light, because she knew that was how he wanted it.

"Fine. It went fine. A Chilly Lilly's franchise is just what they're looking for."

"Well, that's good to hear." It sounded just like what it was: an inanity. But what else could she do? Inanities were all she was allowed to share with him—until tomorrow.

Eve turned and flipped her hair over one shoulder, showing him her back. "Zip me up?" He didn't immediately answer. She glanced back at him. "Jordan?"

He seemed to shake himself. "Sorry. Sure." Slowly, he approached. She felt his thumb brush the bare skin above the strapless wisp of black lace she wore for a bra. He slid the zipper upward. "There."

She turned and smiled into his eyes. "Thanks."

"You're welcome." He was smiling back. "Ready?"

She nodded, feeling her anticipation rise higher still. Maybe without so much to be careful of, he would let down his guard.

"Your eyes are shining," he said.

She allowed herself a low laugh. "You know me. I love a night out."

The night glittered.

The stars shone thick over the Tahoe Rim, and the snow on rugged Mount Tallac sparkled beneath the moon. From her side of the back seat, Eve looked out the window and imagined that the whole of the Tahoe basin beckoned them on into the heart of the wintry darkness. The lake itself, glimpsed now and then through the trees on one side of the highway, shone blue-black beneath the stars.

When they arrived in South Shore, they found that millions of tiny white lights adorned all the businesses along Lake Tahoe Boulevard. "We string 'em up at Thanksgiving in honor of the holiday season," they were told when they asked if things were always lit up this way.

They ate really fine Italian food at a restaurant on Emerald Bay Road. Matt ordered two bottles of wine, and made toasts, one after the other.

"To marriage...to happiness...to a decent fixed-rate mortgage...to finding an orthodontist you can trust..."

Of course, they had to drink to every toast. By the time they got through the antipasto, the evening was glowing even more than it had previously.

Jordan, sitting to Eve's left at the square table, seemed to loosen up more and more as the excellent dinner progressed. Whether he realized it or not, he was letting down his guard, reveling in his role of doting bridegroom once again, going far beyond affection and attentiveness—which was just fine with Eve.

He took her hand and kissed it once, for no reason she could fathom. Not that she needed to fathom it. He could kiss her hand all he wanted. She loved it; she always had. His eyes gleamed at her over the rim of his glass every time Matt made a toast. More than once his leg brushed hers.

Nancy mentioned that she'd never seen two people more in love than Jordan and his bride, and then she and Matt clasped hands and looked at each other with knowing, sentimental smiles.

The wine loosened Nancy's tongue a little. "I don't mind saying, now I see you two are doing just fine, that we've all been a little worried since yesterday."

Jordan lifted an eyebrow at his third cousin's wife.

"Since I was discovered sleeping on the couch by Great-Uncle Niles, you mean?"

Nancy glanced apprehensively from Eve to Jordan. "Er, yes. That's what I mean."

Eve, the anxiousness that the lovely evening had banished rising again, looked at Jordan. In response, he gently snared her hand, turned it over and kissed her palm. His lips were marvelously tender, his breath warm across her skin.

Eve sighed, not caring that Nancy and Matt could hear the soft sound. She remembered he'd kissed her palm that night on the beach, when he had proposed—and she'd kissed his the night at her house, when she had made him take the ring she'd bought for him.

He looked up, into her eyes. "It wasn't anything, was it, honey? A minor argument that got out of hand."

For a moment, she felt a tightness in her chest. How could he say that, call her declaration of love and commitment a minor thing? But then she relaxed. What else could he say, and not tell more lies, or arouse more suspicion?

She gave him a tremulous smile. "We worked it out. That's what matters."

He leaned toward her. Their lips brushed gently above their clasped hands.

Matt and Nancy watched them indulgently for a moment, then Nancy proposed a toast of her own. "Eve and Jordan. May you never lose the magic you've found. And may you always work out your problems, together."

They raised their glasses. Eve memorized the moment, the soft radiance of candlelight, the dark shimmer of wine in a glass, the single velvety blood red rose rising from the crystal vase in the center of the table.

Best of all there was Jordan, smiling that smile she loved, looking at her with tenderness and desire in his eyes.

The dessert cart came by. Eve chose something sinfully chocolate. Jordan asked for a bite. She fed it to him on her silver fork.

After the meal, they went on to Stateline. They gambled at Harvey's and Caesar's, and caught the show at Harrah's South Shore Room. Eve gave herself up to the glitter and the glamour of the night and—wonder of wonders—Jordan seemed to be doing exactly the same.

When she hit the jackpot on the progressive slot machines, she clapped wildly and let a whoop up to the ceiling. Then she saw him a few feet away, watching. Their eyes met. And everything—the bright lights, the people, the clatter of her winnings as they tumbled from the machine, the loud clanging of the bell that told the whole casino someone had hit the jackpot—it all ceased to exist. There was only herself and Jordan, sharing a smile and an intimate glance across a crowded room.

Shortly after that, she moved on to lose most of what she'd won at blackjack. Each time the dealer raked in her chips, it seemed she saw Jordan, not far away, shaking his head in teasing sympathy. And as her pile of chips shrank, he even came to lean over her shoulder, to run a caressing hand along her neck and whisper tender encouragements in her ear.

The wine they'd shared at dinner had produced a rosy glow. Champagne, in the casinos and before the show, kept that glow from fading. Nancy and Matt urged the "newlyweds" to indulge themselves; this was their special night, neither was driving, they could let themselves go.

To Eve, as the hour grew late, it seemed that the

evening was a magical spinning top, turned gently at first by a giant hand and then picking up speed, until it was whirling, giving off sparks, a spinning dance of music and laughter and shimmering lights. She herself twirled at the center, with Jordan somehow always close by, leaning near during the show, rubbing her bare arm with his finger, or murmuring something low and sexy in her ear.

Outside, the night was cold and still, as if waiting. Once, when they left one casino and walked on to the next, Eve paused on the sidewalk, gathering her warm coat close about her and gazing up at the sky. Here, amid the bright lights, the stars were not the brilliant jewels they had seemed above the mountains during the drive from Malachite Junction. Here, the night sky took some of the light from the pleasure palaces that surrounded them, so that the sky itself seemed to glow. She remembered, though she saw no clouds, that the newspaper had promised new snow sometime tomorrow night.

"Hurry up, honey. Let's get back inside where it's warm." Jordan pulled her onward to the next grand, huge casino, where all was light and warmth, excitement and gaiety.

The longer the magic spun out, the less Eve wanted it to end. But even she began to wind down a little after midnight. By two, when she and Jordan finally climbed into the back seat behind Matt and Nancy, she realized she was ready to call it a night.

The effects of the champagne still lingered, making her feel relaxed and pleasantly drowsy. And when Jordan settled her head against his shoulder, she smiled at the scratchy feel of his heavy winter coat.

"Comfortable?"

"Um." She felt his lips, cool from the night air, on her forehead. His gloved hand smoothed her hair.

The next thing she knew, there was cold air across her legs, and a brisk breeze on her face. She lifted her heavy eyelids and saw Dora's friendly yellow house.

"Are we home?" Her own voice sounded so drowsy, so peaceful and content. And then she giggled, "Jordan!"

"Put your arms around my neck."

She didn't argue. He scooped her up, shut the car door with his foot and carried her up to the front steps. Matt and Nancy, chuckling about something between themselves, brought up the rear.

At the door there was a little mix-up; Jordan stepped aside and Nancy fumbled for the key. Eve stirred and told Jordan he could put her down.

"Why don't you just enjoy the ride?"

She giggled some more, feeling foolish and giddy, loving every minute of it. Then she rubbed her cheek against his shoulder. The arms that held her tightened, pulled her closer against his strength and warmth. She glanced up, catching her breath as she recognized the lambent flame in his eyes. His mouth curled in a slow smile.

And she knew what was going to happen the moment they were alone.

"Got it," Nancy said then. The door swung wide.

Jordan carried Eve over the threshold. There was a flurry of "thank-yous" and "good nights." And then Jordan was bearing her up the stairs to their room.

Logically, Nancy and Matt must have followed them up. But Eve couldn't have said if that was so. She'd forgotten the other couple completely. She'd forgotten everything, but the strength in Jordan's arms as he carried her, the beat of his heart that she swore she could hear even through their heavy coats, and the shattering moment at the threshold of the house, when he'd looked at her and she had seen that, at last, she would know the ecstasy of his touch once more.

Nothing's settled, nothing's solved, some faraway voice in the back of her mind kept chanting. Eve tuned out that voice. For what did it matter? If it all came down to nothing—Please, God, let that not be—at least she would have the memory of this last perfect night.

Jordan entered their room, pushing the door shut behind them with his foot, as he had done at the car. He carried her to the end of the bed and set her down. Her silly legs felt like rubber. She wobbled a little when her toes touched the floor.

He chuckled and steadied her, somehow getting behind her, so that his hands were on her shoulders and she was leaning back against his solid strength.

"Too much champagne?" he murmured in her ear.

She shook her head. In that moment at the threshold, any last lingering fuzziness had been utterly seared away.

"Good," he said softly, his lips against the side of her throat.

Eve moaned a little and let her head fall back, arching her neck for him, giving him the length of it, to kiss and fondle as he would. He laid a line of soft kisses up from the collar of her coat to her ear and he stroked where he kissed with his gloved hand. She shuddered a little and rubbed herself back against him, eager for more.

He would not be hurried. He parted her coat, slid it back off her shoulders and down her arms. She shivered when the coat was gone, though the room was comfortably warm.

He left her, taking the coat and hanging it with his in the closet, and shedding his gloves. She waited, feeling each of her heartbeats, the deep, needful throb of them, the hunger for what was to come.

He went to the side of the bed and flipped on the small lamp there. The lamp gave off a soft glow. His eyes were dark and deep as he looked beyond the bed to where she stood, waiting for a word, a sign, from him.

"Are you still on the Pill?"

"Yes." She allowed her mouth to curl into a pensive smile. "I'm an optimist. I also brought my black negligee, just in case."

She saw the answering quirk of his own mouth. "I remember that negligee. But I doubt we'll be needing it tonight."

"We won't?"

"No, we won't."

There was a soft, breath-held silence. In the muted glow of the lamp, he watched her. Then, slowly, as if she moved in a dream, she smoothed her hair aside and removed her diamond earrings. She turned, feeling his eyes on her back, and walked to the vanity bureau. There was a little china dish there. She dropped the earrings in it. They made a cheerful clinking sound, one that echoed in the waiting silence of the room.

She didn't move from there; she waited. And she heard him approach. And then he was standing behind her again, in his midnight-colored evening clothes, broader, stronger, taller than she was. She felt the bigness of him, the maleness. A heated shiver passed along her every nerve.

He ran his hands up her arms, a whisper of touch. Her skin burned in the wake of such a light yet consuming caress. His hands met on her shoulders, spanning her collarbone. She felt his thumbs on the top of her backbone, just above the zipper of her black dress.

Then his hands went their separate ways. One caressed her throat, kindling her senses and soothing her at the same time, while the other took her zipper and pulled it down.

"Oh…" It was her own voice, soft and aroused. The back of her dress was falling open. She felt the air on the tender skin between her shoulder blades.

He peeled the dress forward, so that it slipped over her shoulders and fell to her waist. She hitched in a breath. In the mirror, the skin of her belly, between her strapless bra and her half-slip, looked smooth and very vulnerable. She could see a little pulse beating there, at her solar plexus, like some tiny defenseless animal trapped inside her body and frantic to get out.

She felt apprehensive, suddenly, at the coming intimacy. She whispered his name. "Jordan?"

"Sh, honey. Don't worry. This is just you and me, just the two of us, together…."

"Oh, Jordan…"

"We're good together. We always were, right from that first night. Remember?" His eyes, steady now with tender reassurance, met hers in the mirror. She remembered. How could she ever forget? A night like their first night was something a woman held in her heart forever.

For Eve, that night had been a first in more than one way; it was their first time together and the first time for her since she'd had Lisa. She'd been nervous about doing this so-intimate thing with this incredible man.

She'd been nervous about her body as well, hoping it would please him, knowing it was not as smooth and flawless as it had once been.

But she'd discovered soon enough that her nervousness was wholly unnecessary. He slowly and ardently aroused her, touching her everywhere, his eyes burning with such blatant desire that she forgot her apprehensions and simply responded. It had been an unforgettable night, like all the other nights that followed.

Now, his eyes still holding hers, he touched that little frantic pulse at her solar plexus. She gasped. He clasped her waist for a moment, steadying her.

Then his hands moved higher. He cupped her breasts. She moaned. With his thumbs he rubbed the white fullness above the demicups of her bra, dipping in to tease her nipples, which ached and hardened at his touch, longing for more.

She thought, right then, with a purely feminine smile, that she could actually *feel* her inhibitions burning away, like morning dew on a rose evaporating to nothing with the bright kiss of the sun. She arched for him eagerly, making no pretense of modesty now, not caring that she looked naughty and wanton in the mirror. She forgot the mirror, closing her eyes and letting her head drop back against his chest.

"This is what I've wanted to do," he muttered in her ear, "all these damn nights since you ended it. To touch you again, to love you again..."

She moaned, her mind murmuring, *Yes, Jordan. Oh, yes,* but too overwhelmed by sensation to give the words sound.

One of his caressing hands slipped behind her and made short work of the clasp on her bra. It fell away. Though her eyes were closed, she knew her breasts were naked in the mirror for him and she found she was nothing but glad.

His hands cupped her fullness without the barrier of lace and he toyed with her, rolling her nipples gently, agonizingly, between his thumbs and forefingers, while she moaned and rubbed herself back against him, awash in a sea of desire.

He kissed her neck—soft, teasing kisses that drove her crazy with wanting to turn and get her mouth beneath his. But he held her firm.

His pleasuring hands slid along the curve of her waist to her dress and half-slip. He pulled them down, stretching and gathering, until they were at her ankles. Then he bent, scooped them up, and laid them across the dresser on top of her discarded bra.

She stood in her black silky panty hose and her satin evening shoes. He said, "Step out of the shoes." And she did, nudging them beneath the vanity chair with her toe. Then he peeled down the panty hose. She braced her hand on the dresser to lift each foot, so he could whisk the nylon away.

And then she had nothing, not the slightest bit of lace or satin, to protect her from his sight. He stood again, behind her, still fully clothed.

And he began to stroke her, from the flare of her hips, up the gentle curve of her waist and back down again. He called her beautiful. She believed him, seeing herself as he saw her, finding no flaw now in the depth and softness of her breasts, or the faint, silvery arrows of the stretch marks that gave evidence of the two children she'd borne.

He called her beautiful, and she knew she was, in her own special and individual way. The imperfections of her body were part of her beauty; they told who she was, a girl no longer, a grown woman who had twice let new life come through her.

Jordan caressed her, working his magic on her, igniting her senses as he always could, taking her higher with just a whisper of touch than she had ever thought it was possible to go.

He stroked her shoulders and cupped her breasts. Then his hand moved lower, to the womanly heart of her, and she thought she would die of the wondrous pleasure that he brought.

She let her head fall back against his chest, not even trying to get his mouth to take hers anymore as she felt his fingers entering her. She arched eagerly toward them. He muttered incitements and encouragements against the tangle of her hair.

How long he did those wonderful things with his fingers, she didn't know. All she knew was that, suddenly, she was soaring up and over, her whole body shimmering, glittering and then falling away in a shower of light and fulfillment back to earth, back to the world.

She went lax against him, spent—and yet somehow still aroused. His arms enfolded her, the black of his evening clothes shocking and wonderful against the pale vulnerability of her naked skin.

"If I could...lie down..." she managed to whisper.

He lifted her then, as he had when he carried her from the car, swinging her high against his chest and taking her to the bed where the soft lamplight made a slightly brighter glow. He laid her down.

Sighing, she lifted her arms above her head and stretched a little. He gazed at her, his eyes heavy with desire.

And then he was undressing, with a cool efficiency that belied the heat in his eyes. She watched as he pulled off his tie and tossed his jacket away. He removed his cuff links, then his shirt, his socks, his shoes, the black evening slacks, everything.

And he stood before her, naked as she. His big body was hard and muscular in the glow from the lamp. He was magnificent, the man she wanted, the man she loved.

He smiled. She smiled back, lifting her arms.

He came down to her, lay alongside her, and began all over again to stroke and arouse her. But this time, she gave touch for touch, hungrily, boldly, returning kiss for kiss.

His mouth came down on hers. She lifted toward it eagerly, moaning. Their tongues met and mated as his hand found her again. She was liquid and ready.

She reached to encircle him, found him fully aroused. She stroked him and he moved against her ardent hand. And then he was kissing a trail down her neck to her breasts, which he licked and suckled as she cradled his head and crooned heated encouragements, writhing in pleasure as he took her higher and higher still.

His mouth moved lower. He kissed her belly and then lower still, opening her, tasting all her secrets, until she knew she would die of pure, unalloyed rapture. She felt her eager, heated body rising toward climax once again.

Frantically, she clutched at his big shoulders, not wanting to find fulfillment without him a second time. He shrugged off her touch, determined, it seemed, to give her the ultimate pleasure once more before he joined her.

But she was insistent. She wanted the good, heavy weight of him. She wanted all of him. Right now.

She took his head between her soft hands and she urged him up the length of her body. At last, he surrendered to her sweet insistence. He rose up. She opened herself, avid and welcoming. He came into her, burying himself all the way with one long, deep thrust.

He groaned her name. She took the taste of herself off his lips and gave it back to him, kissing him with slow, sweet, long kisses, as both of them knew that wonderful, total connection, a man and a woman, joined at last for the ultimate dance of love.

He lifted his hips, a long, slow slide out of her welcoming heat. She moaned, a pleading sound, and he returned to her once more.

Over and over he withdrew and then came back, until she cried aloud with the sweet agony of it, until she feared she would shatter with pure ecstasy. Inchoately, she wondered how she had lived these last barren days without this beauty, this miracle, this total immersion in him and their passion. And she knew that she was shameless when it came to him, that she would do anything not to lose him again.

He took them higher. From slow and sensuous, the rhythm turned hard and hungry. She went with it, tossing her head back against the pillows, moaning her ecstasy at the ceiling, coming to the edge of the world once more.

She thought of the spinning top that had been this magical night, of the giant hand, twirling it, faster and faster, until all reality centered down to a hot whirl of heat and sensation.

He cried her name. She answered, *yes...*

And he surged hard into her, spilling himself. She felt the sweet simultaneous miracle happening, her own fulfillment reeling into being with his. She clutched him close; he held her tight.

They went over the edge of the world as one being, fearless and passionate. Together. Complete.

Ten

Jordan shifted a little, settling himself more comfortably on the bed.

Eve lay, sweet and satiated, beside him. Her head rested on his arm, her hair was spread out across his shoulder, soft as spun silk against his skin.

Seconds ago, he had reached over and flicked off the light. Now the room lay in nightshadow. The moon beyond the window had gone down long before their return from South Shore.

His body felt deeply at peace. His physical need for her had, after too long, been fully satisfied. For a while.

He stared up into the darkness, admitting to himself that the inevitable had happened. He'd made love to her. Now he had to deal with what he'd known he'd have to face as soon as he put his hands on her again.

He wasn't going to be able to walk away from her, not in any permanent sense. Somehow, she had become a part of him. And to leave her would be to cut himself in half.

"Jordan?" Her voice was soft, hesitant.

"Hm?"

"Are you...okay?"

He turned his head, looked toward the wall. Damn her. She always knew, always sensed...

"Jordan?"

"Yeah. I'm fine."

She was quiet for a moment, sighing a little and cuddling her soft, luscious body closer against his. But he knew she would not be quiet for long. He could feel her internal struggle, as she tried to frame the questions in such a way that he would answer her, rather than putting her off once again.

He decided he might as well help her out. It all seemed pretty inevitable now, anyway. It was pointless to go on keeping it up in the air.

He smoothed her hair with a hand and brushed a light kiss on her temple. "Okay, honey. What's on your mind?"

She made a small sound in her throat. "Oh, Jordan." She shifted to her side and levered up on an elbow, so she could look at him as much as possible through the gloom. "I know we agreed not to talk until tomorrow evening, but..."

"But what?"

"I, well...now that this has happened, I'm wondering if..."

She was having such a hard time, he couldn't take it. He wanted to end it, to let her off the hook. He moved, lifting himself up enough to brush her lips with a kiss. Then he stretched out again, lacing his fingers behind his head. "Don't worry. We'll be married."

He heard her small gasp. "We will?" She bent over him, peered at him nose to nose, as if she must have mistaken what he'd said.

He chuckled. "You said you were willing."

"Well, I am. Really, I am. But you—"

"I what?"

"You said you wanted to wait. You wouldn't talk about it until Sunday."

"This changes things. You just said it yourself. We'll be married as soon as we can arrange it. Fair enough?"

"Yes." She kissed his nose, then lay back down beside him again. He knew what was in her mind; she wanted more. She wanted tender expressions of undying devotion. She longed for all those loving promises that he'd given her that night on the beach when he'd first proposed.

But things had been different that night. She'd never denied him anything then, and the idea that he might ever lose her had not even entered his mind.

Much had happened since then. He'd been forced to face the fact that he could lose her. In fact, he had lost her. For a while. And her defection had brought home to him the very truth he'd always lived by: when you cared too much, you set yourself up for hurt.

But in spite of his own deepest truth, he had been unable to give her up. And now they were going to be married after all. And he felt—conquered, somehow. As if she had beaten him in some deep, unexplainable way. Declaring undying love right now felt to him like nothing short of overkill.

"Jordan?"

"What?"

"Are you...all right?"

"As all right as I was the last time you asked me three minutes ago."

"Jordan, something is bothering you."

"Look. Don't tell me how I feel. I said we'll be married and we will."

There was silence, a wounded silence. Then she asked, "What about your family?"

"What about them?"

"Would you mind if we told them?"

"Told them what?"

"That we're not really married. But that now we will be, very soon."

"What for?"

"Because I've already come to care for them. I care for them a lot. And I don't like lying, especially to people I care about."

"Hell, Eve," he muttered, moved in spite of himself. In four short days she'd built a connection with his family that, in some ways, was closer than the one he shared with them.

"Please, Jordan. Let's tell them everything."

He considered her request. But he had to reject it. There'd be too many questions, too many worried glances if they told the truth right now. His nosier cousins, like Louise, would go into a feeding frenzy of gossip at the news.

He said, "No. I think the best thing to do is go on as we are for now. We'll tell them *after* we're married and give them less chance to wonder if we'll really go through with it."

She said nothing for a moment. Then, "All right."

"Good."

But she wasn't finished. "There's one more thing."

"What?"

"Wesley. You're going to have to talk to him about why he misbehaves so much whenever he's around you. I tried to talk to him yesterday morning and got nowhere. He completely stonewalled me. But I'm certain that he needs to know you won't...desert him like his father did."

Jordan felt his gut tightening. He doubted he'd be very good at trying to get through to a confused four-year-old. More than likely he would bungle it when the moment came. But he supposed, somehow, it would have to be done. "Okay. I'll talk to him."

"Thank you." He could hear the relief in her voice. Then she rose to a sitting position. He looked at her and caught his breath. Her tawny hair fell across her cheek. Her breasts seemed to gleam in the dimness, white and full, inviting him. He wanted her again.

It didn't surprise him. He always wanted her. She was so open, so full of life and enthusiasm. She was like no woman he'd ever known. She hadn't had an easy time of it, he knew, when that stupid jerk she'd married left her. But somehow she'd managed to take care of her children, to build a business and—most miraculous of all—not to grow bitter or hard. She was not an innocent; she was a grown woman. Yet still she could look at life through the delighted, wondering eyes of a child.

His family adored her. Hell, so did he.

She started to slide off the bed.

"Where are you going?" His voice sounded gruffer than he meant it to.

"Just to get my robe."

"Forget that." He took her arm, pulled her down on top of him and felt what he'd wanted to feel, her soft breasts crushed against his chest.

She pushed at him, but not too hard. "What is this?"

He put his hands in her hair, cupped her face and brought her lips right down to his. "Just me, honey. Wanting you."

"Again?" The word shimmered with frank delight.

"Always."

She sighed, her breath warm and sweet against his mouth. "You're right."

"About what?"

"I don't need my robe." She giggled, a naughty sound.

He lifted his head enough to capture her lips. The giggles stopped as he felt her body go liquid and pliant over his.

He kissed her. She kissed him back. He felt his need growing quickly, his maleness aching and hard.

He slipped his hands down, to guide her legs out so she straddled him. His hardness was right against the womanly center of her. He moved, sliding down, and then with one quick thrust, up into her.

She gave a long, sweet sigh as she felt him enter. "Oh, Jordan…"

"Yeah, honey?"

"I love you, Jordan." She kissed him some more.

They began to move together, in a rhythm that was slow and deep, like currents beneath the surface of a calm sea, unseen but no less strong for their invisibility. It went on and on, never ending. Jordan gave himself up to it, to the feel of her surrounding him.

He stroked her smooth, satiny back and when she sat up on him, he cupped her breasts, loving them with his hands. She let her head fall back, loose and languid on the stem of her neck.

Her hips began to move more rapidly. He knew what was happening; she was reaching toward her release. He smiled at the feel of her. She moved harder and faster, lost in her own world of pure sensation, utterly swept away.

He watched her, loving what he saw. She moaned and tossed her head, her hips rising and falling swiftly in erotic pursuit of sweet completion. At last, she gasped and cried out. Then she found what she was seeking with one long, luxurious moan. Finally, a secret, blissful smile on her lips, she fell against his chest.

He held her close. Gently at first, he began to move to his own rhythm. Once he felt her willingness, her soft receptivity, he was lost. He moved faster, letting go of all control. She went with him, urging him on, making him wild with his pleasure of her, until he tossed his head against the pillows, groaning out loud as his own climax came.

After that, he kept her secure against his body until his heart could slow a little, until he could bear to loosen his hold. Eventually she left him, slipping away gently and disappearing into the bathroom for a time.

"Eve?"

"Yes?" She was back, as if his mere wish for her had brought her there.

"It's late." He rolled off the bed, pulled back the covers and climbed in, holding them up for her.

She gave a low chuckle as she glanced at the clock. "Is it ever. Past four." She slid in beside him. "We'll be sorry at the crack of dawn, when the kids come pounding on the door."

"It was worth it."

"Yes," she said softly, "I have to agree that it was."

He pulled her against him, curving himself around her, thinking that this was a damn sight better than last night and the night before.

She cuddled up close to him, sighing. He smoothed her hair, kissed her shoulder.

Sleep came, swift, deep and sweet.

It was a gust of wind, buffeting the chestnut tree and making it scratch against the window, that woke Eve. Her eyes flickered open. For a moment, she lay very still, absorbing everything, bringing the world into focus.

The light from outside, though definitely daylight, seemed gray. That meant it was probably overcast. And there was a certain feeling in the air, that charged, heavy feeling that came before a storm. She could hear the wind whipping around the eaves. The storm the newspaper had predicted must be coming in.

She frowned a little, in her cozy nest of covers, with the man she loved curled close against her back. Today they were supposed to return home. Would the storm cause a problem with their flight?

Oh, well. Her lips curved in a smile. It wouldn't be too terrible to be snowed in here at Dora's for an extra day. Worse things could happen. She would call Rosie and tell her not to worry. They'd play more canasta. Watch more football. Niles would cook a splendid dinner. And this bed was just dandy, now that she and Jordan could truly be in it together.

She sighed in contentment, but was careful not to sigh too loudly. She could feel Jordan's steady breathing against her hair. At her back, his chest expanded and contracted in the slow rhythm of sleep. She didn't want to wake him yet. After all the recent tension-filled nights, she was sure he could use every moment of rest he could get.

She lay on her side, facing the nightstand. The clock

said past nine. It was later than she'd thought. Some kind soul—Dora or Carla, probably—must have taken charge of the children so that she and Jordan could steal a few more winks.

She closed her eyes again, thinking maybe she'd just take advantage of this lovely opportunity to drift right back to sleep. But it didn't work. Now that she was awake, her mind didn't want to turn off.

She could hardly believe it. She and Jordan were getting married, after all. Just as she'd hoped and prayed. The gamble of coming here, of pretending she was someone she wasn't for the sake of his family, had paid off.

Very soon, what they shared wouldn't be counterfeit in any way. She'd be Jordan's true bride. It was all going to work out for the best. She was buoyant with joy.

Outside, another gust of wind blew the branches against the glass. Without knowing she did it, Eve caught her lower lip between her teeth.

She still worried a little about a few things. Like the fact that Jordan had agreed to marry her and yet said nothing of love. But then, she knew he was probably still a bit wary of her, because she'd once called their wedding off.

Time, she thought. Yes, time would take care of that. He would slowly grow to trust her again. Then he'd feel free to express the love she'd seen in his eyes last night.

She was also sure that, over time, he and Wesley would make peace with each other. Jordan had already promised to have a talk with Wes. Yes, it would all work out just fine.

Eve lay for a while, watching the minute hand of the clock, knowing that the hand was moving, though it seemed to remain still. And then she realized that she was a little keyed up, actually. A little anxious to get on with the day.

Carefully, so as not to disturb the sleeping man who was wrapped so cozily around her, she managed to extricate herself from his warm embrace and slip out of the bed. He groaned softly once, as she escaped him, and then settled down again. She tucked the covers gently around him.

Then she found clean clothes and tiptoed to the bathroom, where she quickly showered and dressed. When she came out, she crept around the room, gathering up their scattered evening clothes. She was just hanging her dress in the closet when Jordan spoke.

"'Morning." It was a soft, drowsy sound.

Eve turned to smile at him. "Good morning." Lord, he looked good, all rumpled and sleepy. She wanted to climb right back into that bed with him.

He must have read her mind. "Why don't you come back in here with me? It's really…warm in here."

She allowed herself a low chuckle. "If I do that, we'll never get downstairs."

"Hm. An interesting suggestion."

"But not a viable one."

"And why not?"

"Because your family have been angels. They've looked after Wesley and Lisa all last night and this morning too, judging from what time it is. They are saints, I swear. But there's a limit, even to what one can expect of a saint. And the limit comes pretty quickly when you're talking about two children under five."

He looked regretful, pulling himself to a sitting position, and raking his hair back with both hands. She watched, feeling the pleasant heat in her midsection as the blanket fell away and she could see his beautiful chest, the sculpted shape of his arms. He yawned and stretched. Then he smiled. "Hell. All right. But come here."

She was deliciously wary. "What for?"

"I said come here."

Cautiously, she approached. When she reached the side of the bed, he instructed, "Bend down here."

The pleasant warmth in her midsection flared hot. She couldn't help thinking about last night, about the way he'd touched her, the way she had touched him....

"I mean it, Jordan." Her voice was woefully unconvincing. "We really do have to—"

"Bend down."

Sighing, she did as he commanded. He lifted his hand and cupped the back of her head. He kissed her, slowly and sweetly. She felt her bones melting.

And then, just when she thought she was going to have to sink down beside him and do what she longed to do with him, no matter how inconsiderate it would be to his poor saintly family, he let her go.

Her eyes, which had drooped languidly shut, flew open. "You are a heartless man, Jordan McSwain."

"Just wanted you to know what we're missing."

"Tonight..." she promised.

"If I can manage to wait that long." He threw back the covers, revealing so much masculine splendor that she wanted to groan out loud. "I'll take my shower and meet you downstairs in fifteen minutes."

His muscular backside disappeared from view as he nudged the bathroom door shut behind him. Eve, staring after him, let out a long and rueful sigh.

"Good morning," Dora said, when Eve entered the sunroom. A chorus of like greetings came from around the big room. Eve smiled and said good morning in return.

"Mommy, Mommy!" Lisa cried from Alma's lap. Eve went and kissed her, and offered to take her from Jordan's grandmother.

"No, she's fine, dear. Really."

"Are you sure?"

"Gammy," Lisa murmured adoringly, and grabbed Alma's thumb.

Alma smiled down at the child. "I'm positive. I love having her right here."

"Mom, are you sick or something?" It was Wesley, trying to tug on her snug stirrup pants.

She bent down and kissed him. "No, dear. I'm not sick. I'm just fine."

"You stay in bed a lot lately."

Nancy and Matt, who were sitting at the table eating breakfast, chuckled in unison. Nancy said, "Your mommy stayed up very late last night. So she had to sleep in a little later, to make up for it."

Eve looked at Nancy, and Nancy gave her a grin. Eve remembered last night, recalled Jordan bearing her up the stairs in plain sight of Nancy and Matt, and she blushed a little.

But even in her embarrassment, she saw how Nancy looked at Matt, and Dora looked at Niles. She didn't miss Carla's knowing smile, either. Eve thought they all seemed very pleased with themselves, as if they'd engineered something quite gratifying.

Kendrick, playing with the dominoes, said, "Come on, Wesley. We got to build a hangar for my jet."

"Oh, yeah. Cool." Wesley hurried to Kendrick's side.

Eve went to the coffeepot on the kitchen counter and poured herself a cup.

"Breakfast?" Niles asked.

"Jordan will be down in a few minutes. We'll figure out something then."

"Good enough."

Eve took her cup to the table and sat down. She glanced out the circle of windows at the leaden sky. "Looks like snow."

"So says the weatherman," Matt confirmed.

"Eve, dear?"

Eve looked at Alma across the table. "Hm?"

"Could you take Lisa now? I think I must make a little trip to the lavatory."

"Of course." Eve collected her daughter and carried her back to her chair. Slowly Alma pulled her walker in front of her and pulled herself up. Dora offered to help.

Alma brushed her away. "I'll manage. Don't fuss over me, Dory."

"I only want to help."

"I know. But I'm just fine." Huffing a little, not looking nearly as "fine" as she kept claiming, Alma tottered off to the small half bath beyond the short hall leading to the back stairs.

"Honestly," Dora muttered under her breath.

Carla patted her hand. "She's a lot like you, Mother. Independent."

"But she's not well. I worry."

"Worrying won't do a bit of good."

"I know, I know."

Eve smiled. After warning Lisa not to touch, she sipped her coffee. The conversation continued around the table. Matt and Nancy talked about what time they were leaving—probably as soon as they could get packed up. They hoped to beat the worst of the coming storm. In the corner, the two little boys flew their toy jets and made airplane sounds. Carla spoke of her two-thirty flight. They expected her at the clinic in Austin tomorrow morning at nine.

Eve was feeling good, satisfied. The weekend was drawing to a close, having turned out just the way she'd dreamed it might. Absently, she kissed the silky crown of Lisa's head, and Lisa giggled and squirmed in her lap.

In spite of the gray sky outside, Eve felt sunny and warm here in the bosom of the family that would soon truly be her family, too. Yes, it had all worked out just fine.

And then she heard Dora gasp. "Jordan! Jordan, what is it?"

Nancy said, "Jordan?"

Eve, nonplussed at the sudden charged tension in the air, slowly turned her head to see what the others were staring at.

Jordan stood in the doorway to the hall that led to the back stairs. His face was absolutely white, except for the slight blueness around his mouth.

"Carla." His voice was a croak. "Carla, you must help…"

Carla stood. "What is it, Jordan? What?"

"It's Alma. Oh God, please. I can't feel her pulse…."

Eleven

Alma lay sprawled faceup across the threshold to the bathroom, her walker caught half-capsized, canted against the wall.

"Get this out of the way." Carla's voice was calm, very controlled. She gestured at the walker.

Jordan lifted it carefully free of the still figure and then shoved it into a small nook beneath the back stairs. When he turned around again, Carla had already knelt and was calling over her shoulder, "Mother! Get an ambulance."

Jordan, feeling numb and powerless, stayed at the foot of the stairs to keep out of Carla's way. He stared down at the back of Carla's head as she put both fists on Alma's chest and gave a hard, brutal shove.

Jordan had to look away. He knew Carla did the right thing, but he could have sworn he heard brittle ribs cracking. He saw Eve then, in the sunroom, holding Lisa, with Wesley clutching her hand.

"Take the children to the front of the house!" he shouted, louder and harsher than he meant to do.

"Don't you yell at my mommy!" Wesley's little face was scrunched up in rage.

"Sh, hush, come on, Wesley…" Eve turned to lead him away. "Grandma Alma's very sick…."

"Gammy! Gammy?" Lisa was asking, bewildered, lost.

Behind him, Jordan heard that awful punching sound again as Carla shoved at Alma's chest. He closed his eyes. When he opened them, Eve had passed from his range of sight.

How long Carla worked at her grim duty, Jordan had no idea. But finally he heard her mutter, "Good. Come on, Alma. Good girl."

He turned and looked down again. Carla said, "I have a pulse."

Minutes after that he heard the siren coming closer, until it was in front of the house. The paramedics came in through the garage. They hustled him out of the way.

He retreated to the door of the sunroom and lurked there, hating his own uselessness. The paramedics set right to work, checking Alma's vital signs and asking Carla a thousand questions, which she answered in a clear, composed voice.

Then they were placing Alma on a gurney and taking her away. He asked to ride in the ambulance with her, but Carla was a much better choice. After all, Carla was not only a relative, she was a physician's assistant as well.

Jordan watched the ambulance doors close behind the gurney. Then he whirled and raced up the back stairs.

He grabbed his wallet and his keys and then pounded down the front way, shoving his arms into his coat as he went.

He was flinging open the front door when Eve called to him from the arch to the living room. "Jordan, do you want me to—"

He didn't let her finish. He turned, gave her a hard, commanding glance. "Just stay here."

"All right." Her voice was calm, her gaze level. Behind her, he caught a glimpse of Wesley, glaring at him. She added, "Please drive carefully. It's icy out."

"I will." He spun away, flipping his collar up, and rushed out the door as the first snowflakes of the storm swirled into the yard.

All that day, Jordan refused to leave the hospital. Carla, due at her clinic, had to fly home. But Nancy and Matt stayed on, as did several other members of the family. Those who could manage it postponed their departures. They all wanted to be there, just in case they might be needed.

Eve called Rosie.

Rosie knew something was wrong right away. "What is it?"

"Jordan's grandmother's had a cardiac arrest."

"Is she—?"

"Still alive, so far."

"Thank God. How is Jordan holding up?"

"As well as can be expected, I guess. To tell the truth, I've hardly spoken to him since it happened. I'll be driving over to the hospital soon. I'll know better then."

"Well, don't even think about things here. I'm managing just fine. Handling all the bookings—and enjoying the peace and quiet.''

It was heartening, Eve realized, to hear her friend's voice, sounding so normal and everyday. She indulged in a little teasing, ''Oh, come on. You miss us.''

''Well, maybe just a little....''

''As soon as I know more, I'll call. But it will be at least tomorrow, I'm sure, before we can leave.'' Eve glanced out the windows, where the snow was coming down. ''And it's snowing here, so that may complicate things, too.''

There were more reassurances from Rosie, and one veiled query about how things were going ''otherwise.''

Eve glanced around the room to see that no one was listening. Then she murmured, close to the phone, ''We're getting married, *really* married, right away.''

''Great,'' Rosie said heartily. ''So it all worked out after all.''

Eve answered, ''Yes, it did. Just fine.'' But somehow, she felt apprehensive about everything now. She wasn't sure why. It was something about the flat deadness in Jordan's eyes as he flew out the door to follow the ambulance. He'd seemed very far away.

Eve shook herself. And how else should he seem? He'd been scared out of his wits for his grandmother. Of course he'd seemed far away.

''Eve? You still there?''

''What? Oh, yes. I'm here—and I do have to go now. Thanks for everything, pal.''

''No problem. Keep me posted.''

''I will.''

Eve hung up just as Nancy came in through the garage from her turn at the hospital.

''How is she?'' Eve asked.

"Stabilized. Conscious and lucid now, but very tired."

"Then she's really going to be okay?"

Nancy nodded. "Yep. That's the word."

Eve, sank into the straight chair by the phone. "Thank God." She asked the next question on her mind. "How's Jordan?"

Nancy's gaze slid away. "He's been with her almost the whole time, ever since Carla left."

"But is he okay?"

"Well, sure. He's fine. Just under a lot of stress."

Eve gave Nancy a probing look. "Nancy, what are you *not* telling me?"

Nancy sighed. "Oh, I don't know. You know how Jordan is. One way or the other, he doesn't let people get too close."

"Nancy, please. Just say what you're thinking."

"Well, when I got to the hospital, I asked him how things were going. He growled at me to ask the damn doctor. And then, when we were told she would pull through, he just gave this disbelieving grunt and turned away. Like he couldn't let himself trust that he wasn't going to lose her." Nancy crossed the room to Eve's side and put a hand on her arm. "Maybe if you go…"

Eve borrowed Nancy's car. Because of the snow, it took her nearly a half hour to negotiate the ten-minute drive to the hospital. But at last she was parking in the small visitors' lot and stomping up to the main entrance.

The woman at the front desk pointed out the waiting room. Jordan was sitting there, a solitary figure on a blue plastic chair. Eve thought she'd never seen anyone look so alone. He caught sight of her when she entered. And he frowned.

In spite of the way his expression seemed to warn her off, she took the chair next to him. "Jordan? How is she?"

He looked at her distantly. "Eve, there is no reason for you to be here. You should have stayed with the kids."

"Nancy's watching them. We're taking turns. She told me they said Alma was going to be all right. Is that true?"

"That's what they say. They sent me out."

"Why?"

"They wanted to run some tests, they said. And they're moving her, to ICU."

She stared at him, trying to make sense of him. Of the strange, cold way he spoke. "Jordan, are you all right?"

"I'm fine, Eve." He sounded like a robot.

"Jordan, I—"

"Look, Eve, I told you I'm fine, and I am. My grandmother is the one who's sick."

"But you sound so—"

"I am fine." Can dark eyes look icy? Jordan's did, and his tone was glacial. "And I don't want to talk about anything right now, Eve. Understand? I just want to sit here quietly, and wait until they'll let me back in with her. Can you handle that, or not?"

Eve looked at him for a moment, puzzled and hurt. And then she reminded herself once again of the great strain he was under. "All right. I'll just sit here with you, then. Quietly."

"There's no need."

"All the same, I will stay."

And she did, for well over an hour. It was an hour of silence between her and Jordan. Finally a nurse came in and said Alma was sleeping peacefully. She gently suggested that there was nothing more to be done. It would be dark soon, and with the storm, perhaps they should go on home for the night.

Jordan said, "Can I see her? I won't wake her. I just want to see her, see she's okay."

The nurse reluctantly agreed. "Follow me. But I warn you, she won't know you're there."

"Fine." He stood up and followed the nurse.

Eve quietly took up the rear. She wanted to be with Jordan and to reassure herself about Alma, but she sensed that if she said anything, he'd turn and order her to stay behind.

The intensive care unit was like a compound. The nurse rang a bell for admittance. Then she led them to Alma's room where Alma lay on her back, looking more frail and otherworldly than ever, with tubes running everywhere, her head covered in a plastic cap, her gown that awful hospital green. Over the bed a screen monitored every beat of her heart. Eve glanced at Jordan, who stared at the thin figure as if he could will the heart that had stopped never to do a thing like that again.

Eve understood what she was witnessing—pure masculine frustration. He hated having to sit helpless before this thing that was so far beyond his control. She put her hand on his arm in a gesture of comfort and support.

Jordan looked at her as if he'd never seen her before. Then he dropped his arm out from under her touch and pulled up one of the two chairs in the room. He whispered to the nurse, "I'll just stay here. I'll be quiet."

The nurse studied him for a moment. Then she whispered back, "Really, Mr. McSwain. She's very likely to sleep through the night."

"It doesn't matter. I want to stay."

The nurse appeared resigned. "Very well. We'll have an extra bed brought in so you can stretch out."

"Thank you." He looked at Eve. "Go back to Dora's. Tell them I'll be here through the night and I'll call if there's any news."

Eve hated to leave him. But she had the children to think of. After the frightening events of the day, she knew she really should be there to tuck them into bed herself. "All right. But I'll come back, as soon as I've put Wesley and Lisa to bed for the night."

"There's no need."

"But I—"

"Stay at Dora's, Eve." He was still whispering, as she was, but the whispers were growing in volume.

"Jordan, I—"

The nurse interrupted them, her own whisper firm. "This is ICU. If you have something to settle, please do it in the waiting room."

Jordan shook his head. "There's nothing to settle. Go on, Eve."

Eve stared at him, longing to grab him and shake him until that distant coldness left his eyes. And then she made herself smile. "All right, darling." She went on tiptoe and kissed his cheek. "I'll go."

The nurse's tense expression relaxed. Jordan dropped to the chair to take up the long vigil. Eve turned and went out the door.

Both Wesley and Lisa were cranky when she got back to them. They sensed the tension and worry all around them and had no idea what to make of it. Eve lavished attention on them, touching them often, telling them how much she loved them, as she fed them and readied them for bed.

As she tucked Wesley in, he asked in a small voice if Grandma Alma was going to "be dead." "No," Eve answered. She explained that Alma was very sick. Her heart had stopped for a little while. But Cousin Carla had made it start again. And now, the doctors were pretty sure Alma would be okay.

Wesley whispered, "She's not my real gramma anyway, is she?"

Eve, perched on the edge of the bed, looked down through the darkness at her son's small face. Sometimes, she thought bleakly, being a mother was the toughest job in the world—especially recently, when she'd complicated things all the more by pretending to be what she wasn't: Jordan's wife.

"She's your step-great-grandmother," Eve said at last, knowing it wasn't much of an answer. It wasn't even true—yet.

"What's that mean?" Wesley was not satisfied.

"Well, I'm your mother, right?"

"Right."

"You and I are in the same family."

"Uh-huh."

"And Alma is Jordan's grandmother. She and Jordan are in the same family. Right?"

"Okay."

"So, when Jordan and I...get together, then our families...get together, too. And since Alma is Jordan's grandmother, she then becomes your step-great-grandmother. Understand?" It was a weak, fragmented explanation.

And Wesley knew it. With the eerie emotional radar young children often seem to have, he homed right in on the central point. "You and Jordan...get together? How do you do that?"

"We, um, get married."

"Married. Like a mommy and a daddy?"

"Yes. That's right. Like a mother and a father."

Wesley was silent for a moment. Then he said in a low, intense voice, "He's not my daddy."

Eve's heart sank. This was not going well. But she dare not back out of it now. "No, sweetheart. He's not your daddy. He's...he'll be your stepfather."

"No. He's not my daddy. He's not. He's mean. And he leaves."

"Wesley, Jordan hasn't left. He's just at the hospital. Tomorrow, he'll be back with us. He hasn't gone anywhere."

"I don't care. He talks mean to you."

"You mean today, when Grandma Alma was so sick?"

Wesley nodded.

"He was worried. Worried about Alma. He wasn't being mean on purpose. I promise you that."

Wesley turned his face to the wall.

"Honey—"

"He's not my daddy."

"Wesley..."

"He's not." She saw the shadows of his lashes on his cheeks as he pressed his eyes closed.

Eve bit her lip and looked at her son's stubborn profile. This was working no better than the last time she'd tried to talk to him about Jordan.

Lord, what on earth should she do? Should she make Wesley talk about Teddy Tanner? But what could she say? *Your real father loves you. Honest. He just doesn't have any time for you, because he's completely wrapped up in himself and his career...* Gee, that would sound just great.

And where would she go from there? In her mind she saw Jordan as he'd looked when she left him at the hospital: stern and withdrawn. He'd promised he'd speak with Wesley about this, but in his current state of mind, how convincing could Jordan possibly be?

And what was desertion, anyway? Wasn't there more than one way to abandon someone you loved? Jordan could marry Eve and take on the responsibility for helping her raise Lisa and Wes—and still never let her and her children get too close to him. In the true sharing of hearts, he could hold himself aloof.

Eve loved him so much that she knew she could bear that. She could be satisfied with what he was willing to share of himself—and hope that someday he might be willing to share more. She was an adult, after all. She could respect the emotional boundaries of another and learn to make a life around them.

But could she ask that of her children? Ah, it was the same old question. After one father had abandoned them, had Eve the right to give them a stepfather who wouldn't let them get too close?

She bent near her son. "Wes?"

"I'm tired now, Mom. I'm going to sleep. You go away."

Eve sighed and let the hard subject go for the night. She brushed her lips across Wesley's cheek. "I love you."

He kept his head turned away, his eyes closed. But he said very softly, in the by-rote way that well-trained children do, "I love you, too."

She tucked the covers closely around him, then stood up. She bent briefly to kiss Lisa, who was already asleep in her nest of pillows on the other bed. Then she went to her own room.

She turned the rocking chair toward the window and sat down in it. She looked out at the darkness—at the chestnut tree now rimed in white as the snow steadily continued to fall.

It was still pretty early, a little past eight. Perhaps she should go downstairs with the others, share comfort and companionship with them for a while, before returning to this room that seemed far too empty tonight. Or perhaps she should just get ready for bed, lie down alone and will the hours to pass.

Eve stared out at the night, at the softly drifting snow. She didn't want to do either of those things. Not tonight, not when her son needed promises she couldn't make. Not when Jordan had sent her away from him, at a time when most people reached out for connection with those they loved.

He'd told her to come back here. To stay here. To wait.

Eve stood up. She was not going to wait. There was too much at stake here tonight for her to do what he'd told her to do.

Twelve

———

"**W**hat the hell are you doing here?"

Eve looked up from the magazine she'd been thumbing through while she waited for the hospital staff to inform her "husband" that she wanted to speak to him. "How is she?"

"Sleeping peacefully. No change. I asked you a question."

"I'm here to be with you."

"I don't need you. Really. Everything's fine."

Eve scanned his face. There were shadows beneath his eyes. She ached for him, for his loneliness and for his inability to reach out. She thought of her son, turning his small face to the wall, murmuring "Go away, Mom...."

She said, "If you don't need me, fine. But maybe *I* need to be here."

His golden brows drew together. He had no answer for that.

She forged on. "May I come in her room with you? I just want to sit with you. I want to wait with you for her to wake up."

He stared at her for a moment. Then, "What about Wes and Lisa?"

"They're in bed. Dora and Niles and Nancy and Matt are all there, all looking out for them. I'm sure they'll be fine."

He raked a hand back through his hair. "No. You just go on back."

"Why?"

"I already told you why!" He must have realized he was almost shouting, because he fell silent for a moment and darted a guilty glance around the room. Then he spoke again, and what he said cut her to the core. "I don't want you here."

She forced herself not to flinch. "Why not?"

He turned away—to collect himself, she was sure. Then he faced her once more. "I don't want to argue with you. Just let it be, all right? I want to go back to my grandmother and I want you to return to Dora's as I asked you to do."

"No."

He blinked. "What?"

"I said no." She stood up and grabbed his hand. "Come on."

He was too stunned by her sudden action to jerk away. "What the hell are you up to?"

"Let's find a place where we can talk."

He did pull away then. "No. This is ridiculous. I have to get back."

"You will soon enough. But right now, you're going to talk to me. Intimately, and in depth."

He gave her a withering look. "Damn it, Eve. This is neither the time nor the place."

"With you, it's *never* the time or the place." She grabbed his hand again. "Now, come with me. Or I'll set up such a ruckus, I'll get us both thrown out of here."

He stared at her, unmoving for a moment. And then something in her expression must have communicated to him that she meant what she said. She would get them thrown out if he didn't go along.

"All right, Eve." His shrug was infinitely weary. "If you think you have to do this…"

Before he had a chance to reconsider, she started off down the corridor to the admissions desk and beyond. Pulling him along, she glanced through open doors and peeked around corners. But she could find nowhere where the two of them might be alone. She thought of asking the woman at the front desk, but she feared giving him a moment's pause wherein he could change his mind. Seeing the exit to the parking lot, she headed right for it.

"What the hell?" he demanded behind her.

"Nancy's car." She had driven it to the hospital, since Jordan had used the rental car. "We can talk there." A gust of freezing wind hit her in the face as she shoved through the heavy outside door.

"This is ridiculous. We'll both end up with pneumonia."

She ignored his muttered complaint and dragged him across the parking lot until they reached the car. Then she had to let him go long enough to fumble for the keys. But at last she had them. She yanked back the passenger door. "Get in."

"What's the point of this?" He glared at her. The snow swirled all around him, dusting his shoulders with whiteness, clinging and melting in his hair.

She looked at him, unflinching. "I said get in."

His eyes were as cold as the frigid air around them, but at least he did as she said. She shut the door to keep him there, rushed around to the driver's side and slid behind the wheel. Then, not looking at him, she turned on the ignition and got the heater going.

Thankfully the warmth began at once, curling up around their feet, melting the ice on their boots. Eve stuck her hands out to the vents to warm them—and to give herself a moment to figure out what in the world she was going to say to him now that she had him captive.

He didn't wait for her to find the words. "Say what you have to say. I want to get back inside."

Eve rubbed her face, which was wet with melting snow, and brushed her hair with her hand. These futile grooming gestures were only a stall, and they both knew it.

"Eve, this is pointless." He leaned on the door handle.

"No!" She reached over him and grabbed the door. "Wait. Hear what I have to say."

She was stretched across him, holding onto the hand rest. And she could feel the way he flinched, as if the closeness of her body offended him. But at least he didn't make any more moves to get the door open.

She retreated to her own seat and then knowing she could stall no longer, she began, "Alma's going to be all right, Jordan—and so will you and I, if you'll let us.''

He wouldn't even look at her; he stared at the snow crystals that were piling up on the windshield. ''Of course we'll be fine,'' he said in his robot's voice. ''And, yes, I heard the doctors, too. I know they said she'd be all right.''

''But you don't believe them.''

He turned to her then, his expression dark as the night outside. ''It doesn't matter. What will happen will happen. Have you said what you wanted to say?''

''No, Jordan. We've got to get to the bottom of this.''

He faced the windshield again. ''There's nothing to get to. No bottom to reach. We've settled things between us. We'll be married. Everything will be fine.''

''No, everything will *not* be fine, not as long as you're hurting like this, Jordan. Not as long as you keep insisting everything is fine when fine is the last thing it is. Not as long as you keep your heart locked up inside you, where no one can touch it.''

His face was set and hard. He stared straight ahead. She took in a breath and told him softly, ''I love you, Jordan. With everything that's in me. I love you so much.''

''Fine,'' he muttered tightly. ''Fine.'' He put his elbow up, against his side window, braced his fist against his chin and resolutely continued looking straight ahead.

She could feel his pain, coming across the seat at her in agonized waves, a pain he insisted on pretending he didn't have, a pain she knew she must somehow break through if they were ever to have any real hope of intimacy with each other. She forced herself to go on, to batter at his crumbling defenses, though she knew all he wanted was for her to let it be.

"I...I was wrong, to call off our wedding, and I'm sorry now that I did it. But as I said then, I just didn't know you well enough. I didn't understand that the worst thing I could do to you was to back out on my promise to you. I had my own fears. After what happened with my first marriage, I was afraid to rush into marriage again. I didn't trust my own heart. But I found out how wrong I was to doubt you the minute I saw you with Alma. I understood then that you weren't a man who'd ever run out on your commitments."

"I told you that."

"I know. But I was too afraid. I had to see it for myself. And I was afraid of other things, too. I was sure there was really nothing that you could need me for in your life. I thought I wouldn't be your equal. But I was wrong, Jordan. All I have to be is willing, and there'll be times when I'll be the strong one, the one *you* can lean on. Times like now...." His knuckles were white against his clenched jaw. She reached over to soothe his tight fist with a gentle touch. "Oh, Jordan. Please. You need me now. And it's okay to need me. That's what we found each other for. That's what loving is for."

"Stop..." It was a guttural sound, ugly in its rawness. He jerked away from her touch.

"No." She grabbed his arm, desperate now to reach him. "I won't stop. I won't ever stop. Alma is going to live now, but the time will come when she won't. And if you don't let someone else love you, if there isn't someone you can trust to turn to when you really do lose her... Oh, Jordan. How will you get through it when that time comes?"

"Stop. No more," he commanded, grabbing for the door handle again, trying to shake her off.

She held on. "I love you, Jordan. I won't leave you again. Please trust me."

He whipped around to look at her then. His face was ugly, distorted with a rage he'd called up as a last resort to cover his hurt and his fear. "Let me go, damn it!"

And then he was shoving open the door, swinging his long legs out onto the snow-covered asphalt. Eve refused to give up. She slid across the seat and went after him. Flinging herself from the car, she lunged forward and grabbed for him. By some miracle she caught his sleeve.

"Damn it, Eve. Let go!"

But she had him; she wouldn't let go of him. She threw herself against his chest and looked up into his face. "Please, Jordan. Please, let me love you. Let yourself love me back...."

The snow blew on her face, caught in her lashes, so it was hard to see what she thought she was seeing: the tears in his eyes, the slight quiver to his mouth. But then, with a guttural moan, he was grabbing her against him, burying his head in her hair, crushing her so hard to his body that she thought all her bones would break.

"Damn you," he muttered, "why couldn't you leave it?" He sobbed, a deep and wrenching sound. "Damn you, Eve..."

"Yes," Eve murmured, clutching him close. "Yes, hold me, I know..."

"I didn't want you to see this...to see me like this.... A man should be strong."

"You *are* strong," she crooned. "It's okay. I know..."

"God. I feel like I'm seven years old again." His voice was hoarse against her ear. "I don't want her to die."

"I know, my darling," she soothed him. "And she won't, not now. They've said she'll make it this time."

He pulled back enough to swipe at his nose with his sleeve. "Lord, this is insane." He tipped his head back to the angry sky. "We can't stay out here. Come on. Back to the car." He grabbed her hand and led her back to the open door.

Once inside there was a moment when they looked at each other, and neither seemed to know what to do or say next. But she reached out, touched his cold, wet cheek.

And the touch was all it took. He grabbed her close again, and kissed her wet hair, her cheeks, her chin, everywhere. She kissed him back, and held him close and whispered over and over that she loved him, more than anything, that she would always be there.

Then, pulling back enough to meet her eyes, he began to talk. He told her things she already knew, but this time he told them from the heart. He confessed that his mother's distance from him had bewildered him. He admitted that he'd wondered, as a very small boy, if there was something wrong with him, something not right about him, that his mother didn't love him, and his father was never around.

"And then my mother died and I went to live with Alma," he said. "And she made up for a lot of it, she really did. It was as if, at seven, I finally found out what having a mother could be. She was...everything, can you understand that?"

"Yes," Eve said. "I can."

"And I feel like if I lose her..." He didn't seem to know the words to go on.

Eve smiled a gentle smile. "She's the only one who

never abandoned you, isn't she? Your mother left you. And your father left you.''

Jordan nodded. ''When he died five years ago, it was like hearing a stranger had died. I hardly knew him.''

''He abandoned you,'' Eve said. ''And…so did I, didn't I?''

He said nothing; he didn't have to. The sad and tender light in his eyes said it all. He smoothed a strand of damp hair away from her face.

She raised her chin. ''I won't ever desert you again, Jordan. I swear to you. I hope you can believe me.''

He smiled then, a smile she didn't quite know how to read, and he lightly brushed her lips with his.

Eve returned to Alma's room with him. They sat together, holding hands, drifting in and out of sleep, until near dawn. Then Eve kissed him and left, promising to be back as soon as she'd fed the children breakfast. Jordan tried to stay awake after she had gone, but he'd had too little sleep in recent nights. He faded off.

And when he woke, he found his grandmother watching him.

Alma smiled. Jordan thought that the sun came out with that smile. He called the nurse, who came in, checked Alma's vital signs and scribbled on the clipboard at the end of the bed.

As soon as the nurse left, Jordan scooted his chair up and took the thin, liver-spotted hand.

''How do you feel?''

''Tired.'' Her voice was thready. She seemed to wince with each breath—a result, no doubt, of the two broken ribs she'd acquired when Carla administered CPR. ''But much better than yesterday.'' She managed a chuckle. ''That was a close one.''

"I know. But you made it through.... I love you, Grandma."

"And I love you."

They remained for a few minutes in companionable silence.

Then Alma surprised him. "Is Eve here?"

Jordan looked at his watch. "She should be. She said she'd be here around eight. It's nearly eight-thirty."

"I'd like to see her. Alone."

He wanted to ask why, but that seemed the wrong thing to ask a woman who'd just barely escaped death; right now was the time to give her anything she asked for. And she was asking for Eve.

He bent and kissed her wrinkled cheek. "I'll check at the front desk."

"Thank you, dear."

He got up and went out, down the hall and through the door that was locked against the rest of the hospital. Eve looked up as he entered the waiting room.

"Hi. I was just going to ask the nurse to tell you I was here." She smiled, but it looked forced. Beside her sat Wesley, with his hands clenched in his lap and a scowl on his face. She cast a glance at the boy and then looked back at Jordan. That glance, and Wesley's mutinous pose, told him everything.

Eve went on, "Wesley asked to come, but he is not behaving very well." She measured out the words carefully, a mother keeping her head when her child refused to keep his.

Jordan turned his eyes on the boy. "What's the problem, Wes?"

Wesley didn't even move. He stared straight ahead.

"Wes?"

Still no answer. Wesley was blatantly ignoring him.

Eve sucked in a dismayed breath. "Wesley, Jordan asked you a question." Wesley continued to scowl at the opposite wall. "Wesley."

Jordan decided to forget the boy for a moment. He gave Eve Alma's message. "She's awake. She's asked for you. She wants to see you alone."

"What for?"

Jordan shrugged. "I haven't the faintest idea. But go on in." He allowed his gaze to flick over Wesley. "I'll take care of Wes."

"But—"

"Go on."

She stared at him for a moment, biting her lip. Then, "All right. I'll be back soon."

Jordan sat beside Wesley, who was still glaring straight ahead. "No hurry. Wes and I will be just fine."

Once Eve had disappeared down the hall, Jordan asked, "Would you like to see Grandma Alma, Wes?"

No response.

Jordan kept his cool and tried again. "I'm not sure they'll let you into ICU, but I can take a crack at it as soon as your mom gets back. What do you say?" He patted the boy's leg.

Wesley jerked away. "Don't touch me."

"Wes, I—"

"Don't talk to me. Shut up."

Jordan drew in a slow breath. "Wes—"

"I hate you."

Jordan gaped at the boy for a moment, not wanting to believe he'd heard those hurtful words. But he had. There was no ignoring them.

Nor could Jordan pretend any longer that this problem with Wesley would just work itself out. Something had to be done between him and this boy, if they were ever to have any hope of finding a common ground.

The moment when more was required of Jordan than a hug and a treat had come. And he doubted he'd be equal to it.

But then he thought of Eve last night, demanding he open up to her, swearing she'd get them kicked out of the hospital if he didn't let her have her say.

Jordan smiled. And Wesley saw that smile. Though he didn't drop his defiant pose, his small brows drew together in dread.

Jordan stood up. "Come with me, Wes."

The boy folded his arms and stuck out his lip. "No."

"What did you say?"

"No!" Wesley was truculence personified, but his eyes shifted nervously away.

Jordan saw little choice. He bent and scooped up the boy.

There was a gasp of outrage and shock, and then the shouting and squirming started. "You put me down! I hate you, let me go, I want my mommy!"

Pretending he didn't see the concerned looks that shot between the other people in the waiting room, Jordan strode purposefully toward the front desk. Wesley, tossed over his shoulder, kicked and beat at him, shouting how he hated him, insisting, "You're not my daddy, put me down!"

Taking a cue from Eve, Jordan shoved through the doors to the parking lot. He confronted an icy, overcast morning. He had to trudge through last night's snow to reach the rental car. He went right to the driver's side, managed to get the door open, and pushed the child in across the seat. Then he slid in himself.

Wesley grabbed for the passenger door handle. Jordan said quietly, "Don't you dare."

Wesley froze, studied Jordan's face for a moment, and then apparently concluded that Jordan meant what he said. He subsided into sulking, crossing his little arms and glaring out the windshield at the steel gray sky.

Jordan looked at the boy, wondering what the hell to do next, recognizing the true irony in the situation. Last night it had been himself in Wesley's seat. Eve had been the one trying to reach out, to make connection, to heal the invisible wounds of silence and denial.

And how had he felt then? Torn. Ripped in two. He'd wanted her to leave him alone. And he'd wanted her to grab him and hold him and swear she'd *never* let him go.

He said carefully, "I'm going to marry your mother, Wes. And the four of us, you, me, your mother and Lisa, are going to all live together. We'll be a family."

Wesley said nothing. He glared out at the gloomy day.

"It will happen, Wes. No matter what you do."

Wesley's lip quivered.

"You can fight it all you want, but that's how it will be. The four of us. A family."

"No!" Wesley turned on him, his little face a twisted mask of rage and rejection. "You're not my daddy! I hate you! You went away! You leaved! You're mean to my mommy! You yell at her!"

"Sometimes when people are feeling bad they yell, Wes. Like you're yelling now."

"So! So what? You leaved. You leaved, and I heard my mommy crying. I went to her room and I listened at the door and she was crying. She talked to Rosie a lot and Rosie said to call you, but I didn't want her to call you. I wanted you to just stay away, stay gone away! You said you liked us, but you didn't like us. And pretty soon, you'll leave again!''

"No." Jordan felt his own throat closing up. He looked at this boy, and he knew exactly what he was feeling. He knew what it was to be left, he'd once been left himself. "No, I won't leave!" He was shouting himself now.

"You will!"

"I won't!"

"You will…"

"No, I won't. I swear I won't.…"

"Liar, you're a liar.…" Wesley reached out then, flailing wildly, wanting to hurt because he himself hurt so much.

Jordan responded without having to think. He reached out too, and wrapped his arms around the now-sobbing little boy. He pulled the small body close to his own. He held on, as Wesley tried to pound and punch at him, wailing wildly, crying out his anger and his pain.

Jordan whispered through the struggles, in a fierce and determined chant, "Listen to me, Wes. Listen. I know I left before. But I will never leave again. I'll be here. I am not going away. No matter what you do, I will never leave.…"

He went on in the same vein, hardly knowing what his own words were, only opening his heart and letting whatever wanted to be said come out. And slowly, Wes grew quiet. The small fists relaxed, the arms went limp. The boy sagged against the big body of the man.

"But what if you die?" Wes asked between hiccups.

"If I die, I will be gone, that's true. But that would be the only way I would leave you. And I'm not going to die for a long, long time. Until way after you're a grown-up yourself.''

"You sure?"

"I can't be absolutely sure, but I can be *almost* absolutely sure.''

Wesley thought about that, his head cocked to the side. Then, saying no more, he slid back to the passenger side of the car and swiped at his nose with his hand.

Jordan popped open the glove compartment, where Eve had stored a box of tissues. "Here.'' Wesley obediently took the tissue and blew his nose. Finally Jordan said, "I think we should go back soon. Your mom will be wondering where we've gone.''

Wesley sniffed once more, nodded and then opened his door. They tramped through the snow side by side and reentered the hospital.

It was right after the door shut behind them that Jordan felt Wesley's hand groping for his. Jordan knew then what it was to be a happy man. Next to having Eve Tanner in his arms, he'd never felt anything half so terrific as the tentative touch of that small hand on his.

Eve entered Alma's room quietly. She met the dark eyes so much like Jordan's, and she smiled. Alma smiled in return and gestured at a chair that was pulled up close to the bed. Eve took it, as well as the hand Alma held out to her.

Eve looked down at Alma's face against the white pillow. The harsh light from above exposed every wrinkle, dealt cruelly with the loose skin of her neck, the pouches beneath her eyes.

Still, Eve thought, Alma McSwain had a beautiful face. A strong, good face that radiated self-knowledge and tolerance for others. A face to love—as Eve's daughter had—on sight.

"Eve, I..."

"Yes?"

"I'm so glad...that Jordan found you."

"Oh, Alma," Eve sighed. "I'm glad he had you."

"I've made my mistakes."

"Everybody does. And you've meant the world to him. You taught him how to love."

Alma shook her head. "Please, dear. Don't flatter me."

"I'm not. I'm completely sincere."

"Well..." Alma wrapped her other hand around Eve's, as if she drew strength from the younger woman's touch. "It's good of you to say so, but the fact remains that Jordan has always kept other people at a distance."

"Yes, I know...."

"I thought he'd never get close enough to another human being to make a life with her. And I'd accepted that, I really had. But then he met you..." Alma lifted Eve's hand to her lips and kissed it. "I wanted to talk to you alone, to tell you myself..."

"Yes?"

"I wanted you to know that my grandson couldn't do better than a woman like you, Eve. You are exactly what I've always wanted for him. I hope you two really do get married someday. But that will have to be your decision, and the rest of us will have to live with it, either way."

Eve didn't manage to suppress her gasp. She had to clear her throat before she could speak. "You've known—the whole time?"

Alma managed a dry chuckle. "Not for certain, until just now."

"But you suspected...."

"Yes."

"But how...?"

"Completely by accident. I was worried about him when he called the night you were supposed to have been married. I called him back at that hotel he'd said you'd be going to at South Shore. They told me that the McSwain party had cancelled. I knew then that there was something going on I didn't understand, but I decided to mind my own business and stay out of it.

"But then, on Thanksgiving night, there you were describing your Tahoe honeymoon, when I was pretty sure you hadn't even been there. And more than that, over the last few days, I couldn't help but notice that something wasn't quite right with you two. A certain...tension, a distance. And then there was the morning Niles found Jordan on the couch...."

"Oh, Alma. This is terrible. We didn't want to upset you, and look what—"

Alma stemmed her protests with a wave of her hand. "My heart stopped on its own, young lady. You and Jordan had nothing to do with it. Certainly I'd like to see you two married, but I'm not fool enough to have heart failure over it if it doesn't work out. Understand?"

"Yes." Eve knew she was right. "Yes, I do."

"Good. Now take care of your problems between yourselves, as young people must always do. And don't go blaming us old folks if things don't work out."

Cousin Louise, Great-Aunts Camilla and Blanche, as well as Camilla's second son, Ronald, were all in the waiting room when Jordan and Wesley returned.

Louise, impatient as ever, started making demands the minute she caught sight of Jordan and Wes. "Jordan. There you are. They told us Eve's with Alma now. We'd all like to visit briefly. And we don't have all day."

Jordan assured her that as soon as Eve came out, he'd see what could be done.

"Well, good," Louise declared. She glanced beyond Jordan's shoulder. "Oh, dear. It's Dora and Nancy. With the children, too. What can they be thinking?" Jordan turned to see the two women. And Kendrick, Phyllis and Lisa, as well.

Nancy, bustling forward, volunteered, "Don't worry. I'm only dropping off Dora. I thought I'd go over to Aunt Denise's and take all the kids along—including you, Wesley, if you want to come."

Jordan smiled down at Wesley. "What do you think?"

"Well, maybe I could see Gramma Alma first?"

Louise piped up, "I'm sure they don't allow children in ICU. What are you people thinking of? And what about the rest of us? We were here first."

But Lisa had heard her favorite name. "Gammy? Gammy? I see Gammy?"

"Me, too," Kendrick announced. "I want to see Auntie Alma, too."

Baby Phyllis, as yet unable to speak real words, shouted something that sounded like, "Gwammy, yum!"

Louise was appalled. "Honestly, a hospital is no place for all these children. Nancy, you should have waited in the car and sent Dora with a message, instead of dragging them all in here. I find it impossible to understand how you could be so…"

There was more in the same vein, but Jordan effortlessly tuned it out. Eve had appeared from the hall to ICU, and he had eyes only for her.

Eve stopped in midstep and blinked in amazement when she saw her son and the man she loved standing side by side. She stared at Wesley, who looked trustingly up at Jordan.

She knew then that the boy and the man had reached their own private understanding.

And then Jordan was smiling at her. The gleam in his eyes told her that the best was yet to come.

He said, "The road to South Shore is probably closed after the storm. But I'll bet we could get through to Reno."

"What in the world is going on here?" Cousin Louise demanded to know.

"Louise, stay out of it," Blanche warned.

"But, Mother, I—"

"Gammy, Gammy, I see Gammy!" Lisa was demanding, and the other children were chiming right in.

Eve heard none of it. At that moment, she heard and saw nothing but the big man with the dark eyes and gold hair.

She nodded. "Yes, I'll bet we could get through to Reno."

"You'll marry me," he said. "Today."

"Yes. Absolutely. I will. Today."

"Well, I never!" Louise sniffed. "What in heaven's name is going on here?"

But Cousin Louise's outrage was lost on Eve and Jordan, just as the soft gasps of Dora and Nancy went unheard. Even the pleading of the children to be allowed to visit Alma didn't reach them right then.

Eve crossed the tile floor without feeling that her feet

even moved. Jordan's arms came around her, strong and warm. She lifted her mouth. His lips closed over hers.

The kiss was sweet, full of promise and commitment.

"I love you, Eve Tanner," he said when he raised his head.

"And I love you, my darling. I can't wait to be your wife."

Epilogue

Two years later, for Alma's ninetieth birthday, Dora gave another reunion. Jordan brought his family: Wesley and Lisa—and Eve, six months' pregnant.

After the big birthday dinner, when everyone gathered in the living room to swap family stories, Cousin Louise wasted no time in demanding, "How about you, Jordan? Tell us about how it once happened that you and Eve were married…and then *not* married…and then married again."

Blanche was heard to murmur, "Now, Louise, maybe Jordan doesn't want to go into all that."

"Well, Mother, *I* want to hear."

"I know, but—"

Jordan cut in, "It's all right, Aunt Blanche."

The whole family breathed a collective sigh of relief as Jordan winked at his grandmother across the room and took Eve's hand.

''Listen up, everyone,'' he announced. ''Because I'm only telling this once.''

And with that, Jordan McSwain embarked on the tale of how he found a wife and a family of his own, when he'd sworn all he needed was a counterfeit bride.

*   *   *   *   *

Dear Reader,

Marriage: Ball and chain. One-way ticket to jail. That giant sucking sound in a guy's wallet. Bachelors committed to remaining uncommitted can be a little squeamish and melodramatic about matrimony. Sometimes it takes a life-changing event to make a guy start thinking right. In *Millionaire Husband,* my tightwad day trader hero is determined to remain free of the ties that bind until his ulcer ruptures and the heroine rescues him. She's independent to a fault, but she could use some help since she's adopting three children.

I wrote this story because both the hero and heroine needed to make some changes, and I loved being right with them as they fought themselves and each other, but eventually grew. Technically, their union began as a marriage of convenience, but despite their difficult situation, they have a chance to find a special part of themselves, each other and love. Isn't that what good marriages do for all of us?

Wishing you the best of love,

Leanne Banks

MILLIONAIRE HUSBAND

Leanne Banks

This book is dedicated to the stock jock
with *cojones*, brains and heart.
Thank you for everything!

One

Another day, another hundred thousand dollars. With the exception of the nagging pain in his abdomen, Justin Langdon was feeling pretty pleased as he climbed the steps to Edward St. Albans Elementary school. The *St. Albans Chronicle* didn't call him their top stock jock for nothing. Popping two antacids, he thought the beautiful thing about the stock market was that a shrewd man could make money when it went up and when it went down. Justin believed in doing both.

After a childhood spent at the Granger Home for Boys, Justin had worked a day job and put every penny he had on making money in the stock market. His tightwad days of eating beanee weenees had paid off, and he was now a multimillionaire. He was damn sure he wouldn't be eating cans of beans any-more. If his financial success occasionally rang hollow, he didn't dwell on it. Besides, two of his highly successful alumni buddies from the Granger Home for Boys had talked him into joining them in a secret, tax deductible, charitable foundation, the Millionaires' Club.

Justin still had moments of doubt over his commitment to the Millionaires' Club, but he would do his duty. He walked through the hallway of the aging elementary school toward the sounds of young children. Justin's charity assignment was to investigate the after-school program to determine whether the Millionaires' Club should donate and how much.

Absently rubbing his stomach, he rounded the hall corner and peered into the noisy classroom. A curvy woman with a mop of red curly hair and dressed as a *J* led the youngsters in a song of words starting with the letter *J*. Was this Amy Monroe, the director of the program? Her feminine curves and one hundred and fifty watt smile nearly distracted him from the fact that the red costume clashed with her hair. She gestured and danced for the children, encouraging them when their volume grew. He'd never seen so much enthusiasm inside one single person before.

"Jack, jam, Japan, jar!"

Justin's stomach clenched and he frowned. It must be the noise, he thought, but he couldn't deny Miss Monroe's effectiveness. He was almost tempted to join in the chorus too.

Amy spied him and waved at him. "Come in and join us," she called, then smiled at the children. "Join starts with—?"

"*J!*" they chorused.

Justin moved into the room and slid into a too-small chair. His stomach seemed to nag him more than usual, but he pushed the pain aside, telling himself it was the result of overexposure to so many noisy children at once.

Justin didn't hate kids. From his upbringing, however, he'd learned that a wife, ex-wife and children constituted the biggest sucking sound a man could possibly experience in his bank account. That lesson had been driven home to him month after month when his divorced mother received the child support payment from his dad and subsequently shopped till she dropped. She and Justin always ended up with more month than money left, eventually necessitating his move to the Granger Home for Boys. Justin had vowed never to put himself or anyone else he cared for in that position again in his life. That meant no marriage and no kids.

Amy Monroe's curves distracted him again. His no-marriage rule didn't mean no dating, he told himself, remembering his good friend Michael's advice for him to drag himself away from the computer and get out more.

"See you Thursday," she said, dismissing the class. "We're doing *K* then."

Justin stood as the kids stampeded past him. A hush immediately descended on the room, and he met Amy's gaze. "You're Amy Monroe, the preschool special-program coordinator," he said.

She nodded. "And you're Justin Langdon. I received a message that you might be coming to observe, but no explanation." She gave him a curious glance. "Do you have a child you want to enter into the program?"

"Oh, no. I'm doing some research on your program. You looked like you were getting through to them," he said. "I'd like to hear more about it. Can I take you to dinner tonight?"

Amy Monroe felt a sliver of temptation and ignored

it. She also ignored the fact that Justin Langdon's intelligent gaze perked her interest. She ignored his chiseled bone structure and the curve of his lips that hinted at sensuality. She told herself not to think about how his broad shoulders promised strength and protection. She ignored the hum of electric awareness shooting between them. She ignored all these things because she had to ignore them. Although Amy couldn't remember the last time she'd joined a handsome intelligent man for dinner, she knew she had no room in her life for dates. She shook her head. "I'm sorry. Tonight's bad."

He shrugged. "Tomorrow night then?"

"Tomorrow's bad, too. Actually every night for the next year is probably going to be bad."

He blinked. "Why?"

"Three reasons," she said and decided to kill all the interest at once. "Their ages are five, three and three. My kids," she said, because since her sister and brother-in-law had died eight weeks ago, Emily, Jeremy and Nick had become her kids.

Justin Langdon blinked again. If she didn't know better, she'd swear he even turned pale with disbelief. "You have three children," he said. "I didn't see a ring—"

"Oh, I'm not married. I've never been married."

"I can see why you'd be busy, then." Justin rubbed his stomach absently. "Is there a restroom?"

"Sure, right through that door," Amy said, pointing to the rear of the room. She grew concerned at the odd expression on his face. "Are you okay?"

He made a vague sound and headed for the restroom.

Amy frowned. She realized children frightened many men, but she hadn't expected his look of near-nausea. Shrugging, she quickly put the classroom in order so she could leave. Hearing a strangled cough, she felt a tinge of uneasiness. "Mr. Langdon," she called, knocking on the door. "Justin, are you all right?"

He coughed again.

Her uneasiness growing by the second, she knocked again. "Mr. Langdon, are you decent?"

"Yes, but—"

Amy pushed open the door and saw that the man's handsome face had turned ashen. He held a paper towel in his hand stained with bright red blood. "Nose bleed?"

He shook his head. "I coughed."

Alarm tightened her chest. She didn't know what the blood meant, but she knew it wasn't good. "You need to get to the hospital."

Justin protested the pushy woman for about forty-five seconds until he felt the urge to cough again. Then he focused his energy on not coughing and fighting the light-headed feeling that settled over him like a thick fog. In the occasional moments the fog lifted, Justin noticed Amy Monroe drove her Volkswagen Beetle like a bat out of hell and swore in a very un-teacher-like fashion at drivers who moved too slowly to suit her.

Pain burned through his gut, stealing his breath and sense of humor. He felt her quick glance of concern.

"Breathe," she told him.

"In a minute," he muttered, hating the combination of pain and fuzziness.

"No," she said. "Breathe. You're tensing up. That makes the pain worse. It's like childbirth. If you breathe, you can stay on top of it."

"You should know," Justin said and drew in a ragged breath. Lethargy dragged at him. He felt as if someone was pressing two hundred pound weights on his eyelids. If he could just rest for a few minutes…

"Mr. Langdon! Justin!"

Wincing at the pain, he didn't open his eyes. "What?"

"We're almost at the hospital."

He'd never felt so tired. It occurred to Justin that he should thank her for bringing him. He struggled to open his mouth, but couldn't. Frustration swirled inside him.

The car jerked to a stop and he felt a flurry of activity. He heard voices.

"—coughing up blood," Amy Monroe said. "I think his stomach is hurting."

"…ulcer. He may need surgery," a male voice said.

Justin tried to protest, but again he couldn't. He focused all his energy on opening his eyes and found himself staring into Amy Monroe's worried gaze. He opened his mouth. "Thank—"

She put her finger over his lips and shook her head. "Save your strength. We were all put on this earth for a reason. You're one of my reasons today. Breathe," she said and brushed her soft mouth against his cheek.

Justin felt himself wheeled over the pavement through the doors. The pain mounting, he stopped fighting and allowed his eyes to close. The hospital faded away and his world turned dark.

"Emergency surgery," he heard a woman say, and then he heard no more.

A vision wafted through his mind. His good friends Michael and Dylan shook their heads. "So young," Michael said.

"What a waste," Dylan said. "All he did was work and worry about money."

Michael's wife Kate took his hand. "He never really got it," she said sadly. "I think he was right on the edge, but he never really got it."

Got what? Justin wondered.

"He fought it," Dylan said.

Fought what? Justin wanted to know.

Michael nodded. "I can't believe he didn't have a will. He would turn over if he knew how much the government was getting of his fortune."

Will! Panic sliced through him. He'd never made a will because he'd always assumed he had time. He broke into a cold sweat. Was he dead?

Kate wiped a tear from her eye. "I wish he could have had more. It feels like such a waste. I can't imagine getting to the end of my life and knowing I could have made a difference, but didn't. I can't imagine never loving someone. It's such a waste," she said and Michael took her into his arms.

Justin wondered if he was dead. All the things he'd intended to do later raced through his head. Worst of all, however, was the incredibly empty feeling that engulfed him. His throat tightened with dread. Had his life really been all for naught? He'd been so busy trading and adding to his wealth, adding to his financial security that he couldn't even see anything, let alone anyone else.

What had he done to make the world a better place?

The regret felt like a tidal wave, drowning him with a thousand should-haves.

If you're out there, God, I'm sorry. I've screwed up big time. If you can give me a second chance...

Ridiculous notion, Justin thought. If Justin were God, why would he give Justin a second chance? What had Justin done to deserve another chance?

Well, hell, Justin thought. Maybe God wasn't a self-centered jerk like Justin was. Maybe God was smarter and better than he was. Maybe God was nicer. Maybe God believed in second chances.

If you can give me a second chance, I'll try to figure out the real reason you put me on this earth and get it done.

Justin wished whoever was putting fifty-pound bags of cement on his eyelids would stop. He frowned, concentrating with the effort to open his eyes.

"Looks like he's waking up," a familiar voice said. Through the fog of his mind, he tried to place the voice.

"Hey, Justin, welcome back to the land of the living," another familiar voice said.

Justin blinked and looked into the faces of his two friends, Michael Hawkins and Dylan Barrows.

"You gave everyone a scare," Michael said, his observant gaze crinkled with concern. It occurred to Justin that Michael seemed more human since he'd married and become a father.

"I know you've been dragging your feet on this after-school reading program donation," Dylan said, "but was surgery really preferable?"

Justin felt a grin grow inside him. He gave a rough chuckle. Pain sliced through his side. He swore under his breath. "Show some mercy, Dylan."

Dylan shook his head. "You look like a truck ran over you."

"Thank you," Justin said wryly.

"No, really," Dylan said, his face growing serious. He gave Justin's arm a quick squeeze. "You need to take better care of yourself. I don't want anything bad to happen to you. Even if you are a cheapskate, you're a good guy.''

A fleeting image of his Scrooge-like dream oozed through his mind and his humor faded. ''Maybe not good enough,'' he muttered to himself.

''I hate to run, but I booked this charter last week,'' Dylan said regretfully. ''I'll rest easy knowing you're okay.''

''Charter to Rio or Paris?'' Justin asked, mildly curious. Dylan was always running here or there. At times, it almost seemed as if Dylan was running from himself.

''Neither. The Caribbean. Weekend in Belize. Maybe you can go with me when you're feeling better.''

''Blonde or brunette?'' Justin asked.

Dylan cracked a grin that didn't extend to his eyes and waved his hand. ''Neither this time. I invited Alisa Jennings, but she turned me down flat. Third time this month.''

''For someone with a healthy ego, you seem to have none where she is concerned.''

''Glutton for punishment, I guess. I'll just do a little fishing and diving and a lot of thinking.'' He glanced at his gold watch, then back at Justin. ''Take care, bud. I'll see you when I get back. You too, Michael.''

As soon as Dylan left, Justin met Michael's gaze. ''Dylan? Thinking?''

''He's pretty hooked on Alisa.''

''I'm surprised he didn't just go on to the next one. Dylan always seems like he's got a string of women waiting for him.''

''I think he and Alisa were more involved than he admits.''

''That's what I always thought,'' Justin said, fighting a sudden weariness.

"But enough about Dylan. You look like you're ready to drift off again, so I'll leave—"

"Just a minute," Justin said. "I, uh…I guess I could have croaked."

"Yeah," Michael said with a nod.

His chest tightened and he brushed the sensation aside. "I thought about everything I hadn't done."

"Like going to Belize?" Michael asked with a grin.

Justin shook his head. "No. Important stuff." Strange emotions tugged at him and he shrugged. "You seem like you're at peace. Why?"

"Oh, that's easy. Kate and the baby. When it's all said and done, everyone and everything else might leave, but I know I'll still have Kate." He paused. "And I like what I'm doing with you and Dylan. It's fun and more." He chuckled to himself. "Kate says the three of us suffer from a fraud complex about our wealth. I guess giving some of it away makes me feel less like a fraud." Michael studied him. "You need to rest," he said. "You'll be okay."

Distantly aware of Michael leaving his room, Justin struggled with the haze settling over him. He thought about what Michael had said and shook his head. He couldn't believe his purpose had anything to do with being a husband and father. Closing his eyes, Justin decided he would just have to keep looking.

Three weeks later, Justin still had a gnawing sensation inside him but, thank goodness, it had nothing to do with an ulcer. Needing to thank Amy Monroe for getting him to the hospital, he found her address and drove to her house after the stock market closed. He pulled into the driveway behind Amy's Volkswagen. He scanned the area and noted the large older two-story home in a neighborhood filled with oaks, weeping willow trees and kids, at least a dozen kids.

Snatching the bouquet of roses from the passenger seat and getting out of his car, he climbed the small, slightly tilted porch and rang the doorbell. A little girl with lopsided pigtails quickly appeared and stared him up and down. "A man is at the door," she yelled at the top of her lungs.

Just then, two toddler boys raced to the door and stared at him. One poked his thumb in his mouth. Twins, Justin noted, thankful again that fatherhood was not part of his purpose.

Amy appeared, dressed in shorts that emphasized her long shapely legs. Affectionately ruffling the hair of one of the twins, she glanced at the flowers and Justin in surprise. Her gaze searched his and she smiled.

Justin's heart gave an odd, unexpected jump.

Amy opened the door. "Come in. I called the hospital a few times to make sure you survived my driving. How are you? Was it an ulcer?"

"I'm much better," he said and nodded. "Yes, it was an ulcer. After surgery, the treatment was antibiotics." He had felt sheepish when he'd learned his emergency could have been prevented with a simple prescription.

"Guys hate going to the doctor, don't they?" she mused.

"This one does," he said and extended the bouquet of roses. "These are for you. Thank you for saving my life." Flowers weren't nearly enough, but Justin wasn't stopping there. He had other plans for Amy and her after-school program.

"You're welcome," she said, taking the roses in her arms. The two tykes wrapped their arms around each of her legs.

Justin couldn't blame the little guys for wanting to be close to her. She radiated a combination of optimism, feminine strength and nurturing that would draw boys, both little and big, and she wore her undeniable sensuality like a spellbinding exotic perfume.

She glanced down at the boys. "Oops. I've forgotten my manners. Justin Langdon, allow me to introduce my kids, Jeremy, Nick and Emily. Smell the beautiful roses," she said dipping the bouquet to pint-size level, then she turned to Emily. "Would you mind getting me a vase with water, sweetheart? There's one under the sink. Dinner's almost ready, so everyone needs to wash up."

Faster than a speeding bullet, the twins detached themselves and tore out of the room.

"Me first!" Nick said.

"*Me* first!" Jeremy said.

"Chicken and dumplings is one of their favorite dinners," Amy explained. "Comfort food. We're very big on comfort food since my sister and her husband died."

Justin frowned. "Your sister died recently?"

Amy nodded, sadness muting the lively glint in her brown eyes. "And her husband. The children lost mom and dad in one day."

Justin digested the new information. "They're not your children?"

"They're mine now," she said firmly. "And they're staying with me regardless of what any social worker says about my age or anything else."

Justin got the uncomfortable impression that there was a story here, a story he'd just as soon not hear.

Emily reappeared and tugged on the hem of Amy's shirt. Amy bent down while the little girl whispered to her. Amy's smile emanated amusement and a hint of challenge. "Emily wants to know if you'd like to join us for dinner. The food should be safe, but our dinner table, uh, culture, may test your ulcer medication."

Justin glanced at two pairs of brown eyes and was surprised at his visceral response to both. Emily's gaze held a tinge of sadness that tugged at him. He couldn't help remembering long-buried feelings of abandonment from his own childhood, and the knowing provocative dare in Amy's eyes affected him in a wholly different way. He could learn about the after-school program, he told himself, justifying his immediate decision.

"I'd love to stay," he said, getting a sly sense of satisfaction from Amy's double take.

"You're sure?" she said, and he had the odd sense she was really saying *Are you man enough for this?*

Justin felt the click inside him. It was a quality he kept hidden from most people, a deadly serious determination to meet a goal, to prove himself. He'd experienced the sensation only a few times in his life and learned it was like flicking a lighter in a room filled with gasoline. It was what had won him a scholarship to college and what had kept him going during his years of eating cans of beanee weenees before he'd made his first million.

Something about Amy Monroe brought the same flame to life. She was a woman with sunshine in her eyes, a body with dangerous curves and even more dangerous dependents—children. He didn't know why, but he had the inexplicable urge to show Amy he was man enough for anything she might need.

Two

"I'd like to expand the program to at least five more elementary schools in this district," Amy said, responding to Justin's question about her after-school program at the same moment she saved Jeremy's cup from a spill. "I'd really like to make it county-wide, and if you want to know what I wish before I blow out the candles on my birthday cake, I'd love to see this spread all over the state, then the whole country." She paused, studying Justin's face. She knew some people felt overwhelmed by her dreams, but she sensed he understood at the same time he was amused.

"Amy, the Empress of Literacy," he said.

He made it sound more sexy than mocking, but perhaps that was just because *he* was sexy.

"I can't deny it," she said. "Two and a half hours per week could make a huge difference in the lives of the children who participate in the program."

"What do you need to make it happen? Money?"

"That would help," she said. "Teachers interested in helping with the program would find it more inviting to know their time and experience would be rewarded. The program also needs more exposure. It would be great if we became the darling of a women's organization, or a corporate sponsor decided to take us on, but since I became a mom," she said, smiling at Nick, Emily, and Jeremy, "I've had three of the best distractions in the world living with me." She noticed Nick squirming in his seat. "Bathroom?"

The little boy nodded. "I don't wanna miss dessert."

"Scoot. I promise to save some for you." After Nick left, she met Justin's inquiring gaze. "He waits a little too late sometimes," she explained. "Are you allowed to eat chocolate?"

His lips twitched, and his eyes flickered with a dangerous sensuality. "I'm allowed to eat anything I want," he said in a low voice that made her wonder what it would be like to be the subject of his undivided attention.

Distressed at her thoughts, Amy bit her lip and banished a wayward provocative image from her mind. If this was how she reacted to being dateless for six months, how would she act after a year? She cleared her throat and stood. "Good, then you can have a piece of the candy bar cake Emily and I made this afternoon."

Nick skidded into the room. "I'm back."

"Did you wash your hands?"

The little boy paused too long.

Amy chuckled and patted his head. "Finish the job and use soap."

"Are you a teacher like Aunt Amy?" Emily asked Justin.

As curious as her niece, Amy glanced over her shoulder to watch his response.

He shook his head. "I trade stocks."

"Which brokerage?" Amy asked.

He gave a casual shrug. "I trade online."

She gave him a second glance. He didn't look like a gambler. "What do you do when the market goes down?"

"When the market goes down, I short stocks."

Amy frowned as she placed a slice of cake on a plate. "Short?"

"I'm not gonna be short," Nick interrupted. "I'm gonna be tall."

Justin chuckled. "This doesn't have anything to do with height. Shorting a stock technically means you borrow the stock at one price hoping to replace it at a lower price. You place your order at a hopefully high price, then get out when it goes down. It's called shorting a stock."

"I've never heard of it."

"Only in America can you make or lose money on something you don't technically own. It's not for the faint of heart," Justin wryly said.

"Oh, makes for ulcers?" she asked.

He paused. "Partly," he grudgingly admitted. "But not making money at all would make more ulcers."

"What's an ulcer?" Emily asked.

"It's something in your tummy that makes it hurt," Amy said.

"When my tummy hurts, I throw up," Jeremy said, then eyed the cake and quickly added, "but my tummy doesn't hurt now. My tummy is smiling because it's going to get cake."

"My tummy is smiling bigger," Nick said.

"Is not," Jeremy said.

"Is too," Nick said.

"Is—"

"If your tummies don't shut up, you might not get cake," Emily pointed out.

Complete silence followed. For sixty seconds.

The doorbell rang.

"Is not," Jeremy whispered.

"I'll get it," Emily said, bounding from the kitchen.

Amy frowned as she set plates of cake in front of each twin. "Who could that—"

"It's Ms. Hatcher," Amy yelled from the foyer.

Amy's stomach sank.

She felt Justin's curious gaze on her. "Hatcher?"

"One of the social workers," she whispered. "I don't think she likes me."

He stood. "Why do you need a social worker? You're the closest living relative, aren't you?"

Amy nodded. "Yes, but my sister didn't have a will, so it's complicated." She glanced at the cake and winced. "She won't approve of the cake."

"Cake?" Justin echoed in disbelief. "What's wrong with cake?"

Amy shoved her hair from her face with the back of her arm. "She'll find something."

At the sound of heavy footsteps, Amy greeted the social worker with a bright smile. "Ms. Hatcher, what a surprise. We were just having dessert. Would you join us?"

The older woman gave a sharp glance to the boys and the messy chocolate cake. The boys' faces and hands were covered with chocolate. She sniffed in disapproval. "Sweets at this time of night will make it difficult for the children to sleep." She looked down her nose at

Amy. "And it's unsafe for little Emily to answer the door. You should know better."

"I was cutting the—" Amy began and stopped. She didn't know why Ms. Hatcher so easily succeeded in making her feel inadequate. Amy had been trained to teach, and although she hadn't been trained to mother, she was determined to be the mother her niece and nephews desperately needed. "I'm sure you noticed that Emily may answer the door, but she doesn't open it unless she knows the visitor. Is there anything else I can help you with?"

"The health department will be making an inspection next week," Ms. Hatcher grudgingly reported.

Amy felt a trickle of relief. Progress, at last. "That's great news. That means we're one step closer."

"There are other steps in the process," Ms. Hatcher reminded her, glancing at Justin.

He extended his hand. "Justin Langdon. I met Amy through her after-school program. I'm sure you're familiar with the impressive results of her work."

Surprised at the alliance he offered, Amy met his green gaze and sent him a silent thank-you.

"I'm aware that Ms. Monroe has set a full plate for herself," Ms. Hatcher said. "You may see me to the door," she said to Amy.

Amy followed the woman to the foyer and endured Ms. Hatcher's lecture. After the social worker left, Amy leaned against the door. It was amazing how one person's presence could suck all the joy out of the air. Amy resented it. She didn't understand what Ms. Hatcher had against her. Although their first encounter hadn't been stellar, the woman couldn't seem to get past it. Amy knew the woman didn't approve of her. She disapproved of Amy's youth and the fact that she wasn't married.

She seemed to disapprove of everything about Amy, yet the woman clearly didn't have valid grounds to prevent Amy from gaining custody of the children. The only thing Ms. Hatcher could do was make things difficult for Amy, and that was what the woman was doing.

Amy sighed and returned to the kitchen. The twins were licking their fingers and Emily had eaten the frosted perimeter and left the un-frosted center on her plate. All three faces were smudged with chocolate, all three content. Amy's heart twisted. Heaven help her, she loved these kids.

"We hated it," Justin said in a deadpan voice, lifting his empty plate and meeting Amy's gaze with a knowing look in his eyes. "You should have given us gruel instead."

"What's gruel?" Emily asked.

"Yucky, gross soup," Amy said, her lips twitching at Justin's joke. "Now you need to prove Ms. Hatcher wrong and get ready for bed."

All three groaned in unison.

"Why is that lady always so cranky?" asked Nick.

"She's mad at Aunt Amy because Aunt Amy slammed a baseball into her windshield and broke it," Emily said.

Amy felt Justin's intent gaze. Heat rose to her cheeks. "I apologized and paid for the repair," she felt compelled to say.

"She's still mad," Emily said, sadly shaking her pigtails.

"She needs to eat more cake," Jeremy suggested. "Can I have one more piece?"

"May I," Amy corrected. "And no, sweetie, you may not. First person ready for bed gets to pick the first bedtime story."

The three stampeded from the kitchen, leaving the room in abrupt silence.

Justin chuckled and shook his head. "You broke her windshield the first time you met her."

"It was an accident," she said, clearing the dishes from the table. "And it was technically before I met her." She shrugged. "How was I supposed to know she was going to pull into my driveway?"

"She reminds me of someone," Justin said.

"Named Atilla?" Amy asked, turning on the faucet to rinse the dishes.

"Close," he said. "I thought a house had already fallen on her."

Amy smiled at his reference to the witch in *The Wizard of Oz*. "I'm sure that somewhere underneath her gruff exterior—"

"—lies a heart of stainless steel." His expression turned serious. "Can she prevent you from getting custody of the kids?"

Amy felt a ripple of unease. "I don't think so," she said. "She can just make things difficult. She doesn't approve of me."

"Any reason besides the baseball?"

"I'm too young, too employed, too single." Amy figured she would remain single for the rest of her life, and that was fine.

"And you smile too much," he said in that deadpan voice that made her smile at the same time her stomach danced. "You laugh too much. And her biggest objection is probably that you aren't ugly enough."

Not ugly enough. A forbidden pleasure rippled through her. "I'm not?"

He shook his head and stepped closer. "You need warts and an extra eye."

"You suppose she would like me then?"

"Maybe," he said. "You still might not be ugly enough even with warts and an extra eye."

She looked into his green eyes and wished she had a little more time and just a smidgeon more freedom. He was the most interesting man she'd met in a long time, and his mere presence in her house reminded her she was female. Amy heard Nick gargle. She had no time and no freedom, so she'd best just store up this moment for a rainy day.

"Thank you for coming tonight, Justin Langdon," she said and following a wayward impulse, she kissed him. Her mouth should have landed on his cheek. Instead, she pressed her lips against his surprised mouth. In two seconds, she caught a hint of his fire, his musky scent, and the taste of chocolate. The combination was seductive. She pulled back.

"Do you kiss every man whose life you save?" Justin asked.

Surprised at herself, Amy struggled for breath. "I don't save many lives. I used the Heimlich maneuver on a first grader when he tried to swallow an entire hot dog and he cried on me." She bit her lip. "Thank you for putting in a good word for me with Ms. Hatcher."

"Aunt Amy!" the twins chorused.

Regret and relief warred inside her. "I need to go. Can you let yourself out?"

He nodded, looking at her thoughtfully.

"G'night," she said. "And don't get your shorts in such a twist that you get another ulcer." She left him and the dishes, knowing the dishes would be there when she returned, but he would not.

Three stories, five songs, and lots of hugs later, Amy tucked first the boys, then Emily into bed, and softly closed the door. Sinking against the hallway wall, she crossed her arms over her chest and drank in the peace in the silence and darkness.

She struggled with the weariness that tried to settle on her shoulders. "I can do this," she whispered. "I can be what those children need me to be." Although Amy had always considered herself a fighter, strong enough for herself and anyone weaker, she was surprised at how tiring being a mom was. She was even more surprised by the loneliness.

Pushing away from the wall, she resolved to keep her weariness to herself. In time, it would fade. She hoped it would fade. Rounding the corner to the kitchen ready to face the dinner dishes, she stopped short at the sight that greeted her. She'd been right about one thing, wrong about the other. Justin Langdon was long gone. But he'd done the dishes.

Her heart twisted. She skimmed her fingers over the clean counter. Justin was an enigma. She found him extremely compelling. Another time, she might try to solve some of the mysteries she saw in his eyes. Amy thought of the kids and shook her head. In another life.

Justin climbed the steps to the front door of his town home in his well-lit, well-patrolled, quietly affluent neighborhood. He strode through the door and listened to the silence. After the noise and chaos of Amy's home, his house felt a little too quiet.

Justin scowled. That was impossible. Her home symbolized everything he'd always wanted to avoid in his life. Dependents. He'd filled out countless tax forms answering "None" to the question "How many dependents?" Justin had always been determined to keep his answer at the nice safe, round number of zero. As a kid, he'd been disappointed so much by those who'd claimed him as a dependent that he never wanted to be in the position to disappoint.

He felt an odd uneasiness when he thought about Amy and her situation. She was taking on a lot of responsibility without much visible means of support. The memory of his promise to the Almighty wafted through his mind like a feather. Justin still knew he needed to find the reason he'd been put on this earth. Could it be related to Amy and the kids? His stomach clenched and he shook his head. That would involve the *D* word—dependents. Walking down the hardwood floors of the hall to his den which housed state-of-the-art video and stereo systems, Justin reached for an old James Bond DVD. With its Italian leather furniture and soft light, the room oozed comfort. He could easily imagine the sight of Amy lounging in his den, her lips inviting, her curves seductive. When she'd kissed him, he'd felt a ripple shoot to his groin. Her combination of power and sensuality alternately aroused his admiration and his baser instincts. He remembered she'd smelled like apple juice and sex.

A fleeting image of Amy's rugrats, cute though they may be, running wild in his peaceful domain made him twitch.

Justin shook off the images and slid the DVD into the player. He'd done her dishes and he would donate a tidy sum to her after-school program, but he was certain there was nothing else in the cards for him and Amy.

Over the next week, Justin pushed Amy from his mind and returned to his daily routine of trading on the stock market. At odd times during the day, however, her smiling face would sneak into his mind, her laughter would ring in his ears, and the remembered sensation of her lips against his would make his mouth buzz. Knowing he was scheduled to meet with the other members of the Millionaires' Club soon to deliver an update, he left his home office as soon as the market closed and drove to meet her at her after-school program. He rounded the corner just as she was finishing her class.

"*P* words," she said, dressed in pink and purple for obvious reasons. She wore a giant pipe cleaner shaped into the letter *P* on her head. Something inside him lightened at the sight of her.

"Pretty!" yelled one little girl.

"Pirate," called a boy.

"Pancake," yelled another.

And so on until Amy held up her hands. "I think you've got it," she said. "It's time for us to *part*," she said, grinning as she emphasized the last word. "You've been practically perfect. Ask your parents to talk to you about the letter *Q*. Bye for now."

She glanced around the room as the little ones left and her gaze landed on Justin. She met his eyes for a long moment that hit him like a gut punch. He walked toward her.

"You've surprised me again," she said. "Just please tell me you're not having a recurrence of your ulcer."

He shook his head. "I'm still clear," he said, then remembered the original purpose for his visit. "I asked you about your program a few times and what the financial needs were, but you never answered."

She nodded, the *P* pipe cleaner bobbing on her head. "And you never told me why you were interested."

"I know someone who may be interested in helping."

She brightened. "Oh, that would be great. A blank

check would be great, too," she joked, then her eyes clouded. "A new social worker would be terrific."

"Ms. Hatcher still causing problems?" he asked.

Amy absently pulled the makeshift *P* hat from her head and sighed. "Every time I think we're making progress, she throws something else in front of me. I'm starting to wonder if she really can prevent me from adopting the kids."

Seeing her discouragement, Justin felt an odd need to fix her situation. He shouldn't care, he thought, but for some strange reason he did. "I have some connections. Would a different lawyer help?"

"I think I need to be about ten years older and married," she said wryly. "Got any miracles in your pocket?"

Miracle. The word jarred him. He swallowed over a knot of tension in his throat. Miracles were too closely associated with the man upstairs for Justin's comfort. "So you're saying that if you were either ten years older or married, you would have no problem with gaining custody of the children?"

"Both would be nice," she said. "But either would probably work at the moment."

"You would give up ten years for those kids?" he asked incredulously.

"Oh, yeah," she said without pause. "A stable loving parent during childhood can make all the difference in the world."

She spoke as if she'd experienced a stable loving environment. Justin felt a sliver of envy. "Did yours make a big difference for you?"

She paused and met his gaze. "I didn't have the most stable upbringing. I always viewed my background as something I would overcome, and for the most part, I think I have. I want something different for my sister's children.''

In that moment Justin felt a bone-deep connection that reverberated throughout him like shifting plates of the earth's crust during an earthquake. Justin looked into the fire of Amy's brown eyes and had the sinking sense that he was staring into the face of his purpose.

Three

———

"No, no and no," Justin muttered as he entered O'Malley's bar later that night. "This has got to be a joke," he said to himself. To God. "I thought we had this settled. You know more than anyone that I am not a choice candidate for marriage or anything involving kids." Continuing his conversation with the Almighty, Justin made his way to the opposite end of the bar where Michael and Dylan were seated. "I realize you're perfect and you don't make mistakes, but this looks like the makings of a whopper to me."

"Justin, who are you talking to?" Dylan asked.

Justin shrugged. "You wouldn't understand."

"Did you get the research taken care of?" Dylan grinned. "I realize how much you hate to part with your green, but we've been talking about the after-school reading program for months."

"I talked to the woman in charge of the program and she gave me a figure. I think it's low, though."

Dylan and Michael stared at him in surprise.

"Low?" Michael echoed. "Does that mean you think we should kick in more?"

Justin nodded. "Yeah, and maybe we can find a ladies' club or something to sponsor the program. It needs some visibility."

Dylan shook his head. "I never thought I'd see the day when you'd suggest we give *more*. I never thought I'd hear the word *more* come out of your mouth in association with giving away your money."

Justin shrugged. Giving away another thirty thousand bucks was the least of his worries at the moment. "Things change."

Dylan frowned. "What's happening with the market lately?"

"It's up and down like it always is. Why?"

"Are you still doing okay with it?"

Better than okay, actually, Justin thought. "Most days," he said. "Why? Do you need a tip?"

"No, you just seem different."

Justin accepted the beer Michael offered him. "I am different. It's not enough for me to make money and hoard it. It never felt right to spend it for the sake of spending."

"Like me," Dylan said, his eyes glinting with dark challenge. For all his fun and games, Justin knew Dylan had a deeper side.

"Let's just say you haven't had the same hang-ups about spending that I've had," Justin said wryly and took a long swallow of beer.

"I've had more time to spend my inheritance. Up to now, my position on the board of my dear departed father's company has been nonexistent. That's about to change, though," Dylan said, his voice holding a thread of steel.

"What brought this on? The trip to Belize?" Michael asked. "Without Alisa?"

"Belize was great," Dylan said. "No paved roads, not much to do except dive and pet nurse sharks. The breeze blows all the crap from your head. Alisa may be the one that got away, but the seat on the board is mine and it's time I took ownership."

"Watch out, Remington Pharmaceuticals," Michael said, lifting his bottle in salute. "If you guys would get married and have a kid, your lives would be a helluva lot better. Speaking of which, I've got new baby pictures of Michelle."

Justin and Dylan groaned. "Just because things worked out with you and Kate doesn't mean the rest of us should get married." Dylan elbowed Justin. "Right? Justin my man is the poster boy for a forever bachelor. Right?"

Justin paused, hearing *M* words ring in his ears like a discordant bell. Miracle. Marriage. There was a reason both came to mind at the same time. As far as Justin could see, a successful marriage took a miracle.

Dylan elbowed him again. "Right?"

"Right," Justin muttered and took another long swallow of beer. He felt Michael's curious gaze on him and had no interest in answering any more questions. "The after-school research is done, so it's your turn with the medical research," he said to Dylan.

"No problem," Dylan said. "Any other business?"

"None from me except Kate wanted me to invite you two for a cookout this weekend."

"Will Alisa be there?" Dylan asked.

"I don't know," Michael said with a shrug. "I thought you said that was over."

"It is," Dylan said in a cold voice.

"Think you can make it?" Michael asked Justin.

"I'll let you know. You never know when a family emergency can crop up."

Michael screwed up his face in confusion. "But you don't have any family."

"Exactly," Justin said, thinking of Amy and her brood. If he ended up with a family, it would definitely be an emergency. "I've got some charts I need to check. Later," he said and left the bar knowing his two friends were shaking their heads over him.

James Bond didn't do the trick tonight. After Justin studied a few stock charts, he tried a DVD, but his mind kept wandering to Amy. He told himself he would write a check for the after-school program and get the best lawyer he could find, but his thoughts sat on his brain like an undigested meal. He finally went to bed and after an hour of tossing and turning, he fell asleep.

The Scrooge dreams returned with Amy's kids featured as poor and needy. Little Emily never smiled and the sparkle vanished from the twins' eyes. Ms. Hatcher played an evil housemother, but the star fool bore an uncanny resemblance to himself. He was the one who could have changed everything and made life better for Amy and her kids, but his reluctance kept him from it, and he died before he could change his mind. Desperate to gain custody of the children, Amy agreed to marry a man who would kill her spirit.

With sickening horror, Justin watched in Technicolor as Amy took her vows to such a man. Everything within him rebelled. *No. No.* "No!"

Justin sat straight up in bed, his body in a cold sweat. The image disturbed him so much his heart pounded with his fury.

Taking several deep breaths, he cleared his head. He rose from the bed, naked, and walked to his window. He pushed aside the curtain and drank in the moonlight.

He wasn't dead. Amy and the kids were still safe. It had only been a dream. Only a dream.

"Yeah, right," Justin muttered and shook his head. This was no dream. This was a kick in the butt. No more running. Justin knew his purpose was clear. Heaven help him, he was supposed to marry Amy.

"You think we should what?" Amy said, unable to believe her ears as she stared at Justin. He'd called her and asked to come over to speak to her after she put the kids to bed. Although she'd been tired, she agreed.

"I think we should get married," Justin said. "You said you needed a husband to get custody of the children. I'm the one you need."

Her stomach took a dip at his words. "But we don't love each other."

"Exactly," he agreed.

"We don't really even like each other."

"I don't agree with that," he said. "I like you."

Amy dipped her head and covered her face with her hand. "I like you. Let's get married," she whispered to herself. She lifted her gaze to his again. "This just doesn't make sense to me. Why would you do this? I mean, you don't need a green card or anything, do you?"

He shook his head. "No. I'm a U.S. citizen," he said, then looked away. "This is hard to explain."

"Try me," she said.

"You know how you have this strong feeling that part of your purpose in life is to help those disadvantaged preschoolers?"

Amy nodded, but the connection eluded her. "Yes."

Justin stood and shoved his hands in his pockets. He walked restlessly to the other side of her den. "Well, when I had that medical emergency, I had a weird dream and I kinda got the message that there was a reason I'm on this earth and I needed to find out what it was."

"And?" she prompted, still not making any connection.

He turned to face her. "I had another weird dream last night. This one was about you and the kids, and I think—" His jaw hardened. "I *know* I'm supposed to marry you."

"Omigoodness," she said, realization sprinkling through her like a cold rain shower. "You think marrying me is your mission."

"I wouldn't say mission," he said, wincing.

"Then what would you call it?"

"The same reason you gave me when you took me to the hospital. You are one of my reasons for being on this planet."

He spoke with such rock-solid certainty that she blinked. She almost believed him. She would have believed him if the notion had not been so totally insane. "Please don't take this the wrong way, but does your family have a history of mental illness?"

His laugh was short and wry. "No. This is more sane than it appears. You need a husband, and I need to keep my deal with the Almighty."

"I didn't make your deal with the Almighty," she pointed out.

"But you made a deal with yourself to get custody of your sister's children and give them a loving home."

He was right, and Amy wasn't sure she liked him for it. "But I don't really need you to keep the deal I made with myself."

Justin just met her glare with an uplifted brow.

"I shouldn't need you," she said, standing and looking up at him. At the moment, she didn't like his height, and she didn't like the strength in his face. She especially didn't like the fact that he seemed far less rattled by this than she did. "I don't know anything about you. I don't know if you have a criminal record."

"I don't."

"I don't know what your education level is," she continued.

"I graduated from St. Albans with a B.S. in Finance."

"I don't know if you have a drinking problem."

"I don't."

His gaze was so open and level she couldn't not believe him. Desperation trickled through her. "Children are very expensive. You may not make good money. I can't afford to feed and house another person."

His eyes flickered with a touch of humor. "I make okay money."

"Children are expensive," she insisted.

"I make very good money," he said, his left eye twitching.

Amy felt a sinking sensation in her stomach. She would bite her tongue in two before she asked the obvious question.

"I'm a millionaire," he finally, reluctantly said.

Stunned, Amy blinked at him. "Pardon?"

"Million, six zeroes," he said.

She sucked in a quick breath. "But you don't look like a millionaire."

His lips twitched. "How does a millionaire look?"

"I don't know," she said, thinking Justin was entirely too attractive. "Bill Gates?"

"He's a billionaire," he said.

"Oh," she said. "Well, when you get up to six zeroes, who's counting?"

"A billion has nine zeroes."

"It doesn't matter," she said, waving her hand and looking at him sideways. "Are you sure you're not a kook?"

He met her with the most level, sane gaze she'd ever seen. "I'm not a kook. I'm proposing marriage because—"

"—it's your mission."

"Because I believe it's one of the reasons I'm here on earth," he said. "As crazy as it sounds, I bet you can respect that."

She could respect it. "Kinda," she agreed and rubbed her eyes. She felt as if she were in some other-worldly zone.

"Saturday okay?"

Amy sighed. "For what?"

"For getting married," he said in a calm voice.

Her eyes flew open. "That's four days away."

"Did you want to do it sooner?" he asked, again in a voice so calm she questioned his sanity.

Her heart shot into her throat. "No!" She shook her head. "I don't know if I can do this. I don't know if it's a good idea. I'm going to have to think about it."

"That's okay," he said. "I had a tough time with it at first, too."

She eyed him curiously. "What did you do?"

"Shook my head, said no a lot, broke out in a cold sweat."

"You don't look at all upset now," she said, and barely kept the accusation from her voice.

"It's right," he said. "I never thought I would say that, but it is." He leaned forward and squeezed her arm. "Sleep on it, but remember Ms. Hatcher."

"I'll never sleep if I think about Ms. Hatcher."

"I can make her go away," he said in a voice liquid with sensual promise.

Amy felt something inside her shift and quiver. That last statement was the most seductive offer she'd had in ages. Talk about a dream come true. Make Ms. Hatcher go away. "I'll think about it," she told him.

"Name the date," he said as if they could have been meeting for bagels and coffee. "And I'll get it done."

His casual tone belied the formidable look in his eyes, letting Amy know he would accomplish anything he set out to do.

"G'night," he said, and brushed his fingers over her cheek before he walked out the door.

Her cheek burning from his touch, she lifted her hand to cradle it as she watched him walk to his car. A swirl of emotions spun her head round and round. She had joked about needing a husband to pass muster with Ms. Hatcher, but it had been strictly a joke. Or so she'd thought.

All her experiences with Justin had been odd from the beginning. He'd proposed marriage when she had thought a date with him would be nice. Her head began to throb. How could he be so calm? Surely he must be insane.

Pushing away from the doorjamb, she pinched the bridge of her nose. She had never pictured herself mar-

ried. Then again, she hadn't pictured herself mothering
her sister's three children either. Locking the door, she
walked down the hall and peeked in on the twins. Jeremy's covers were already kicked off and his thumb was
tucked in his mouth. Nick slept on his tummy with his
mouth open.

In sleep their rowdiness quieted and they looked so
sweetly vulnerable. Amy's heart caught. They'd lost so
much at such a young age, she thought, feeling the grief
from her sister's death wash over her.

Amy tiptoed to Jeremy's bed and pulled up the
covers. She leaned down and gave him the softest breath
of a kiss. He sighed, and she smiled.

Leaving the room, she closed the door behind her to
check on Emily. Everything inside her tightened at the
sight of the little girl. Emily clutched an old stuffed
teddy bear in her hands. She was old enough to have a
better idea of what she'd lost. Amy could tell Emily
wanted so badly to please. Emily tried very hard to act
like an adult, as if she could handle anything. It was
almost as if she was afraid to cry, Amy thought, as if
she didn't trust the security of her situation enough to
relax.

Amy kneeled beside Emily's bed and gently stroked
the little girl's forehead. Although the idea chafed at her
feminist conscience, Amy suspected Emily would benefit from a man around the house. The solidity and security offered by the right man could work wonders. But
was Justin the right man? Amy wondered.

An image of Ms. Hatcher flashed through her mind,
sending a cold chill through her. Amy frowned. These
children needed her. They needed her love and stability,
and they needed to belong to her.

Amy thought again of Justin's proposal.

A long, long time ago, when she was much younger, she had dreamed of finding a man to love, a man who would provide a safe harbor from the bad stuff life threw at her or him. Then she grew up and realized she had to make her own safe harbor, her own security; and needing a man could actually make her more vulnerable instead of less.

Long before Amy became an adult, she'd preferred to pilot her own ship. The idea of sharing the helm unsettled her. It wouldn't be her top choice.

She glanced again at Emily as she lay sweetly sleeping. Emily hadn't gotten her top choice either, Amy thought, her sister's death weighing heavily on her shoulders. Justin's proposal dangled before her, alternately seducing and repelling her.

Justin's phone rang at 6:00 a.m. Amy wanted to meet him after the kids left. She had called the school and arranged to go in late. Justin pulled into her driveway behind her Volkswagen and threaded his way through the obstacle course of Big Wheel toys on the walkway to her porch. Glancing at his watch, he rang the doorbell. He hoped to make it back to his house in time for the opening of the market. If he was going to bear some responsibility for three children, he was going to need to continue to make money.

Three children. His stomach turned. Heaven help him. Heaven had better help him, he thought, because this sure as hell hadn't been his idea.

Amy greeted him at the door, her gaze wary, her smile absent. The thought struck him that he would have liked to see her smile. She led him into the den and waved her hand at the sofa.

Justin sat. She didn't. She paced, the hem of her flippy skirt emphasizing the length of her bare legs.

"There are too many unanswered questions about your pro—" She faltered. "—suggestion that we marry."

He noticed she couldn't cough up the word proposal. If he'd had any secret romantic fantasies about marriage, he supposed he would have had a tough time with it, too. The only fantasy Justin had ever had about marriage was avoiding it. But since this was the deal from the big guy upstairs, Justin had no choice.

"What questions?"

"Where we'll live, how long we'll remain married, if you like children," she said, looking at him sideways. "I have a feeling you don't."

Justin shifted in his seat. "I don't dislike children. I haven't spent much time around them. As to where we'll live—"

"We need to live here," she said. "The kids don't need any further disruption in their lives. They've been through enough."

He nodded slowly. "I'll need a room for an office."

"I have an extra bedroom," she said and took a deep breath. "If we decide to get mar—" She stumbled over the words and shook her head. "If we decide to do this, I think we should do it for two years, then decide if we want to go our separate ways."

Justin turned the terms over in his head. "That's fine. I can get a prenup worked up to provide for you and the kids."

Amy looked at him in horror. "Oh, no! I wouldn't expect alimony or child support once this was over."

He shrugged. "I think that would be best."

She stared at him a long moment and realization crossed her face. "Oh, because it's your mission?"

Her choice of words grated on him. Amy had the kind of voice that could bring men age three to ninety-three to their knees. And her body— Justin wasn't on his knees, but he damn well wouldn't deny she aroused a distinctly *un*mission-like response in him. "One of the reasons I was put on earth," he corrected.

She nodded. "Okay. I think we need to keep the surprises to a minimum, so you need to know that I'm very independent and I don't take orders or interference well at all."

"That doesn't surprise me," he said, thinking of Amy's interplay with Ms. Hatcher. "I'm not interested in interfering or giving orders. I'm here to provide you with a vehicle to get custody of your sister's children and financial assistance."

She gave a quick nod and looked at him uneasily.

"What else?" Justin asked, impatient.

She crossed her arms under her breasts. "We need to discuss sex."

Four

————

Justin went completely silent. In odd random moments
when he hadn't been fighting the idea that this marriage
would likely kill him financially, if not mentally, he'd
thought about taking Amy to bed. It was no hardship to
imagine her lithe legs wrapped around his hips and her
full breasts massaging his chest while he thrust inside
her. She lived her life so passionately he'd like to see
how that passion translated in the bedroom.

Her brown eyes wide with a mixture of uncertainty
and a sliver of forbidden curiosity, she twisted her fingers together. Despite her bravado, Justin saw the vulnerability underneath. "You've thought about sex?" he
asked, rising to his feet. It occurred to him that his sanity
could well be pushed to the brink living in such close
proximity to Amy and not taking her for his own.

She bit her lip. "Uh, kinda, well, not really," she

quickly amended. "You can sleep in the extra bedroom. It can double as your office."

Justin studied her for a long moment. "We can change that later."

Relief washed over her face. "Yes. Right, later. I mean, we haven't even gone out on a date. I don't know you. You don't know me. We may not want each other," she finished in an uncharacteristically breathless voice. She looked at him as if she'd just told the biggest whopper of a lie and prayed he wouldn't call her on it.

Amy looked as if she'd just offered the biggest dare in the world and wanted to call it back. Justin wondered if the seductive images of sharing a bed with him ever danced across her mind. He knew from her covert, fleeting glances at his body that she was aware of him as a man. If she hadn't felt she needed to save her sister's children and then save the rest of the world, he suspected she might just let herself go. Even Amy must struggle with her needs.

He walked toward her and touched her chin. "You're a beautiful woman," he told her. "I want you. You want me."

Her eyes widened and she swallowed audibly. "That's a little arrogant, don't you think?"

He shook his head. "It's not arrogance when it's the truth. You have a body that could stop and rewind the clock of every man in St. Albans."

Amy felt the tiniest ripple of pleasure, but told herself not to be flattered. "There are lots of bodies."

"Yes, but not all move like yours," he said.

He'd noticed the way she walked. By the look in his green gaze, he'd noticed quite a bit more. Her heart skipped.

"You have a fire inside you. It shows in your eyes,

in your voice, in lots of ways. Men have always liked to play with fire.''

The visual of Justin, naked, touching her, made her feel suddenly hot. Before she knew it, he lowered his head and pressed his mouth over hers. He rubbed his lips from side to side, then slid his tongue inside. She was both shocked and mesmerized by his boldness. He kissed her as if he were opening the doors and windows to a house that had been shut for months. For years?

Amy felt a dangerous delicious temptation to lean closer, to feel the sensation of his hard chest against her breasts, to feel more of him. Her heart hammered. Her mind scrambled. This was crazy. Too crazy for today. She had more important things to do, she told herself. The motivation for his proposal to marry washed over her like a cool spray from Nick's water gun. She pushed away.

"*This* is not the reason you want to marry me," she said. "Technically, you don't even want to marry me," she reminded him and herself. "You want to marry me because you think it's your mission."

"One of the reasons I was put on the earth," he corrected in a curt voice, his eyes as turbulent as her emotions.

"Whatever," she said. "You didn't suggest we marry because of your overwhelming love and passion for me. I won't pretend that you did."

"Just as your agreement to marry me is not based on your feeling that you can't live without me," he said.

"I haven't agreed."

"You haven't? Who's pretending now?"

Amy scowled. At the moment, she didn't like him. She didn't like him at all for being right. "All right, dammit, I'll marry you. For the children. I may be a little attracted to you, but that doesn't mean I'm interested in going to bed with you," she said, and tamped down her loud protesting inner voice of truth. "I have my priorities straight here. I'd appreciate it if you'd do the same. I'm not marrying you to save me or take care of me. I learned a long time ago to do that for myself."

His eyes darkened. "Then we're well-matched. I learned the same lesson."

A dozen questions flitted through her mind. What had forced Justin to learn the same hard lesson she had? She burned to ask.

Justin glanced at his watch. "Speaking of priorities, I need to go. The market opens in fifteen minutes. When do you want to get married?"

Her head spun with his businesslike tone. "I'm not sure. Friday or Saturday," she said. "Or next week," she added at the same time she knew the sooner she did the deed, the sooner she would gain custody.

"I'd rather not do it during market hours," Justin said.

Amy nodded. She may never have envisioned herself as Cinderella, but this was a little chilly for even her. "Saturday, then," she said, grimly reminding herself this was for two years. She would do just about anything for two years to keep her sister's children safe.

"Saturday. I'll be in touch," he said and walked out the door.

Amy could have sworn she felt the weight of a noose settle around her neck.

Amy and Justin met downtown for blood tests and to make application for the marriage license. Before she knew it, Saturday arrived. Amy broke into a sweat. *What was she doing!*

Emily knocked on Amy's bedroom door and bounded into the room. She jumped onto Amy's bed, her eyes sparkling with excitement. "We're getting married today!"

Amy gulped and mustered a smile. "Yes, we are."

"Do you want me to make pancakes for breakfast?"

Amy's stomach shrank at the thought. "Oh, that's a lovely offer, but I'm so excited I don't think I could eat." Excited wasn't the most accurate word choice, but Amy refused to quibble with herself this morning. "Could you make pancakes another time?"

Emily dimpled. "Yeah, when Justin moves in."

Amy's stomach twisted. "Right. Great idea," she said and rose from the bed. "You chose your dress last night and the boys' clothes are laid out on their beds. How would you like your hair?"

"Ponytail," Emily said. "With a ribbon?"

"Can do," Amy said, grabbing a brush from the bureau.

Emily stood in front of her staring into the mirror as Amy brushed her hair. "Are you going to wear a long white dress like my Barbie doll has?"

What to wear had been the last thing on her mind. "Uh, no, sweetie. People who wear long dresses have usually planned their weddings a long time in advance."

"Longer than a week?" Amy said.

Try four days, Amy thought. "Exactly."

"Then what are you going to wear?"

Amy still didn't know. Her brain felt as if it were playing hopscotch. Guessing at Justin's ring size, she'd bought his gold band yesterday. She'd ordered a few flowers from the florist which she planned to pick up on her way to the judge's chambers. She hoped ice cream and the sheet cake she'd bought from the bakery would distract the children from the lack of true emotion surrounding the occasion.

Emily tugged on her sleeve. "What are you going to wear?"

Still at a loss, Amy smiled. "A surprise," she said, and it would be a surprise to herself, too.

"This is what you call a family emergency?" Dylan asked as he entered the hall outside the judge's chambers.

"Any wedding would be to me," Justin said. He'd spent most of the night arguing with the Almighty, trying to convince Him that Justin was not a good choice for this job. It was the strangest coincidence. The thunderstorm had gotten louder and louder the more Justin had argued. When he finally shut up in defeat, so had the storm.

Coincidence, he told himself again, but he knew what he had to do. Marry Amy Monroe.

"I still don't understand this. You made a deal with God." Dylan shook his head. "Are you sure they didn't mess up your anesthesia during your emergency surgery? Maybe your brain was affected—"

"You're here to be a witness," Justin said. "If there's one thing I don't need right now, it's a psychoanalysis from St. Albans's *numero uno* babe magnet."

"Okay, but I have to ask, are you sure she isn't marrying you for your money?"

"I told you. This is not about money. It's about custody." He glanced up and felt a slight easing at the sight of Michael and his wife, Kate.

Michael wore an expression of subdued admiration. "You sure know how to take the fuss out of a wedding. No church, no reception."

"Cheap," Kate added with disapproval.

"Expedient," Justin said, grinding his teeth. "Thank you for coming."

"Oh, my goodness!" Kate said as Amy rounded the corner balancing a bouquet, and holding a hand of each twin. Dressed in a pink frilly dress with a slightly lopsided ponytail, Emily brought up the rear with a miniature bouquet.

Justin's heart stopped. Amy was dressed in a cream-colored lace dress that whispered and sighed over her curves with a hem that kissed her shapely calves. Her hair was pulled up in a topknot with a spray of baby's breath, but a few unruly curls escaped. Her cheeks flushed, she gnawed on her bottom lip in nervousness. She was his bride. The knowledge filled him with surprising warmth.

"The children are adorable," Kate whispered.

Dylan cleared his throat. "Why didn't you tell me she was—"

Justin blinked. "Was what?"

Dylan shrugged. "Well, hell, she's stacked better than the City Library. I gotta tell you," he said with a nudge. "This marriage may not be such a hardship after all."

He had no idea, Justin thought. Amy's gaze finally landed on him, skimming over him from head to toe, then returning to his eyes. If her eyes could talk, they would have said "Are we insane?"

He walked toward her. "You look beautiful," he said, instinctively taking her chilled hand in his.

"Thank you," she said, her gaze dropping to his shirt collar. "You look very nice, too."

He sensed she was trying to hide her apprehension.

"Emily helped," she said.

"You look pretty, too," he said to the little girl.

Emily grinned hugely. "Do you like our flowers?"

"They're almost as pretty as you."

"I gotta go to the bathroom," Nicholas said, shifting from one foot to the other.

Jeremy tugged at his collar. "Aunt Amy says we get cake and ice cream when we get home."

Amy gave a pained smile. "The reward system at work."

"Good idea for the kids."

"And me," she muttered. "I should take Nicholas before we have an accident."

"Let Justin take him," Kate interjected, stepping forward. "I'm Kate Hawkins. This is my husband, Michael, and friend, Dylan. Why don't you guys take the other two children for a drink of water at the fountain while I help the bride?"

Michael's face crinkled in confusion. "Help the bride do what?"

Kate rolled her eyes. "Get ready for the ceremony."

"The ceremony won't take five minutes, so—"

"Sweetheart, would you please take the children to get a drink at the water fountain?"

He blinked. "Sure. Come on," he said to the kids.

Nicholas shifted again. "I gotta go."

Amy didn't want an accident. "So should I."

Justin surprised her by stepping forward and taking Nick's hand. "I'll take him."

Amy paused in surprise. "Are you sure you know how—"

Justin lifted an eyebrow. "I think we can muddle through."

She watched them leave. "It may sound crazy, but I

have a hard time believing Justin has ever helped a three-year-old visit the bathroom.''

"Given his aversion to children, I'd be surprised, too," Kate said.

"Aversion?" Amy echoed, swerving to look at Kate. The slim brunette with curious warm eyes wore an easy air of sophistication.

Kate gave a wry grin. "That was pre-emergency surgery Justin. He seems to have changed. Some," she added grudgingly. "Would you like one last dash to the powder room?"

Amy nodded and walked toward the ladies' room. "So what was the pre-emergency surgery Justin like?"

"Ultracareful. I always got the impression he had no intention of ever getting married or having children."

Amy's stomach began to twist and turn. "He doesn't like children?"

"I can't say that," Kate said. "He's crazy about our baby, Michelle." She sighed. "These three guys have hidden depths. Maybe it has something to do with spending all that time at the Granger Home for Boys. Maybe—"

Amy's jaw dropped. "Justin lived at the Granger Home for Boys?"

Kate nodded, saving the bouquet from Amy's limp hand. "Oh, yes. All three of them lived there. You didn't know?"

Amy shook her head, trying to make sense of the new information. It reinforced her feeling that there was more to him than what he had revealed. If he'd lived at Granger then he had firsthand experience with the reason Amy wanted custody of the children and why she felt so strongly about making a safe place for them.

"But you know he trades stocks and is very successful at it?" Kate asked.

"Yes. When he suggested that we get married, I told him I couldn't afford another mouth to feed and he told me he was a millionaire."

"This has happened so fast I bet he didn't have time to get you to sign a prenup," Kate said, extremely amused by the idea.

"I signed it the same afternoon we got our blood taken. It was more than generous." She met Kate's gaze. "I'm not interested in his money." She hesitated revealing her feelings. "I'm marrying Justin to ease the process for gaining custody of the children. To be perfectly honest, I've never set my sights on marrying any man, let alone a rich man. It always appeared to me that a woman pays in self-esteem and autonomy for that decision."

Kate stared at her in surprise, then smiled. "I think you may be very good for Justin."

Looking in the mirror, Amy felt a swirl of contradicting emotions. In less than fifteen minutes, she would be a wife. "This marriage may not last long," she confessed in a whisper.

Kate gave her a considering glance. "Michael and I didn't marry under the best circumstances and I didn't think our marriage would last."

"You changed your mind?"

Kate smiled. "Michael changed my mind. For what it's worth, Michael says Justin is a stand-up guy. When the chips are down and everyone else has fallen, Justin is the one who'll still be standing by you."

That sounded so incredibly tempting to Amy. Sometimes she felt she'd spent her life being the stand-up woman. Her palms damp, she rubbed them on the sides of her dress. *For the children,* she repeated to herself like a mantra. She licked her lips. "I guess it's time."

Kate looked at her with sympathy in her eyes. "We'd already planned a cookout this afternoon. Why don't we let it double as a wedding party?"

"I already have cake and ice cream at home for the kids," Amy said.

"Bring it," Kate said. "Hey, it's one less meal you'll have to cook. And my little girl will worship your children because they can walk and run."

"Thanks for the offer. Let's get through the ceremony first," Amy said, feeling an overwhelming urge to hike up her dress and run.

"It'll be short," Kate told her in a reassuring tone as she returned the bouquet. "You look beautiful."

Amy and Kate left the ladies' room and encountered the rest of the group in the hallway. Justin caught Amy's eye and strode to her side. "Ready?"

No. She nodded.

"I'm not an axe murderer," he assured her. "Just for my own peace of mind, you're not related to Lorena Bobbit, that woman who cut off her husband's…"

Amy almost laughed. "No. Did everything go okay with Nick?"

"No problem. Just unzipped and put him in front of the urinal and let it fly."

Amy felt a tug on her dress and looked down to find Nick smiling broadly. "Justin showed me a new way to pee. It's a lot better than sitting. Jeremy wants to try it now."

Amy looked up at Justin. "Thank you for your contribution. I think," she added.

"It was nothing," he said. "Guy-thing. You ready?"

No, but I'd really like to get it over with. "Let's do

it," she said gamely and walked into the judge's chambers.

Judge Bishop, a friendly man in his fifties, had just arrived from a morning golf game, jubilant over his score. "This is a great day to get married," he said as he was introduced to Amy. "I shot a score of sixty-eight and left the rest of my foursome in the dust."

Amy pushed her lips into a smile, wondering if she would remember that little tidbit in years to come.

"I'll keep this short, so you can get to the good stuff," Judge Bishop said with a broad wink.

Amy felt her smile falter. Oxygen was suddenly in short supply. Justin continued to hold her hand.

"Do you take this man…" the judge began, and Amy feared she might hyperventilate. Out of desperation, she did something she rarely did except for children. She pretended. She pretended she was talking to an order taker at Burger Doodle.

"…to have and to hold from this day forward for richer and poorer…"

Amy translated, *Do you want mustard and pickles on your burger?*

"I do," she whispered.

"In sickness and in health…"

Do you want fries with that?

"I do," she whispered again.

"Till death do you part?"

And a hot apple pie?

"I do," she said, firmly aloud.

From the corner of her mind, she heard Justin answer the same way she had. The bubble surrounding her game of pretend began to deflate when the judge asked for the rings. Emily bounced to her side with Justin's ring attached to a ribbon on her little nosegay.

With trembling fingers, Amy pushed the band on Justin's finger and repeated the words, "With this ring, I thee wed."

She stared at the wide gold band with the diamond solitaire Justin placed on her third finger and heard his voice repeat the same words. The weight of it was unfamiliar. The metal felt cold against her skin. She was enormously glad she wouldn't have to say anything else because she was too stunned by the ring to make a sound. The ring was definitely not a cheeseburger with mustard and pickles, fries and an apple pie.

She glanced up to find him staring at his own gold band in shock.

"You may now kiss the bride," the judge said.

Justin met her gaze and she had the slipping, sliding feeling that she had just danced with fate, done the polka with eternity. Though she may have pretended it, those were not Burger Doodle vows she'd just made.

Justin lowered his mouth to hers, and all her pretending was over.

Five

Amy felt as if she'd spent the day at the circus, minus the fun. After the ceremony, everyone met at the Hawkins's for a barbecue. The children enjoyed themselves immensely and Amy relaxed a tad until Dylan gave a second toast. It was definitely time to leave. The children were on such a sugar high from the cake and ice cream that they skipped their afternoon naps and ''helped'' Justin move in.

She prepared a gourmet dinner of peanut butter and jelly sandwiches and chicken noodle-o's soup. God finally smiled on her when all the kids tuckered out early and she put them to bed. Leaning against the wall in the darkened hallway, she closed her eyes and let out a long sigh. The only sounds she heard were the faint ticking of the downstairs clock and the rustling of computer and modem cords as Justin continued to set up his office.

She rubbed her thumb over the still unfamiliar wide

gold band on her finger. Needing solitude, but unwilling to go to her bedroom just yet, she walked downstairs and lay down on the sofa in the quiet den.

Moments later, Justin appeared in the doorway. A dark silhouette with broad shoulders, he emanated a quiet strength merely by his presence. Amy wondered if the strength was in her imagination. There was so much she didn't know about him.

"One question," he said, his voice low and intimate in the darkness. "With those kids helping, how do you get anything done?"

She smiled at the dismay in his voice. "The rule of thumb is if you're female, you add an hour to your estimated completion time for every child helping you."

He strolled toward her and looked down at her. "And if you're male?"

"Add eight," Amy said.

"Eight?"

Amy nodded, keeping her head on the pillow. "Eight for every child helping you. It's unfortunate, but men have difficulty focusing on more than one thing at a time. I'm not sure if it's due to hormones or the Y chromosome."

"Where did you learn this fun fact?"

"Oh, it's well known. Ask any married mother." She took a breath and looked up at him, a male stranger in her house. Her husband. Her heart jumped. She closed her eyes, thinking he might not affect her so much if she didn't look at him. "Is part of the reason you offered to marry me because you once lived at the Granger Home for Boys?"

"Kate's been talking."

"A little," Amy said, wondering why his voice felt

like it rubbed over her like a forbidden caress. "It wasn't all bad. You didn't answer my question."

"My experience at Granger may have influenced me, but it wasn't the deciding factor."

"Your *mission* was the deciding factor," she said, reminding herself as much as him.

Feeling his hand close around her ankle, she opened her eyes in surprise.

"Do I have your attention?" he asked.

"Yes, and my foot."

"Good," he said, not releasing her ankle. "If we're going to live together, we need to come to an understanding about a few things."

The slow motion of his thumb on the inside of her ankle distracted her. "What things?"

"Your annoying description of why I proposed to you," he said, holding firm when she wiggled her foot.

"Mission," she said. "What's wrong with that?"

"I said it was part of my purpose," he corrected through gritted teeth.

"Semantics. Would you let go of my foot?"

"When we reach our understanding," he said. His thumb and middle finger formed a human ankle cuff. The sight of his hand on her bare skin disrupted her.

"You want me to call it your purpose," she said.

"That would be better."

"We understand each other," she said, noticing that his finger began its mesmerizing motion again. "You can let go of my foot."

"Not quite," he said. "We don't understand each other yet. We don't know each other."

Amy gave a little test jerk of her foot to no avail. "Your point?"

"We don't have to make this situation a living hell for each other."

She met his gaze, wondering how one of his fingers could make her insides turn to warm liquid. "And how do we accomplish that?"

"We get to know each other," he said in a voice that brought to mind hot nights and tangled sheets.

She wanted to say she didn't have time to get to know him, but he chose that moment to skim a fingertip up the sole of her foot. Her stomach dipped.

"For the sake of peace of mind," he said.

She searched her mind for a reason to disagree, but her brain had turned to sludge. "Okay."

"We start tonight. I ask you a question and then you ask me one."

"Truth or dare," Amy said, not at all sure this was a good idea.

"Just truth," Justin said.

"Okay, ladies first," she said, shifting into a more upright position, ready to ask the question that had been burning a hole in her mind all day. "How did you end up at Granger?"

His jaw tightened. "My mother was unable to care for me."

"Why?" she asked.

He shook his head. "That's two," he said. "My turn. The first time I met you I asked you to dinner. If you hadn't been caring for your sister's children, what would your answer have been?"

Amy squirmed slightly. It was much more fun asking questions than answering them. "Gosh, that was a long time ago, almost two months ago. And I got pretty distracted when you had the ulcer attack," she said, trying to lead him away from his original question.

"What would your answer have been?"

Amy made a face. "Maybe."

"Your answer would have been maybe," he said.

Amy frowned at his disbelieving voice. How had he known she'd been intrigued by him from the beginning? "Okay," she admitted. "Maybe yes."

"I'm not familiar with what 'maybe yes' means. I'm sure it's my Y chromosome. Could you translate?" he asked, massaging her ankle.

Amy glowered at him. "It means yes. You were interested in my after-school program. How could I resist?" she rhetorically asked. She told herself she'd been completely unaffected by his watchful, intelligent green eyes, chiseled facial features and those broad shoulders that looked like they could carry any problem a woman might face. Amy wondered why she felt as if she were back in pretending land again.

He nodded and released her foot. Her ankle felt surprisingly bereft. "Sleep tight, Amy," he said and turned to leave.

Oddly miffed, she sprang up from the couch. "Sleep tight? That's it?"

He glanced around at her with one lifted eyebrow. "I stuck to my proposal. One question," he said. "Did you want something else?"

His voice was like a velvet invitation over her skin. The way he looked at her reminded her she was a woman. She fought the urge to rub away the effect of his touch on her ankle. She crossed her arms over her chest and shook her head. "No. G'night."

After watching him leave the room, she stood there for several moments, trying to regain her calm, but it had vanished like Houdini. She climbed the stairs and entered her bedroom, stripped and pulled on a cotton nightshirt. As she climbed into bed, Amy tried not to think about the fact that a dark, masculine stranger lay just down the hall from her, and that the dark masculine stranger was her husband.

Justin lay in a lumpy bed in a room one half the size of his walk-in closet. His *bride,* who possessed a body designed to make him burn with lust every wretched night of his immediate future, lay approximately twenty-five feet away. He hoped God was very happy.

Justin was waiting for the peace he'd expected in exchange for fulfilling at least the initial phase of his purpose on earth. Instead, when he closed his eyes, he saw Amy sprawled out on the sofa downstairs, her hair a riot, her eyes filled with sensual curiosity. Even her ankles got to him, slim, creamy and delicate. He had wanted to trace his finger up her calf to the inside of her thigh and higher still.

Justin wondered if hell could possibly be worse than being married to a woman who resented you and needed you at the same time. He stifled a groan. Then he thought of the kids and the tight feeling in his chest eased slightly. Even though they were nosey, noisy and expensive, he wouldn't wish his upbringing on them. He admired Amy for her commitment and sacrifice. In a strange way, their shared goal bound them together.

All fine and good, he thought as he rolled over on the soft mattress, but he wondered if the next two years would drive him quietly insane and totally broke. That image kept him awake for hours.

Justin finally drifted into a dreamless sleep. A sound permeated his deep slumber. He buried his head further in the pillow, but the sound persisted. It wrenched at something deep inside him before he even identified it.

A child was crying. Justin sat upright and listened. "Nick."

Hustling out of bed, he ran into the hall and collided with Amy. He instinctively closed his arms around her when she began to fall. She gasped, and he dimly noted her breasts heaving pleasurably against his chest. Her fingers closed around his biceps.

"Omigod, are you naked?" she whispered.

"Boxers," he said, feeling the brush of her thighs against his. Nick let out another sob that would rip the heart from Atilla the Hun. "Nick's crying."

"I know," she whispered, disentangling herself. "He does this every few nights. It used to be every night. I think it's part of his way of working out his grief. I'll take care of it."

She carefully opened the door and moved quickly to his side. Quietly following, Justin watched her touch his arm and whisper to him. "It's okay, baby."

"Aunt Amy?" he asked in a husky voice, giving a hiccup.

"It's me," she said, stroking his face. "You're okay."

"I had a scary dream. I was at Chica's Pizza and everybody left me. I was all by myself and I couldn't find you."

"That's not gonna happen," she said. "You're stuck with me. Do you want to get a drink of water and use the bathroom?"

He nodded. "Can I pee the way Justin taught me?"

Justin smothered a chuckle and stepped forward. "Yep, and I'll help," he said, offering his hand to Nick.

Catching Amy's look of surprise, Justin guided the wobbly child to the bathroom and held him up so he could drink from the faucet, then helped him finish with the toilet. He returned the boy to Amy.

"He has never shown this much motivation to use the bathroom," Amy murmured.

"That Y chromosome comes in handy when you least expect it."

She shook her head, but smiled. "I'll tuck him in."

"What about me?" he asked, figuring he could blame his audacity on the late hour.

"What about you?" she asked.

"When are you going to tuck me in?" he asked. "It's my first night here. I might have a bad dream."

"Count sheep," she said.

Justin wondered how such a woman who was so warm and generous with the kids could be so heartless with him. He knew, however, that Amy resented needing him to accomplish her goal.

And so began the inauspicious, passionless marriage of Amy and Justin. The following day was a flurry of activity with Justin continuing to get *help* from the children setting up his computer. The boys fastened themselves to him like glue, and in the corner of her mind, Amy wondered about them growing attached to him.

That evening, he met her again in the den. This time she was ready for him. She crossed her legs Indian style so he wouldn't work his voodoo on her ankle again. "Why couldn't your mother take care of you? Was she sick?"

He walked behind the couch and touched her hair. She turned her head to look at him.

"She wasn't physically ill," he said. "Or mentally ill in the true sense. She just couldn't manage money. Every month she would receive a check for child support from my father and she would spend it all within three days. Bills piled up, the landlord threw us out, our electricity was cut off too many times to count. She would stay out all night sometimes. A neighbor found out and called social services. Not long after that, I started living at Granger.''

Her heart twisted at the picture he'd drawn of his childhood. Amy's upbringing may not have been a fairy tale, but her mother was usually around even if she'd passed out drunk more nights than not.

''Neglect,'' she murmured. ''How old were—''

He shook his head. ''—one question. My turn. What made you decide you wanted to change the world?''

Her lips twitched. More than one friend had teased her for her crusader orientation. ''I don't have to change the world, really,'' she said. ''Although that would be nice. I can just be satisfied working on my little corner of it.''

Justin shrugged. ''You didn't answer my question. What made you decide—''

Amy waved her hand. ''Okay. When I was about thirteen or fourteen, I observed that there were two kinds of people in the world. People who make a difference and people who waste their lives. I saw too many people waste their lives to know I didn't want that for myself.''

She could see the follow-up questions on his face, but he just nodded. ''Okay, good night.''

The same irritation spiced with indignation she'd felt last night prickled through her. He clearly had more control and less curiosity than she did, blast him. ''Good night,'' she said, trying to keep the edge from her voice.

Justin glanced over his shoulder. ''It'll be a helluva lot better for both of us when you stop being angry that you accepted my help. Sleep tight,'' he said and climbed the stairs.

Amy gaped after him. *Angry! Me, angry?* She had half a mind to chase him up those stairs and show him what *angry* was. While it may be true that she was exasperated with the legal system, and she resented the fact that getting married would make it easier to gain custody of the children, she wasn't angry with Justin. She wasn't pleased she'd had to marry a stranger, and the marriage was turning her life upside down, but her anger was directed at lawyers and a certain social worker. Not Justin. Right.

Monday presented the usual problems associated with the first day of the week. Justin left early saying he would work at his home during market hours until he got the kinks out of his new computer system. Emily missed the school bus, Nick had an accident, and when Amy arrived at school, she faced a class with so many children sick from a virus her classroom should have been quarantined.

That evening Justin didn't arrive home by dinnertime, making Amy wonder if he was experiencing buyer's remorse. Probably sensing her edginess, the kids chose that night for a full-fledged arsenic hour.

Topping it off with a cherry, Ms. Hatcher arrived at the door. Amy just managed to beat Emily to the door. Moving her lips into what she hoped looked like a smile, Amy opened the door and greeted the woman.

"Good evening, Ms. Hatcher. Do come in. You've arrived just at dinner time again," Amy said, cheerfully trying to keep the edge from her voice.

"I nearly tripped over the tricycle on the sidewalk," Ms. Hatcher grumbled as they headed away from the foyer.

"I'm so sorry," Amy said, thinking it was a shame

the woman hadn't broken her neck. As soon as the thought whispered across her mind, she winced, hoping she wouldn't get struck by lightning. "I wish I could offer you dessert, but—"

Amy heard the front door open and close. She glanced past Ms. Hatcher to see Justin. Her stomach flipped. She and Justin hadn't prepared for this. She didn't know whether to kiss him or tell him to leave. A visit from Ms. Hatcher was too important to muddle, and she and Justin hadn't even made plans. "Justin," she said, biting her lip, "Ms. Hatcher is here."

"Hi, Justin!" the twins chorused.

Waving to the boys, he quickly surveyed the scene and walked toward Amy. "Nice to see you, Ms. Hatcher. Has Amy had a chance to share our news with you?"

The woman frowned as Justin put his arm around Amy. "News? What news?"

"We were married over the weekend. You can be among the first to congratulate us."

Ms. Hatcher's eyes nearly popped out of her head. "You're married? So quickly?"

He nuzzled Amy's hair, surprising the dickens out of her. "When it's right, it's best not to wait. Amy and I have each other, and the children have two parents."

"B-b-but, what about your honeymoon?"

Amy stiffened.

Justin skimmed his fingers down the sensitive inside of her arm and laced his long fingers through hers. "I'd like nothing more than to have my bride all to myself, but we thought it would be much better for the children not to leave them for a while." He squeezed Amy's hand a little too tightly as if to wake her from a trance. "Right, sweetheart?"

Amy nodded. "Right. The children have really taken to Justin, and I think it will be wonderful for both the boys and Emily to have a successful male role model in the home." Amy resisted the urge to put her finger down her throat. Give her pearls, heels and a vacuum cleaner and she could have been a 1950s television wife.

"Well, we will need to interview Mr. Langdon and perform our routine check," Ms. Hatcher said, clearly still struggling with her surprise.

Amy battled another dart of anxiety. What if there was something detrimental in Justin's past?

"Feel free. It's important for you to do your job," Justin said and to Amy's ears he might as well have said "Have at it, you nosey hag. I have nothing to hide."

She needed to get Ms. Hatcher out the door. She wouldn't be able to sustain the 1950s television wife persona much longer. "Was there anything else you needed this evening?" she asked.

"Not that I can think—"

"Then let me escort you to the door," Justin said. Amy wondered if he'd noticed her squeaky tone of voice. She suspected he knew how tense she was.

He deliberately pried Amy's fingers from his and took Ms. Hatcher's arm.

"Thank you," she said under her breath and felt her shoulder twitch when the woman turned away. A moment later, it twitched again.

Emily looked at her curiously. "Aunt Amy, why are you moving your arm funny?"

"I don't know, sweetie," she said, rolling her shoulder. "I think I'm a little tense." *Or maybe I'm allergic to Ms. Hatcher.*

Justin returned and met Amy's gaze. "She's gone."

Amy heaved a sigh of relief and rushed toward him. She impulsively hugged him and pressed her mouth against his, then pulled backed. ''I cannot tell you how much I appreciate you showing up at the exact moment you did. Thank you. Thank you. I owe you a big one.''

Justin glanced down her body with a sensual once-over, then seared her from the inside out with a warm, yet challenging gaze. ''How big a one do you owe me?''

Oops. Amy felt her heart skip. She wondered if she'd traded the Wicked Witch of the West, Ms. Hatcher, for the Big Bad Wolf, her husband.

Six

Amy felt a tugging sensation on her shorts. She glanced down at Jeremy.

"What's a honeymoon?" he asked.

Her shoulder twitched again. "It's when the bride and groom take a special trip."

His eyes lit up. "To Disney World?"

"Yes, or the beach. It could be anywhere."

"I think we should go on a honeymoon!" he said.

"Yeah!" Nicholas chorused. "Let's go on a honeymoon."

Emily rolled her eyes in sisterly superiority. "We can't go on a honeymoon, you guys. Kids don't get to go. Just grown-ups."

Jeremy frowned. "That stinks."

"Exactly," Amy said. "We would miss you too much, so we're not going on a honeymoon."

Jeremy's face cleared. "Okay. Do we have any cookies?"

"Did you eat your peas?" Amy asked, glancing at the table.

Jeremy squirmed. "Two of 'em." He slid a glance toward Justin. "Do you eat peas?"

"Yes, I do. Peas make you tall."

Jeremy's eyes widened and he took in Justin's height. "They do?"

Nick smiled. "I'm gonna be tall," he said. "I eat 'em with catsup."

Amy turned away from the kids and whispered to Justin, "Peas make you tall?"

"Can't hurt," he said with a shrug, and nodded toward the kitchen table. "It worked."

Amy turned around to see Jeremy eating his peas. "Amazing," she muttered. "Teaching the twins the boy-way to pee, scaring away Ms. Hatcher, and now getting Jeremy to eat his vegetables." She glanced at him. "I'd almost have to recommend you for sainthood."

"Oh, no," Justin said, raking her from head to toe with another glance that turned up her body temperature. "I guarantee I'm no saint. I look forward to collecting the big one."

Amy tried very hard to prevent her mind from venturing into forbidden territory at his mention of the big one, but she would just bet Justin had.... Her face heated. She definitely needed to chill out. "Ice cream," she said brightly. "Who wants ice cream?"

Later that evening, Amy collapsed on the sofa in the den and closed her eyes. She heard Justin's footsteps and felt his presence in the room, but kept her eyes closed. There was an air of expectancy between them.

She ran her thumb over her wedding band, then lifted her hand in the air. "Why did you get me such a nice ring? You could have gotten me cubic zirconia."

A brief silence followed. "How do you know it's not cubic zirconia?"

Amy popped her eyes open and stared at him. "Is it?"

His lips lifted in a wry half-smile. "No, it's not. I've been called a tightwad, but even I know it wouldn't be appropriate in this case."

She pulled herself up into a sitting position. "In a way, it would be very appropriate," she said. "Our marriage isn't normal."

He raised his eyebrows. "From what I hear, normal isn't always that great. The ring is more a reflection of you. I think you're genuine, so I think you deserve a genuine stone."

Touched, Amy looked down at her ring, and the meaning of the band grew on her. It was one of nicest, sincerest things a man had said to her and it made her feel vulnerable and a bit confused. She slowly lifted her gaze to him again, too aware of her confusing feelings, too aware of the way his jeans fit his body and long legs like a lover's hand. Her fingers itched to trace the slight wave of his hair and the hard line of his chin. Her mind longed to know the secrets behind his eyes. Dangerous, she thought, and searched her mind for a safe subject. "How was your day at the market?"

"Profitable," he said. "My turn. What is a big one?"

Her stomach did a little dip. Not that again, she thought. "It's a relative term. Your idea of big and my idea of big could be very far apart."

"What about duration?" he asked, sitting beside her.

Amy's heart picked up at his nearness. "Again, relative. I would guess no longer than, say, three minutes,'' she said, betting that three minutes of anything with Justin couldn't get her into too much trouble. Three minutes wasn't long enough to— Well, if three minutes was long enough, it wouldn't be very good. Her cheeks began to feel hot again.

''Three minutes,'' he said.

She nodded, mesmerized by the intent look in his eyes.

''Of anything?''

''Within reason,'' she said.

''Okay, I want the big one tonight,'' Justin said.

Her heart stuttered. ''So soon?''

''I told you I wasn't a saint.''

She swallowed. ''But if you use up the big one, you won't have it for later.''

''That's okay. Three minutes,'' he said.

She swallowed again. ''Three minutes of what?''

''One thing,'' he said. ''A three-minute kiss.''

Amy's breath stopped in her throat. ''That's a long kiss.''

''Depends on who you're kissing,'' he said and leaned closer.

Her heart hammering, Amy inched backward.

''Scared?''

Pride roared through her. She lifted her chin. ''Of course not, it's just a kiss. Should I get a timer from the kitchen?''

He chuckled. ''I have a timer on my watch. I can set it,'' he said, and pushed a few buttons on his watch.

Then he looked at her, lifted his hands to slide his fingers through her hair and pulled her to him like a bunch of flowers. As if the clock weren't ticking, as if he were in no rush, he rubbed his lips back and forth against hers, savoring the sensation of her mouth.

She sighed at his relaxed approach. He suckled her bottom lip into his, rimming just the inside with the tip of his tongue. Secret longings twisted inside her. Gently tilting her head, he stroked her scalp with his fingertips while his tongue toyed with hers.

Her breasts glanced his chest and his groan vibrated sensually inside her. Deepening the kiss, he trailed one hand down to massage her jaw.

A burning sensation built inside her. Inhaling his musky, male scent, she struggled with a restless need to take his mouth the way he was taking hers, to touch him, to get closer. She balled her fists to keep from reaching for him at the same time she opened her mouth farther for his exploration.

In a second, the tone of the kiss changed from lazy to hot and compelling. He tasted like sex. Consuming her lips, he slid his hand down her throat to her arm, urging her to touch him.

Her breasts felt swollen and her nerve endings buzzed with forbidden excitement. Her mind clouded with arousal, she leaned into him and lifted her hand to his shoulder. His strength lured her. Amy had told herself she always had to be the strong one, but his power surrounded him like a cloak, and the temptation to lean into him and absorb his power was overwhelming. Justin meshed his chest against hers, and the heat of him aroused her further. His fingertips grazed the side of her breasts, and Amy suckled his tongue deep into her mouth.

She burned. She wanted. He rubbed his thumb in a teasing movement on the outer edge of her breast. She wanted more. She wanted him to slide his hand under her shirt and cup her fully. She wanted him to rub her aching nipple, to take it into his mouth.

His finger edged closer and a moan vibrated in her throat. As if he could read her need, he moved slowly, ever closer to the stiff peak of her breast. So close.

Beyond the rush of arousal crashing in her bloodstream, she heard a tiny pinging sound. Justin paused and swore under his breath. The pinging grew louder. He pulled back, and she fought the instinct to follow his mouth with hers.

The alarm, Amy realized. The alarm had gone off. Three minutes had passed. Her body screaming for more, she disentangled herself and inhaled sharp breaths. The sound of her breaths mingled with his in the darkness like a hot sultry night, emphasizing the thick atmosphere of impending intimacy.

Rattled by the way he'd affected her in just *three minutes,* she stood and wrapped her arms around her waist. She knew without a doubt that the way he tempted her was more than sexual; it was also emotional. The knowledge frightened her so much her hands shook. She clasped either arm to halt the trembling.

Her mind whirled. She had always suspected Justin could be dangerous to her. His combination of strength, intelligence, and the underlying thread of his sexuality was entirely too compelling. She closed her eyes to calm down.

He touched her shoulder and she nearly jumped out of her skin. "Don't!" she whispered and held her breath. She was more sensitive than if she'd been sunburned. "Please don't touch me."

He didn't touch her, but his low murmur was almost worse. "Okay," he said, so close to her ear, she could almost feel his lips again. A shiver ran through her. "I want to do much more than touch you. I want to listen to your body instead of that damn alarm. I want to kiss you all over, but three minutes wouldn't be enough time. Three hours wouldn't be either,'' he said and the sensual promise of his words might as well have been an intimate caress in all her secret places.

"Sleep tight," he said, but it sounded more like a sexy taunt or challenge. Amy suspected she wouldn't be sleeping well tonight. She had grossly underestimated the effect he had on her.

An hour later, Justin rolled over for the twentieth time. He was still aroused. Although he'd sensed Amy was a passionate woman, he'd had no idea her response would burn his control to cinders so quickly.

Every time he closed his eyes, he tasted her lips and remembered the sensation of her tongue. He felt her breasts begging for his touch. He recalled the way her restlessness signaled her arousal. Every little move she'd made had wound his spring tighter and tighter. It would have taken so little to go further, to push up her shirt and stare at her full breasts before he tasted her nipples with his tongue. It would have taken so little for him to push aside her shorts and feel the inviting moistness between her thighs.

She was his wife.

But she might as well not be.

Giving in to insomnia, Justin pushed back the covers, rose from his bed and flipped on his desk lamp. Turning on his computer, he scrubbed his face with his hand. If he couldn't sleep, he may as well study stock charts.

The following morning, Amy felt vulnerable and she was angry with herself for the vulnerability. She shouldn't have gotten so worked up over a kiss. *But what a kiss,* her honest, feminine and currently unhelpful mind said. She banged her glass of orange juice down, and it sloshed all over the counter.

"Oops," Nicholas said.

Jeremy giggled. "Oops."

Together, they chorused, "Oops."

Her frayed nerves stretched tighter when the twins joyfully chorused, "Justin!"

They were always so happy to see him, she thought, and made a face in the direction of the sink. The problem was she often felt just as childishly happy to see him as the children did.

"Good morning," Amy said in a muted voice, noticing that his eyes were a little more narrowed than usual, and his hair was slightly mussed. Maybe he hadn't slept any better than she had, she thought hopefully at the same time she was ashamed for having such dark thoughts. He looked pretty darn good for having had a rough night.

"Morning, boys," he said cheerily, then offered the same muted tone back at Amy with a nod, "Good morning."

"G'mornin', Justin," Emily said in her sweet, sleepy tone as she spooned cereal into her mouth.

Justin returned the greeting. Amy's heart softened and she stroked her niece's hair. "I'll ask the Colemans if you can borrow their piano again today. Okay, sweetie?"

Her mouth full, Emily smiled and nodded.

"Who are the Colemans?" Justin asked.

"A family down the street. They've been kind enough to let Emily use their piano. I think she's interested in taking lessons." Amy hadn't figured out how she would afford a piano or the lessons, but she supposed that was a challenge for another day.

Justin nodded thoughtfully. "I'm heading over to my other home office, and I'm meeting some friends tonight, so I won't be home until late. You guys, give it your best shot to have a good day." He paused and met her gaze. "You too, Amy," he said in a deeper, almost intimate tone that tugged at something deep inside her.

That night, for the sake of sanity, Justin revisited his bachelor roots. He met Dylan at O'Malley's for beer and a burger.

"Michael will be late," Dylan said as he joined Justin at a table perfectly positioned for watching the wide-screen television playing the Baltimore Orioles game.

"Problem?" Justin said.

Dylan made a face. "Yeah, he's getting a home-cooked meal instead of a burger. I wouldn't be surprised if Kate has another baby soon."

"So soon?"

"I think they want a big family," Dylan said, and the look on his face reminded Justin of time spent at the Granger Home for Boys.

"Remember when everybody wanted a big family?" Justin said, taking a drink of beer.

"A big nuclear family," Dylan said. "We wanted Dad and Mom and a bunch of brothers and a sister or two to attract the girls when we were teenagers."

"It may not be nuclear, but you technically have a big family," Justin pointed out. "You're part Remington, so you've got two half-brothers and a half-sister."

Dylan laughed shortly. "Half is the operative word. Nothing would make them happier than if I disappeared.

Especially Grant. He's the oldest and I know he thinks I'm trying to take over the entire company.''

Justin quirked his mouth in a partial grin. For the most part, Dylan concealed his competitive nature with a well-honed, cool untroubled air. "And you're not?''

Dylan gave him a sideways glance. "Careful, someone might find out I give a damn after all. I don't want control of the entire company, just part of it,'' he said in a voice that reminded Justin of a shark.

"No wonder Grant doesn't sleep well at night.''

"Enough about me. How's married life? How are the perks?'' he asked with a sly grin.

"Amy and I haven't known each other very long, so we're not to the perks stage yet.'' He gave a sigh of frustration. "Besides I'm married to a descendent of Joan of Arc, so she doesn't believe she has any human needs.''

Dylan winced. "Sorry, bud. But you know even Joan of Arc burned in the end. How's the rest of it? Are you spending money like water?''

"Not yet,'' Justin said, the prospect of uncontrolled spending threatening a bout of indigestion. "I bought something today for one of the kids and I'm setting up accounts for their college education.''

Dylan raised his eyebrows. "This sounds like the real thing to me.''

"The kids are very real,'' Justin said with a shrug that belied his true feelings. "Kids take a lot of planning. I always knew that. I didn't know they could be fun, too.''

"And Amy?''

Justin thought about how responsive she'd felt last night and wanted to growl. "Amy could be a lot of fun if she'd quit trying to save the world for fifteen minutes.''

''Maybe you can get her to save you,'' Dylan said with a wicked grin.

Amy sat alone in the darkness of her den. The children were blessedly asleep and she was blessedly alone. Justin still hadn't arrived home. She should be welcoming these precious moments of solitude with open arms.

Instead her gaze wandered to the clock. She wondered where he was and with whom. It was none of her business, she told herself and rose to pace the area carpet. After all, it wasn't as if they were married in the truest sense of the word. If his idea of going out with friends included seeing a woman who would meet his needs, then that should be fine with her. In sexual terms, she had no claim on him.

So why did the very thought of Justin with another woman make her heart pound with fury? If Amy looked in a mirror right now, she feared a green monster would be staring back at her.

The force of her emotion for him made it even worse. She should not care, she fumed. ''This is why I didn't want to get married,'' she muttered. ''Caring for a man too much just gets in the way,'' she muttered to herself. ''Feeling too much for a man muddles the mind and saps the energy.''

She glanced at the clock again. Eleven-thirty. She missed their questions. Her day felt incomplete without them. She missed those few moments when she allowed herself to give in to her curiosity about him. And she was frustrated with herself for caring so much.

Taking a deep breath to calm herself, she left the den

and climbed the stairs. This was why she needed to rein in her feelings at all times. Tonight was a perfect reminder. Amy must depend on herself and no one else. Always.

Seven

The following afternoon, Amy found herself in a bind. The preschool children for the after-school program would be arriving any moment and her sitter had called with an emergency. She needed Amy to pick up Emily, Nicholas and Jeremy. Amy's back-up sitter was out of town on vacation.

Although she would almost rather chew nails, she tried to get in touch with Justin, first at his house. To her surprise, she found him at her home instead.

"What's up?" he asked.

Just hearing the strength in his voice calmed her. "I have a problem. My sitter's had an emergency, and I'm here doing the after-school program, so I need someone to pick up the kids from the sitter."

A long pause followed, and she held her breath. Regret seeped in. "Forget it," she said. "You don't—"

"For Pete's sake, give me a minute," he said. "The

market's still open and I've got two possible trades left. I'll place limit orders. Where does the sitter live?''

Amy quickly gave him the address and directions all the while thinking how much she hated asking for his help at the same time she was heaving a sigh of relief. ''I really appreciate this,'' she said. ''I owe you a—'' She broke off before she said ''a big one.'' The big one had gotten her in big trouble last time.

''We'll see,'' he said. ''See ya.''

No sexy tease on the *big one* from him either, she noticed with an odd sense of loss as she slowly hung up the phone. Perhaps he wasn't so interested in the big one with her now. That was good, she insisted to herself over a huge sinking feeling in her stomach. That was wonderful.

She kept telling herself the same thing during the after-school program and while she ordered burgers at the drive-thru. Ordering burgers, however, reminded her of her wedding ceremony. Brushing aside her sadness, she lugged the paper sacks of fast food to the front door and prayed her day wouldn't be topped off by the arrival of Ms. Hatcher. Opening the door, she reminded herself to limit her gratitude to Justin. She didn't need any more of that kind of trouble.

It only took a second for Amy to hear the tinkling of piano keys. For a half-moment, she wondered if it was a recording, but the sound wasn't at all professional sounding. She quickly marched through the foyer to the formal living room to find Emily, and her brothers standing on either side like bookends, playing a spinet piano.

Amy nearly dropped the burgers.

''Emily?'' she asked. ''Where did the piano come from?''

The boys looked up. "Justin!" they chorused.

Emily whipped around on the small bench with a huge smile on her face. "Justin got it for us!"

Justin poked his head around the corner with the phone attached to his ear. He looked at Amy and didn't speak or wave. He just looked at her from head to toe and back again, making her nerve endings dance on end.

Amy took a deep breath and looked at the piano. Beautifully polished and golden brown with white ivory keys, the instrument fit perfectly in the room without taking up too much space. She couldn't have made a better selection. How exactly was she supposed to limit her gratitude on this?

Nicholas sniffed loudly and rubbed his belly. "I smell burgers."

"You can't have any cuz you puked in Justin's car," Jeremy said.

Amy winced. Oops. Men could be particular about their cars. She was surprised Justin was still in the house. She searched Nicholas for outward signs of illness. "Are you sick, sweetie?"

He shook his head.

"He got into the sitter's cookie jar and ate too many cookies," Emily said.

Nick stuck out his bottom lip. "Justin won't let me have anything to eat cuz he said he doesn't want me to get sick again."

Surprised at Justin's wisdom, Amy felt the force of all three gazes on her as if they were waiting for her verdict. "Justin is right. We need to let your tummy settle down before anything else goes in it."

Nick eyed the sack of fast food. "But what about my burger?"

"We'll see. I'll call the three of you in a few

minutes," she said and headed for the kitchen. She rounded the corner and plowed into Justin. Still talking on the phone, he wrapped his arm around her to stabilize her.

Amy caught a mouthwatering whiff of his aftershave, and remnants of the emotions she'd felt when he'd kissed her rushed through her. Tough to hold a grudge after the way he'd come through for her today.

"Okay. I'll check my system tomorrow morning for the correction," he said, then turned off the phone. "My online trading system listed a wrong trade on my account and I just caught it."

His green gaze searched hers, and Amy struggled with a deep vulnerability that swept through places she kept hidden inside her. "What made you get the piano?"

His lips twitched ever so slightly. "Who said I got it?"

She smiled and shook her head. "Well, it's not Christmas, so I know Santa didn't bring it down the chimney. I thought you told me you were a tightwad."

"I am," he said. "This is different."

"How is it different?"

He shrugged with discomfort and took the food sacks from her arms to the kitchen counter. "Emily wanted to take piano lessons, so she needed a piano."

"Needed?"

"In the scheme of things, this wasn't a big deal, so don't make it one," he said, narrowing his eyes restlessly.

"It was a big deal for her and for me," she added, taking a breath and lowering her guard a millimeter. "Thank you."

Nicholas and Jeremy burst into the room, popping the

bubble of intimacy forming between her and Justin. "We want burgers! We want burgers!" they chanted.

"The natives are restless," he said. "Better feed 'em."

Throughout the evening, Amy would almost swear there was an air of anticipation between her and Justin. It grew thicker with each passing minute. At unexpected moments, his gaze would catch and hold hers. Her heart was also doing unexpected things like softening toward him. Amy's emotions swung from attraction and fascination to fear. By the time she put the children to bed, she felt like she was stuck on a carnival ride.

She went downstairs to the den, waiting and wondering which question he would ask her tonight. Which of her many questions about him would she get answered tonight? After waiting several moments, she leaned back on the sofa. Forty-five minutes later she awakened, but Justin was nowhere in sight.

Both disappointed and peeved, she returned upstairs and saw the light under his door. Burning with questions and curiosity, she lifted her hand to knock. She stopped just before her hand connected with the wood. It was better to keep a little distance, she told herself. She needed to rein in her fascination. He might be her husband, but it was in name only.

Justin avoided Amy the following morning. Her eyes might be saying *yes,* but he knew what her mouth would say. *No.* And if he weren't careful, the idea of changing her no to a yes could become an obsession. Could? he thought with a mocking chuckle. Who did he think he was fooling?

Hearing the blessed sound of footsteps departing the house and the door closing, he headed to the kitchen for a cup of coffee. Spying a bag lunch on the counter, he wrestled with his conscience, then grabbed it and darted out the front door.

Amy was buckling Jeremy into his car seat.

"You forgot something," he said, running to her side.

She glanced at him and the bag, then shook her head. "No, I didn't."

Confused, he looked at the bag. "Isn't this a lunch?"

"Yes," she said, sliding into the driver's seat of her Volkswagen.

"Who's it for?"

She met his gaze and her lips tilted in a smile so sexy it affected him the same way it would if she were dragging her mouth across his bare abdomen. "It's for you," she said and pulled her door closed. "Gotta go. Have a nice day."

Justin managed, barely, not to gape as she pulled out of the driveway and the kids waved at him. He glanced down at the bag lunch in amazement. Amy couldn't know that no one had ever prepared a bag lunch for him before.

He opened it and looked inside to examine the contents. Turkey and cheese sandwich on wheat, granola bar and banana. And a note. *No cookies until I know your favorite. Peanut butter or chocolate chip?*

That red-haired witch, Justin thought and felt an itchy, impatient sensation crawl over his nerve endings. He'd gone to bed hard and wanting every night since he'd said his marriage vows to Amy. Ever since "I do" had meant "I don't," he'd been burning in his bed. He hadn't known Joan of Arc could be such a tease.

Both. Thanks, J.

For the third time, Amy looked at Justin's bold scrawl

answering her cookie question and couldn't help smiling. So, she had more than one cookie monster living in her house. She slid the note back into her pocket and stored the information in her brain.

The kitchen timer dinged and she pulled the second batch of cookies from the oven. The aroma of fresh-baked sweets filled the air.

"Is it your mission in life to torture me to death?" Justin asked from the doorway.

Amy turned around to look at him and stopped short. His hair attractively damp and mussed from his recent shower, he wore no shirt and a pair of cotton lounging trousers that tied at the top and rode low on his hips. The sight of his bare torso and abdomen short-circuited her breathing.

"Well, is it?" he asked, moving toward her.

Amy swallowed and shook her head. "No. How am I torturing you?"

"Too many ways to count," he muttered under his breath and nodded toward the cookies. "The smell is distracting."

"They're a thank-you gift."

"For who?"

"For you."

He blinked, then shrugged his impressive shoulders and reached for one of the cookies. "I'm not going to argue, but why?"

"Because you picked up the kids for me and I heard your car sustained damage."

"You're welcome," he said and took a bite of the still-hot cookie.

His chest was extremely distracting.

"What are you staring at?"

Embarrassment rushed through Amy, and she swung

around to avoid him. "Nothing," she said in a high-pitched voice while she quickly removed the cookies with a spatula.

"I don't think so," he said, his hand squeezing her shoulder. Urging her back around to face him, he studied her face. "What's going on?"

"Nothing," she insisted in the same damn unconvincing high-pitched voice.

"I don't believe you," he said bluntly. "Answer my question."

Darn. "If this is truth or dare, I think I'll take the dare this time."

"It's not truth or dare," he said, moving closer. "It's just plain old truth."

Amy sighed and looked past his right shoulder. "It's your chest."

He glanced down. "What's wrong with it?"

"Nothing," she muttered, unhappy with him for forcing her to answer. "That's the problem."

He wrinkled his face in confusion. "I don't get it."

"You don't have to," she said, knowing her cheeks were as red as tomatoes.

He lifted a hand to her face. "You're blushing."

She rolled her eyes. "You're so observant."

Holding her jaw, he studied her for a long moment. She saw the moment the light dawned. "There's nothing wrong with my chest and that's the problem," he echoed in surprise. "You like my chest."

She bit her lip. "I didn't really say—"

She broke off when he lifted her palm to his chest. His warm skin and the thud of his heart against her palm wholly distracted her.

"I can't believe Amy of Arc likes my chest."

"I'm not Amy of Arc," she protested, but there was

no oomph in her words. He moved her hand in a sensual circle over his skin, over the pectoral muscles, then down the center to his belly.

Amy's mouth went dry. "You work out."

"A few times a week." He released her hand, but she couldn't quite find the will to remove it. Meeting her gaze, he lifted his hand to her hair, then circled the back of her nape and slowly drew her to him. He dipped his head and his mouth hovered a tantalizing breath from hers. "What do you want?"

She whispered the only word her lips would form. "More."

Justin's tongue drew a circle around her inner lips. Amy's temperature immediately rose ten degrees. He slid his fingers through her hair and drew her against him trapping her hand against his chest so that she felt his rapid heartbeat.

The sensual pleasure of touching his bare skin made her wish she could feel him against her naked breasts. He slid his thigh between hers and the thin cotton of his trousers both tantalized and frustrated her. There was no mistaking the hard bulge of his crotch rocking against her. Amy slipped her fingers to the back of his neck, urging him on. He drew out every carnal urge she'd never thought she possessed. In the eyes of the law, he was her husband. For Amy he was still forbidden territory, but she was finding him too tempting to resist.

She was consumed with his touch, his mouth, his attention. She wanted him to consume her. He guided her in a sweeping, sliding motion over his thigh that teased her, and turned her damp and swollen. She stroked his tongue with hers, unable to swallow a moan.

He slid his hand down over the outside of her breast

to her waist, then lower to her bottom. He shifted slightly so his masculinity rubbed against her intimately as he guided her in an undulating provocative rhythm. Amy's mind grew hazy with desire.

"What do you want?" he asked against her lips, his breath coming as quickly as hers.

"More," she whispered again.

He dragged his other hand to the hem of her tank top and slowly slipped his fingers up her waist and each rib until he slid one finger just underneath her bra. "Do you want me to stop?"

"No," she said, and he unfastened the front clasp.

"You feel so good," he muttered "I want to taste you."

Amy shuddered at the dark desire in his voice.

He toyed with her nipples, drawing tiny moans from her throat. Suddenly, he lifted her onto the countertop and raised her shirt to reveal her swollen breasts. For a moment, he stared at them, then met her gaze with an expression of barely restrained passion. He lowered his mouth to her nipple and made love to it with his tongue. At the same time he slid his fingers inside her shorts, past her panties to where she ached for him.

"Oh, Amy," he said when he found her swollen. "So wet."

She couldn't recall ever wanting to be the sole source of a man's desire and satisfaction this much before. She couldn't recall feeling so utterly female, so powerful, yet vulnerable within the same moment.

This wasn't just her gratitude over Justin coming through for her. It wasn't her appreciation for the piano. This man called to her in a way no other ever had. She didn't completely understand it, and wrapped in the cloud of arousal, she couldn't begin to explain it even to herself, but she wanted him to know her. As a woman.

She arched her breast farther into his mouth, and Justin slipped his finger inside her. He gently nibbled on the hard tip of her breast, sending a shower of sensations through her.

Swearing, he drew back and scored her with his gaze. "I want to be in you. I want to feel you wet and tight all around me."

She shuddered at the provocative bluntness of his words.

"It's either the kitchen counter, your bed, or my bed," he told her. "You choose."

Her heart fluttered wildly. "Your—" She swallowed over her suddenly dry mouth.

"Good enough," he said and lifting her in his arms, he carried her into his bedroom. With excruciating slowness, he eased her down the front of his body. "Last chance. Are you sure about this?"

Absolutely not, she thought, but more than her body was urging her onward. Doubts, however, slithered and crawled through her mind like serpents. Teetering on the edge of the unknown, she took a deep breath. "What am I to you?"

He stared at her without answering for a long moment. "You're a witch," he said.

Amy's mouth fell open. "A wi—"

"You're the witch who makes me hard and keeps me from falling asleep every night," he said, and the insult felt more like praise.

"You're Amy of Arc determined to save the world."

Irritation trickled through her. "I'm not Amy of—"

"I'm a pretty selfish sonovabitch, so I admire you for it."

Surprised again, Amy swallowed the rest of her protest.

He lifted his hand to her jaw and shook his head. "You are, by some stroke of fate or insanity, my wife. I need to know you. In every way."

His words clicked deep inside her. She couldn't imagine refusing him. Anticipation tinged with the metallic taste of fear filled her mouth. Theirs would be no easy coupling. He would touch her in ways she hadn't been touched, make her feel things she hadn't felt before. There were doors inside her she'd kept locked shut from everyone, and she wondered how she would keep those same doors locked from Justin.

She couldn't begin to answer all her unanswered questions. Except one. "If I'm a witch and I've been keeping you awake," she said, twining her arms around the back of his neck to bring his mouth closer to hers. "Then show me how to put you to sleep."

His eyes lit like twin flames. "This is gonna take a while."

Eight

He led her to the bed and pulled her down on his lap. Lifting her tank top over her head, he pushed her bra from her shoulders so her top was completely bare to him.

"Your breasts have driven me insane," he told her.

Amy glanced down at her chest, expecting to feel her usual detachment about her body. Instead she watched his hand cup her, making her nipple pout. He made her feel so sexy. "I don't usually think about them," she confessed.

"I have," he muttered and pulled her closer to worry her nipples with his tongue.

In the mirrored closet door, she caught sight of the provocative image of his dark head buried in her breast. The sight and sensation provided a double sensual whammy, surprising her with immediate force. That was the tip of *her breast* his mouth caressed.

She had never thought she was a particularly sexual woman. Was that woman in the mirror really her?

He lifted his head and looked at her. Suddenly self-conscious, she ducked her head. She felt caught.

"What is it?" he asked in a low, intimate voice.

"I've never watched—"

Realization crossed his face. He stood and stripped off his lounge pants in one smooth motion. Amy stared at him. His body was unrelentingly male. Tugging her to her feet, he took her mouth at the same time he unzipped her shorts and pushed them down over her hips along with her panties.

He brought her lower body against his, then tilted her head toward the mirror. "Now look."

Her mouth went dry at the soft, sensual image of her body entwined with his.

"Nothing to say?" he taunted, stroking her breast with his hand.

She closed her eyes, but the strong, knee-weakening visual burned in her brain. "You are such a show-off," she said, biting her lip.

"What do you mean?" he asked, his sexy chuckle vibrating against her.

"I mean," she said, "your body is—" She stifled a groan of embarrassment. "Your body is impressive," she hissed through her lips.

"You're impressed with my body? I hadn't thought you'd noticed."

Hearing the smile in his voice, she shot him a dark look. "Liar."

His gaze grew serious. "Don't you know what a turn-on it is knowing such a sexy woman is impressed with me?"

"I'm not a sex—" she automatically started to say before he covered her mouth with his hand.

He shook his head in disbelief. "Teacher, somewhere along the way, your education has been sadly neglected." He rubbed his mouth over hers. "And I'm gonna show you how much."

He took her mouth and the room began to spin. Stroking her tongue with his, he tempted and teased her to respond. She'd thought it would be heat and fury, and maybe it still would be. She hadn't thought he would make her laugh and ache for him at the same time. How did he do that? she wondered.

"Look," he said. "Look at you." He shifted her in front of him. Burying his face in her shoulder, he skimmed his hand over her breast, down over her abdomen, then lower still between her legs.

Through half-closed eyes, she peeked at the erotic sight of his large hands arousing her. But his touch was too distracting, her feelings too overwhelming, and her hunger for him too strong. She turned into him.

"Why won't you watch?"

"I'd rather watch you," she said, and he groaned.

Nudging her onto the bed, he followed her down, kissing her breasts, dragging his tongue over her skin. The tension inside her tightened with breathtaking speed. He dropped open-mouth kisses over her abdomen, whispering words of praise.

When he kissed her intimately, she stiffened.

"I want to taste you," he said, and his words melted her resistance.

His tongue sought her tender recesses while his hands stroked her inner thighs. He found her swollen bead of femininity and caressed her until she began to squirm. She felt hot and needy, full to the point of spilling over.

"Justin," she said, her voice husky to her own ears. She wove her fingers through his hair.

"So close," he said, flicking his tongue over her again and again.

Helpless against his sensual onslaught, she twisted beneath him. He devoured her and the coil of tension tightened excruciatingly. She arched, and a power surge ricocheted through her. She gasped in shocked pleasure.

Justin kissed his way up her body to take her mouth again. The taste of her pleasure on his lips spun her around again. Before she could catch her breath, he pushed her thighs apart and holding her gaze, he thrust inside her.

Amy gasped. Despite her arousal, she felt over-stretched. He was large and hard.

He made a sound that mixed pleasure with exquisite frustration. "Tight," he muttered and swore.

"It's been a while," she confessed.

"How long?"

She breathed and wiggled beneath him, feeling herself slowly begin to accommodate him. "A while."

He swore again at her movements. "How long?" he repeated.

"Do we have to discuss this now?" she asked, distracted by his sensual invasion. "Can't you think of something better to do?"

He looked at her as if she'd just completely shredded his patience. His gaze dark and primitive, he flexed his powerful thighs and pushed deeper inside her, stealing her breath again. He lifted her hands to the wooden posts on the headboard. "Hold on," he told her and began a mind-bending rhythm.

His chest brushed her breasts and he stole kisses with each thrust. She felt the friction of his legs against her thighs. With a long motion, he pulled his hardness nearly all the way out of her. Craving more of him, she arched and flexed around him in silent invitation.

He licked her lips. ''You like the way I feel inside you, don't you?''

She felt him, tantalizingly out of reach, at her entrance. She wiggled.

He licked her lips again. ''Answer me,'' he demanded.

Surrounded by him and her need for him, she felt as if she were at his mercy. It was humbling, liberating, and scary. Though she feared what she might be giving up, she closed her eyes and just for the moment surrendered to her humanness, to her need as a woman. ''Yes,'' she whispered.

Covering her hands on the headboard with his, he took her with all the heat and fury his gaze had earlier promised. He stretched inside her, filling her so completely she felt as if every stroke of his masculinity provided the most exquisite, intimate massage.

She felt his tension rise with the force of a crashing earthquake. His body quaked and rippled as he took her to the top again. Amy fought her release, fought the dizzying oxygen-deprived moment of ecstasy. In a primitive feminine way, she wanted to experience every moment of his pleasure.

She felt it before she saw it. His body stiffened, then he closed his eyes. ''Amy,'' he muttered in a sex-rough voice that called her to come with him. His climax took her over the edge again, and her body joined his in a rocket to the sky, shooting like a star.

Moments passed before Amy could breathe normally. Her head was spinning, her ears ringing as if cannons had gone off. Distantly she felt Justin roll beside her, his chest pressed against her side.

Her heart pounded so hard she was sure he could hear it. She knew she had never given herself so thoroughly, and she couldn't remember feeling this vulnerable in her adult life. Ever. She wanted to be held. Badly.

"Are you okay?" he asked, and she closed her eyes to his inquiring gaze. If he couldn't see her eyes, then he couldn't read her turmoil.

She cleared her throat. "Yes."

"Sure?"

"Yes," she said too quickly. Why did she feel as if she'd splintered into a thousand pieces and all those pieces of Amy would never be arranged in quite the same way again? She suddenly felt the horrifying urge to weep. Gritting her teeth against the feeling, she stiffened her love-worn body.

Justin slid his arm around her waist and shifted her on her side so she was cocooned against him. He surrounded her and even though her mind was racing, some primitive part of her must have trusted him because her body relaxed.

"You blew me away," he murmured next to her ear, a secret that gave her a sliver of ease.

Although she suspected their "blowing away" scales were vastly different, the notion that she'd had a fraction of the impact on him that he'd made on her allowed her to breathe normally.

Several hours later, she awakened, disoriented. What was she doing here? This wasn't her bed. Justin's arm was still wrapped around her, serving as a reminder of their intimacy. Amy shifted slightly and her body reminded her more thoroughly with twinges from their lovemaking.

A silken thread of uneasiness twisted inside her. Something about this was too comfortable, she thought. It would be too easy to slide into a habit of counting on Justin. Even though they had connected in the most powerful, physical way last night, he hadn't spoken any words of love and neither had she. Her heart tightened.

She couldn't love Justin, she told herself. She didn't know him well enough to love him. Besides, if she gave her heart to him, then what would she have left after he left her?

Too disturbed to remain, she held her breath and slowly slid from his bed. Gathering her clothes, she bundled them against her and tiptoed to her room. She tugged on a nightshirt and panties and crawled into bed. She'd thought she would feel safer in her own bed, more like herself. But she still felt shaken up and bothered. Knowing tomorrow would require all the energy and clear-thinking she could muster, she told herself not to think about Justin. She mentally closed every door in her mind to him, and when he still crept in like a warm breeze, she pulled the sheet over her head.

Justin watched Amy from the kitchen doorway as she poured juice and cereal. He wondered why she had left. He remembered the intensity of their lovemaking, however, and combined with her inexperience, he'd guess she was knocked off-kilter.

She must have felt his gaze. She looked up from taking a sip of orange juice and choked. She rose quickly from the table and rushed to his side.

"I— You—" She cleared her throat. "Do you want some orange juice?"

"I can get it myself," he said, catching all the little signs of nervousness, stuttering, high-pitched voice, and fluttery eyelids. Deciding he might as well get it over with, he pulled her into the hallway for a moment of privacy. "You left," he said. "Why?"

She bit her lip. "I, uh…" Her eyes widened helplessly. "Too much," she said haltingly adding, "you."

"At first," he agreed, remembering how tight she'd felt. "But you got used to me."

Color bloomed in her cheeks. "I didn't mean that way." She closed her eyes and shook her head as if this conversation was almost more than she could bear. "I mean the whole thing was too much. I'm not used to making love like that."

"I sure as hell hope not," Justin said.

Her eyes popped open. "And I didn't think it all the way through, the ramifications to the children."

Confused as the dickens, Justin put his hand on her shoulder. "Amy, what are you talking about? Last night had nothing to do with the kids."

Her gaze of distress slid away from his. "Well, I didn't think about sleeping arrangements and how the children would feel about finding us in the same bed."

"Wouldn't that be normal for a married couple?"

"If we were a normal married couple," she said. "But we're not. And I started thinking about what we'll do when the two-year trial period is over and if you leave how much it will hurt the kids."

But not her. Justin fought the stinging sensation he felt in his chest. He swallowed the bitter taste of regret. "Sounds like morning-after remorse."

"Some," she admitted.

"I can move out if that will make it easier," he said, thinking it would make life a damn sight easier for him.

Her eyes widened in fear. "The children."

He remembered and nodded at the bottom line. "It's

okay. I won't leave before the custody issues are re-solved," he said, wondering if it would kill him. "We'll just stay out of each other's way."

She moved her head in an uncertain, helpless circle, but said nothing.

Justin wondered where he could find a pair of blinders so he wouldn't see her twenty times a day. And earplugs so he wouldn't hear her voice. And a clothespin for his nose so he wouldn't catch her scent at odd moments. He wondered how to wipe out the memory of how she'd felt in his arms and tasted in his mouth. He wondered how to erase the visual of burying himself inside her, feeling her let go and let him in.

He didn't know how he'd do it. He just knew he had to.

Amy left a bag lunch on the counter for Justin. When she returned that evening, she found it in the exact same spot she'd left it, uneaten. The cookies she'd made for him were also uneaten. When she caught a quick glance inside his room that evening, she spied a dozen stock charts posted on the wall. Remaining in his room, he didn't show up for dinner or afterward when she could have awkwardly attempted to explain her inexplicable behavior. Perhaps it was best that she hadn't had an opportunity to explain anything since she wasn't so sure she understood too much herself right now.

She only knew there wasn't much she wouldn't do to give her sister's children a secure home and it felt as if Justin could threaten that goal at the same time he was helping to make it happen. He reminded her she was human, that she was a woman. With no effort at all, he made her aware of how much she could want. He added a dimension to her life that was thrilling and distracting.

The distracting part bothered her most. What she needed to accomplish was too important to get waylaid by a passion for a man with compelling green eyes and an inner core of power that drew her like a magnet.

So why was she thinking about him now? she asked herself as she prepared another bag lunch for him. She scowled, then wrapped two cookies in a plastic wrapper and put them in his bag. A vivid memory of Justin, his eyes lit with desire, his body naked as he thrust inside her, flashed across her mind. A rush of heat suffused Amy. Splashing her face with cool water from the water faucet, she decided she might have more in common with Joan of Arc than she'd thought. When it came to Justin, she felt like she was burning at the stake.

Finding the lunch untouched on the kitchen counter again the following afternoon, Amy reached the conclusion that Justin had put her on *ignore*. She couldn't, however, fault him for his treatment of the children. Emily drew some watercolor pictures for the walls of his bedroom as a thank-you for the piano. Amy noticed he praised the little girl for her effort. The boys swarmed around him for attention, and he took them outside to play a quick round of dodge ball.

She glanced at the lunch she'd left him and made a face. No surprise, but so far she was flunking Wife 101.

Justin acknowledged Amy with a quick nod as he headed for his room to bury himself in stock charts. Even in a wacky market, the stock charts made a helluva lot more sense than his witchy wife.

"Kate Hawkins called," Amy said.

Justin stopped. "What did she want?"

"To invite us to a barbecue. I accepted."

He nodded slowly.

"And the local stockbroker's association called asking whether you preferred beef tenderloin or seafood spinach crepes for the dinner where you'll be speaking. I told them beef. When the woman learned I was your wife, she invited me to come."

"You'd be bored," he told her.

She lifted her chin and met his gaze. "I told her to count me in."

Irritated and confused, he didn't bother hiding it. "Why?" he demanded.

"Careful," she said with a smile so sweet it made his teeth ache. "I might get the impression you don't want me to come with you."

"Like I got the impression you don't want to make love with me."

Her eyes widened in surprise and color rose in her face. She walked closer to him. "This is obviously difficult for you to understand, but nobody gave me an instruction manual for how to handle this situation. We don't have a normal relationship, whatever normal is. Believe me, I don't have one tenth your sexual experience, so if making love with you left me feeling totally unwrapped, it shouldn't come as a big surprise to anyone. Excuse me if I needed to catch my breath, catch my *mind!*" she nearly yelled.

Taken aback, he looked into her brown eyes flashing with misplaced indignation. He felt the slow drag of his gut, tugging him toward her again. It would be the death of him, he thought. "You never answered my question about your sexual experience."

"You're right. Unlike you, I could barely breathe let alone think," she fumed and turned on her heel.

He could just let her have her temper tantrum while he returned to his stock charts. In another life, he thought wryly and followed her into the den where she watched the children from the picture window. "How long had it been?"

She slid a sideways glance at him. "Three and a half years," she said in a low voice.

He blinked. "Why so long?"

She crossed her arms over her chest. "I was too busy. I worked while I was in college to help pay for my tuition. Relationships looked messy and I knew I didn't have the time or energy for them."

"Who was it?"

"A guy who was very persistent. He pursued me long enough to catch me at a moment when I was—" She shrugged.

"Weak," he supplied.

"Curious," she immediately corrected as if weak wasn't in her vocabulary.

"Did he satisfy your curiosity?"

She paused a moment. "Yes, but not much else."

Ouch. "Lousy lover?"

"I really didn't have any basis for comparison."

She surprised him again. "Your only lover?"

She nodded. "And last until you."

"You're telling me you've only had two sexual experiences in your life?" he asked, unable to believe it.

"No," she said. "After the first time with him, I gave it two more tries, then called it quits. Being with you was—" she said, taking a breath. "Very different. But you have such a huge—" she glanced at him "—ego, that I'm sure you've heard this kind of thing before."

Bowled over by her disclosure, he struggled with a weird assortment of emotions. He had an odd urge to punch the guy who'd taken her without taking care of her. On the other hand, Justin was fiercely glad he had been the man to show her the pleasure of lovemaking.

He walked to her side and despite the fact that her back looked as stiff as a board, he curled his hand around the nape of her neck beneath her hair. Despite her *cajone*-breaking image, he suspected the woman needed gentleness, something he hadn't offered her so far. "I wouldn't have thought you were so inexperienced," he said.

She glanced up at him. "Why?"

"Well, hell, Amy, you're built like a woman who could pose for a man's fantasy magazine. You laugh and every male within earshot age four to ninety-four is vying for your attention."

"You really think I'm built like a woman who could pose for a men's magazine?"

Justin twitched at the thought. He rubbed his face. "Don't get any ideas. The local school board wouldn't approve and neither would I. I wish I'd known all this."

She took a deep breath. "That's what I've been saying. You don't know me. I don't know you. You don't love me," she said, searching his face. "But we're going to do this for at least two years, right?"

He nodded, wondering if two years would be long enough for him to learn everything about Amy he wanted to learn.

"If we had been dating for less than a month and we made love, would you have necessarily expected me to stay the whole night?"

"After a night like that?" he asked, and he watched her nod. "I would have kept you in bed for three days straight."

Her eyes widened. "Oh." She gulped. "I'm not familiar with the etiquette, so—"

He gently squeezed the back of her neck. "Screw etiquette, Amy," he said as kindly as he could manage. "This was about getting enough of you."

Nine

Amy's stomach dipped and swirled at the expression on Justin's face. She was beginning to feel that every time she was around Justin, she was in over her head. She prayed that wasn't true.

How had they gotten into this discussion? she wondered desperately. How had they gone from a barbecue and stockbroker's dinner to the complete unabridged history of her dismal sex life? Eating glass would have been preferable to telling him about her lack of romance, but Amy had made a deal with herself. If she wanted Justin to answer her questions, and she grudgingly admitted she did, then she would have to attempt to answer his questions.

She cleared her throat. "Can we get back to the broker's dinner?"

"You'll be bored," he told her.

"No, I won't. It will give me a chance to understand more about what you do."

"I can show you charts anytime."

"It will be the first thing resembling a date that you and I have attempted," she said bluntly.

That stopped him. He looked at her curiously. "You want a date?" he asked, sounding surprised.

She stifled a sigh. "Yes."

He shook his head. "I wouldn't take anyone I liked to this meeting. Besides—" he said, breaking off as his gaze skimmed over her breasts and lower.

"Besides what?"

Clearly reluctant, he rubbed his mouth. "Besides, if I were taking you on a date, my mission would be to get you into bed."

His *mission*. At the thought of being Justin's singular sexual mission, Amy felt a shudder ripple through her.

"But not at a stockbrokers' meeting. In the past, I could have picked up a woman there, but—"

Anger shot through her. "Picked up a woman? Is that why you don't want me to go? I might be interrupting your happy hunting grounds."

"I said in the past," Justin told her.

All her doubts clamored to the surface. "Yes, and our marriage is a figure of speech for both of us, so what's to keep you from 'hunting'? For all I know you could be picking up women when you go out with your so-called friends."

He looked at her with an incredulous expression. "Are you jealous?"

Amy's fury increased tenfold. She sucked in a quick breath. "I am not jealous," she insisted. "But if you're going to seduce me, I might need to be concerned about safe sex."

His eyes darkened and Amy quickly gleaned that she'd insulted him. "I'm not the one sneaking away from your bed in the middle of the night," he told her. "And if you were so concerned about safe sex, then why didn't you mention contraception the other night?"

Amy swallowed. "I'm on the Pill."

"Why?"

It was none of his business. "Because my periods are irregular!" she said through clenched teeth.

He paused a long moment. "Okay," he said. "You can come to the stockbrokers' dinner and meeting if you want."

Too peeved to be reasonable, she barely resisted the urge to kick him. "Never mind," she said with a sniff and went outside to play with the kids.

Justin felt the breeze from the door swinging in his face and thought about ripping it off its hinges. She was going to drive him insane, he thought. If his friends had been true friends, they would have locked him up and thrown away the key when he'd said he was getting married.

First she tortured him by not making love with him, then she blew him away by making love with him. Then she'd insulted the daylights out of him by sneaking away like a thief. When he tried to keep a sane distance, she insisted on attending a boring stockbrokers' meeting with him. She'd flattered him beyond measure when she'd told him she could neither breathe nor think after he'd made love to her, then she might as well have kneed him in the groin when she'd suggested he was *hunting*.

He swore under his breath. The only thing he'd been hunting for was his sanity. He glanced out the window watching her twirl Nick around in her arms. She was an angel and she was a mistress. She was exquisitely soft and unrelentingly tough. She was impossible to manage, and if he did what was best for him, he would get the hell out of her looney bin.

But heaven help him, now that he'd had her, he wanted her again.

Over the next few days, Amy was snooty to Justin in a friendly way if that were possible. She turned her nose up at him at night, but she always left a bag lunch for him. When he didn't eat it, the next day she left a Post-it Note on his monitor reminding him to eat lunch. That little Post-it Note gave him an odd, warm sensation. He tried to recall the last time anyone had given a damn whether he ate or not and he couldn't. That night they planned to join the Hawkins's for a barbecue, and Justin found himself looking forward to the casual gathering. He wryly wondered if his bride might unbend enough to talk with him in the presence of other people.

"It's not nice to hold a grudge," Amy could hear her mother say in her mind.

It may not be nice, but it's safe, she respectfully replied. Much safer to hold a grudge and keep her distance. It was difficult, however, to bear ill will toward the man when he made Emily giggle with a silly joke. He pulled into the long driveway of the Hawkins's home and the children immediately clamored to get out. Amy released Nick's car seat belt while Justin took care of Jeremy's. Emily climbed out with a large bag of chips in her hands.

"There you are," Kate Hawkins called, walking toward them with her baby in her arms. "Michelle's been waiting for you."

"May I push her in the swing?" Emily asked.

Kate smiled and smoothed Emily's bangs. "Of course you can, angel."

The boys dashed forward. "Can we swing?" Nick asked.

"It's all yours," Kate said, pointing to the swing set. "Michael was determined to get the outdoor gym up for the baby even though she's not ready for it yet. I'm glad someone will enjoy it this summer." She glanced up at Amy and Justin and a wicked glint shimmered in her eyes. "Justin, you look remarkably at ease considering you're a family man, now. I expected twitches and shakes and ulcers."

Amy was the one experiencing twitches. "He's actually very good with the children."

"Wonders never cease," Kate said.

Justin gave a long-suffering sigh. "You're never going to forgive me for what I said at O'Malley's that night you overheard me, are you? Would it help any if I mentioned I've never seen Michael happier and you're the cause of it?"

Kate's face softened. She reached forward and gave him a hug. "Of course I forgive you. Something tells me you're facing your own challenges now." She glanced past them. "Oh, here comes Alisa. I'll be right back."

"I bet Dylan will turn cartwheels when he finds out Alisa's here," he muttered.

Amy watched Kate greet a slim woman with long straight blond hair. She glanced at Justin. "Dylan doesn't like Alisa?"

"They go way back," he said, carrying the food from the car.

"How far back?"

"Back to the Granger Home for Boys. Her mother was the cafeteria manager and Alisa used to steal cookies for some of us. She and Dylan developed a heavy-duty crush as teenagers. Dylan keeps asking her out, but she won't have anything to do with him." He cracked a half-grin. "As the stomach turns. About the stockbrokers' dinner," he began.

Amy lifted her chin. "Never mind."

"You're not gonna get snooty again, are you?"

She stopped midstep. "I'm never snooty."

He stopped and looked at her. "Yes, you are. You've been snooty since we talked about the dinner."

"I have not."

"Yes, you have," he said with maddening calm.

"I have not," she insisted.

He shrugged. "Then prove it."

She swallowed her trepidation. "How?"

"Kiss me," he dared her.

Her heart flipped over. She swallowed again. "Your hands are full," she said in a weak protest.

"My mouth is free."

She stifled a sound of *help*. She wasn't prepared to turn to brainless mush tonight, and she knew kissing Justin would affect her that way.

"Amy," Kate said, providing a ready distraction, "I'd like you to meet Alisa Jennings."

"Saved by the bell," Justin murmured.

Amy felt a rush of relief and turned toward Kate and the blond woman. "Gotta go," she said to Justin, quickly leaving his side.

"Amy, this is Alisa Jennings, and she met Justin when he was—" Kate broke off, waiting for Alisa to fill in the blank.

"Probably around ten," Alisa said, extending her

hand to Amy. "I must congratulate you on getting a ring on Justin's finger. He's been antimarriage as long as I can remember, so you must be very special to make him change his ways."

Amy's stomach turned. Alisa obviously didn't know the circumstances surrounding her marriage to Justin. "Uh, I'm not sure I—"

"—well, you know what a good woman can do," Kate interrupted tongue-in-cheek and put a comforting hand on Amy's arm.

Alisa smiled. "Yes, I've watched what you've done with Michael."

Kate glanced at Amy. "See how smart she is? That's why I wanted you to meet her."

Amy couldn't help smiling at their female camaraderie.

"Plus she has all these stories about Michael and Justin when they were kids."

Her curiosity piqued, she met Alisa's friendly gaze. "Really? What do you remember about Justin?"

"He always worked, sometimes more than one job. He worked with the cleaning crew at Granger until he was old enough to get a better paying part-time job," Alisa said. "And he was the best money manager of any kid at the home. All the other boys would buy candy or sports equipment with their extra money." Alisa shook her head. "Not Justin. He saved it. Everybody was always trying to hit him up for a loan," she said with a grin. "But Justin set a limit of two bucks and he wouldn't lend any more until the previous loan was paid."

"Let's move toward the picnic tables," Kate said. "Did they call Justin a tightwad back then, too?"

Alisa's face softened. "No. One year, there was this

kid who wanted to visit his family for Christmas, but they didn't have enough money for him to come home because his father was very sick. Justin paid for his bus ticket.''

Kate stopped with a surprised look on her face. ''Really? I would never have thought—''

Amy's chest grew tight at the image of Justin, as a child, sharing his very hard-earned money that way. Overwhelmed by a need to defend Justin, Amy had to interrupt. ''I haven't seen this tightwad side of Justin,'' she blurted out, and bit her lip. ''He describes himself that way, but I don't believe it. He bought a piano for Emily two days after I made an idle comment about her wanting to take lessons. And the after-school program I run has just received an anonymous donation.''

Kate nodded in the direction of her husband. ''Same thing happened with the home for unwed pregnant teenagers where I volunteer. When I asked Michael about it, he was evasive. Sometimes I wonder if the three of them have been doing something together, but whenever I start to ask, he—'' She paused and smiled. ''He distracts me.''

Alisa cracked a grin. ''Isn't that one of the qualities of a good husband? The ability to distract?''

''Perhaps,'' Kate said. ''Have you found anyone distracting lately?''

Alisa's grin fell. ''Not really.''

''Kate,'' Michael called. ''Your mom's on the phone.''

''Oh, and there's Dylan. Excuse me,'' Kate said.

''I thought he wasn't coming,'' Alisa said under her breath after Kate left.

''Pardon?''

Alisa waved her hand in a dismissing gesture. ''Nothing. Dylan and I were close as kids, but we're not at all now.''

"Justin told me the two of you had a crush as teenagers," Amy said. "He also said Dylan keeps trying to get your attention now, but you won't have anything to do with him."

Alisa's mouth tilted in a sad, wry smile. "Justin always had a knack for pinning the tail on the donkey. The way I look at it is history has already repeated itself where Dylan and I are concerned, and it doesn't need to repeat itself again. We met again in college and he—"

Amy could see Alisa's eyes deepen with pain and even though she didn't know the woman, she felt the hurt echo inside her. "It didn't go well," she finished for her.

Alisa met her gaze and Amy had the sense that she'd just made a new friend. "Right," Alisa said and gave Amy a kind, but assessing glance. "I have a feeling Justin may have found exactly what he needs in you."

Amy looked across the yard at Justin, her *husband*. Her stomach dipped at all he was and wasn't to her. What if fate was involved between them in some strange, crazy way? What if this was about more than custody and the kids and Justin's deal with God? What if somebody somewhere had put them together because they were meant to be married?

The wayward thought danced lightly through her mind like a butterfly, but the implication hit her like a two-by-four. Fate? Meant to be? Those terms sounded awfully close to fairy tales, she thought, and she had given up on Cinderella before she hit twelve years old. Plus there was her history of nonromance.

But what if there really was a man in this world for her, and what if it was Justin?

Amy closed her eyes. Then heaven had better help them both.

The evening was a companionable time filled with children's chatter, lots of food, and threatening storm clouds. The sky finally burst open, and the group went scurrying toward the house.

Nicholas glanced back, pointing at the table in horror. "The cupcakes! I didn't get one!"

"I'll get them." Amy darted back to rescue the cupcakes, but Justin beat her and snatched the plastic container. Grabbing her hand, he tugged her out of the downpour to the closest dry spot next to the house.

Justin's hair was plastered to his head, raindrops dripped off his chin.

Amy shook her head and laughed. "You're so wet."

"And you think you're not?" He shook his head and sprayed her.

Amy lifted her hands to shield her face and laughed again. "Stop!"

She pushed her drenched hair away from her face and looked up to find his gaze lingering on her breasts. Glancing down, she saw that she was just as wet as he was. The rain had turned her T-shirt nearly transparent as it molded faithfully to her breasts. Embarrassed, she crossed her arms over her chest. "Oops."

His gaze met hers with a trace of something that looked very close to possessiveness. "Yeah. If there was a wet T-shirt contest, you would definitely win, but I don't want anyone else seeing you like that." He pulled his shirt over his head and transferred it to her.

It was such a chivalrous, protective gesture that she didn't know what to say. With the rain pouring down just two feet away, she stood there staring into Justin's eyes and a dozen feelings rose within her. Bare-chested because he'd just given her his own shirt, this was the same man who had survived the Granger Home for Boys and had given his money to a kid so he could visit his parents. This was the same man who always knew the bottom line, and this was the same man who had made love to her with a force stronger than the rain. Her husband.

Unable to stop herself, she stretched up on tiptoe and kissed him. She slid her arms around his neck and with her kiss, she tried to tell him things she wasn't able to articulate to herself let alone to him. She tasted his surprise and desire, and she felt the familiar insistent urge inside her for more.

He pulled back and studied her with hooded eyes. "What was that for?"

Speechless while her body hummed, and her mind and heart raced, she tried to make her brain work. "A thank-you," she improvised. "For giving me the shirt off your back."

He paused again, pushing her hair behind her ear. "Maybe you can return the favor sometime."

Later that night after the kids were tucked in, Justin found Amy downstairs looking out the window at the full moon. "I wondered if you'd come tonight. You've been pretty busy with your stock charts."

"It's getting near the end of the trading season," he told her, but he knew he'd been avoiding her. As he looked at the way the moonlight glimmered on her hair and he remembered the provocative image of her nearly naked breasts, he wondered if he should be avoiding her again tonight.

She looked at him curiously. "Trading season? I thought the stock market was open year-round."

"It is, but there's a theory that the best time for trading is between October and May. Since it's almost May, I keep a close watch on my short-term positions."

"What do you like most about trading?" she asked.

He enjoyed being the object of her feminine curiosity. "I like the illusion of control. I have no control over the market, but if I study stocks and apply different theories to the charts, then I find my percentage of wins goes up."

"Do you celebrate when you win?"

He shook his head. "Not usually."

She studied him for a moment. "You don't usually celebrate when you win because you win all the time."

"More often than not," he said.

She pushed away from the wall and pointed her finger at his chest. "If you're so good the stockbrokers want you to come talk to them, then 'more often than not' must be an understatement."

Capturing her hand in his, he lifted her impertinent finger to his mouth and gently nipped it, watching her eyes widen. "There's a fine line between confidence and overconfidence in trading. The difference can cost you a fortune. The reasons I've been successful are that I know the difference and I focus on the discipline and process of trading."

He darted his tongue out to taste and soothe her forefinger. As her gaze locked with his in sensual expectation, Justin wondered what it would take for a woman like Amy to fall for him. He wondered what life would be like to have a woman like Amy loving him. Dangerous thoughts. It was the kind of thing he'd never allowed himself to wish. He was pretty damn sure it wouldn't be wise to start wishing now.

She stepped closer so that her body barely brushed his every time she breathed. "You're like a book I never thought I wanted to read, but once I opened, it was hard to stop. Every time I learn something about you," she said in a low, husky voice tinged with frustration, "I want to know more."

She was so inviting she reminded him of a flower waiting to be plucked. In the corner of his mind, he remembered how she'd reacted the time they'd made love, but he allowed himself a kiss. Gently pushing her back against the wall, he lowered his mouth to hers, and she immediately responded by opening her lips and twining her tongue with his.

Her instantaneous, sensual response affected him like an intimate stroke. Aroused, he played with her mouth, tasting her and allowing her to taste him. With each stroke of her tongue over his, a visual formed in his mind of her kissing her way down his body. Her hair skimming over his bare skin, her hardened nipples taunting him with random touches in her movement down to his thighs. Even now, he could feel the tips of her on his chest.

His hands itching to touch her, he slid his hand under her T-shirt and cupped her breast. Her sexy sigh in his mouth was too irresistible an invitation and he slipped his other hand underneath her shirt so that he touched both breasts.

Amy moaned and undulated against him. Instinctively he pressed his arousal between her thighs and when she opened her legs, Justin began to sweat. He knew how she felt, how she tasted.

He felt one of her hands circle the back of his neck,

urging his mouth against hers, as if she were hungry for him, as if she couldn't get enough.

The notion sent a firestorm throbbing through his blood. He rhythmically slid his tongue into her mouth and she suckled him in the same way her body would squeeze his hardness if he were taking her.

She moved restlessly against him and he felt her hand slide down to touch him intimately through the fabric of his shorts. He couldn't withhold a groan. He wanted her naked. He wanted her mouth on him. He wanted her.

"Touch me," he urged in a low voice against her sexy open mouth.

With unsteady hands, she unfastened his shorts and cupped his aching masculinity in her hand. The touch of her caresses made him feel as if he would burst. Looking into his gaze with eyes dark with desire, she rubbed the honey of his arousal with her thumb and lifted it to her tongue.

The sight was so erotic it nearly made him crazy. "I want to take you," he told her. "I don't care much where or how. I just want to take you now."

Everything about her was one big delicious, inviting *yes*. Justin slid his hands down to her hips. It would be so easy to push down her shorts and find her wetness. It would be easy to lift her and wrap her thighs around his hips. It would be so decadently easy to thrust inside her tight wet femininity.

His mind and body throbbing in anticipation, he took her mouth as he began to unfasten her shorts.

Distantly he heard a high-pitched sound outside the room. He was so intent on Amy that he let it slide. However, he heard it again. A child's broken sob.

Despite his raging arousal, the sound tugged at him. It cost him, but Justin pulled back to listen.

"Aunt Amy," Nicholas cried from the top of the stairs. "I had a bad dream."

Justin ducked his head and inhaled deeply. He could feel her body humming with the same need he had. He took another deep breath. "You need to go," he murmured.

Ten

An hour and half later after a chilly shower, Justin still burned for her. But he wouldn't go to her. Prowling his small room, he felt caged. As much as he wanted her, his *wife* was an incredibly complex creature. Bold and shy, she somehow also managed to be both fearless and vulnerable. Justin didn't want her running out on him again. When he made love to her again, he wanted her waking up beside him.

He wondered how their relationship might have progressed if they hadn't married for the reasons they did. He tried to picture dating Amy, but it was damn difficult with three kids, as good as they might be. He wondered again what it would be like for her to give her heart to him.

His chest grew tight at the thought. He'd never wanted a woman's heart before. Her body, her attention, maybe, but not her heart. That got messy. But hell, marriage was about as messy as a man could get. The problem with wanting Amy's heart was that he suspected if she gave her heart, she would want him to give his in return. Justin would almost rather give his wallet.

"Have fun," Amy called after Justin as he left for the stockbrokers' dinner. He looked almost as good in a tux as he did naked.

He made a face. "I'm speaking."

She shrugged. "Well, then break a leg."

"I'll try not to. Later," he said and the door closed behind him.

Amy immediately turned to the kids. "I'm going out tonight, so a sitter will give you pizza."

"Woo-hoo pizza!" Nicholas yelled.

Emily was more reserved. "Who's the sitter?"

"Jennifer Stallings. I think you've met her. She lives down the street and she's very nice and experienced."

Emily nodded hesitantly.

Concerned, Amy bent down and gazed at her niece. "What is it, sweetie? Do you feel sick?"

Emily shook her head. She hesitated again. "You won't get in an accident, will you?" she asked in a low voice.

Amy's heart twisted and she pulled Emily into her arms. "I have every intention of not getting in an accident. I know it's hard not to feel scared, but we can't lock ourselves at home. Not you or me." She pulled back and gazed into her niece's pensive face. "I tell you what. I plan to be home by around midnight at the very latest, and when I get home, I'll pop in and give you a kiss. Okay?"

Emily relaxed slightly. "Okay. Where are you going?"

"To surprise Justin," Amy whispered.

Emily's eyes widened. "Is it his birthday?"

Amy chuckled. "No, but he's giving a speech, so I'm going to surprise him by showing up to listen to him. Could you keep an eye on your brothers while I get ready?"

Emily nodded, and Amy raced to her room and jerked open her closet door. Her clothing selection for a dinner party was dismally limited since during most of her life she dressed like an elementary school teacher. Fanning through her hangers, she finally chose a black sleeveless sweater-and-skirt combination. With heels and her trendy new faux pearl necklace, she should pass muster.

She didn't want to embarrass herself or Justin. Doubts niggled inside her. What if he wasn't pleased to see her in the audience? What if the reason he had discouraged her attendance was something other than boredom? Like a more experienced woman. Her stomach knotted at the thought.

Nerves rising to the surface, Amy dressed and applied make-up, smearing her eye shadow and reapplying. Horrified when a blob of mascara fell beneath her eye, she quickly blotted it, then approached her hair which balked at every effort she made to tame it.

"Why don't you put it up on top of your head like you did for the wedding?" Emily asked from the doorway.

Amy shook her head at herself and smiled at Emily. "Out of the mouth of my favorite girl. Perfect solution. What would I do without you?"

Emily beamed beneath her praise. "Do you want me to pick some flowers in the backyard?"

"Dandelions," Amy murmured picturing the backyard. Not weeds. She spritzed her hair with water, then scooped it up off her neck and began to pin it in place.

"Thanks Em, but I have a few sparkly bobby pins I might use instead this time. Maybe you can help put them in?"

Emily did indeed help with the pins and Amy would have to say the five-year-old had far steadier hands than she did tonight. After giving the sitter instructions and kissing each child twice, Amy left.

The meeting was held at an exclusive club in downtown St. Albans. Amidst the luxury automobiles, she handed her car keys to the valet driver who looked at her car askance. Nerves and irritation bubbled inside her. "It's a classic," she said with a smile. "Make sure you take care of it."

She walked into the opulent lobby decorated with chandeliers, statues, and fountains and she located Justin's dinner party. Almost all the round tables of eight, including Justin's table, were filled. After a thorough search, she found one spot at a table near the center of the room and sat down.

Although she felt terribly out of place, she picked at her food and tried to remain invisible as the dinner conversation swirled around her. Stealing glances at the head table, she saw that Justin was seated between two beautiful, perfectly polished women who probably had not needed the assistance of a five-year-old to fix their hair. They were everything she wasn't, she thought and fought not to feel diminished. The brunette, Amy noticed, kept touching him. She fought a terrible tug of envy.

"It's packed tonight," the middle-aged man with the hideous tie beside her said. "Everyone wants to hear what St. Albans's premier stock stud, self-made millionaire has to say. I say he's been damn lucky and has just missed the speed bumps most of us hit."

Indignant on Justin's behalf even though the brunette was sitting entirely too close and he was smiling too frequently, Amy clamped back a hasty retort.

The young man on her other side shook his head. "I have to disagree. Haven't you heard? He's been trading for years. He didn't make his fortune overnight or with one big trade."

"You sound like a Langdon groupie," Mr. Bad Tie said.

The young man shrugged. "I'm intrigued, like about three hundred other people who are here tonight. If he can share his secret, I'll be more than happy to cash in on it."

Mr. Bad Tie grunted. "If it were that easy, everyone would be doing it," he said then turned to her. "Allan Walters. I haven't seen you before. Which firm are you with?"

Taken off guard, Amy blinked before she shook the man's hand. "I'm not with a brokerage. I teach—"

"—business or marketing," he finished incorrectly for her with a nod of approval. "It's good for anyone teaching business to be exposed to this kind of thing, but I hope you tell your students this is rare and people can lose the money as fast as they make it."

"Needs to retire," the young man beside her murmured for her ears only.

"I hear Langdon goes through women like penny stocks," Allan said with a sigh as he eyed Amy's cleavage. "One of the luxuries of being young and wealthy."

Insulted, Amy bit her tongue, then counted to ten. "You seem to know a lot about Mr. Langdon. Have you met him?"

"No, but word gets around if you know what I mean."

"So, most of the basis for your opinion is rumor," Amy clarified.

Allan with the bad tie adjusted his tie. "Well, it's clear he plays the field. Look. He's got a woman on either side of him tonight."

"The only thing that's clear is that the seating for his table is arranged male, female, male, female," she said and tried to tell herself she was totally correct even though a part of her worried.

"Well, I know the guy isn't married because it would have been in the newspaper."

"I can't tell you much about Mr. Langdon's past romantic life, but I'm pretty sure he doesn't get his stock tips from the newspaper or rumor mill. Perhaps that's part of the reason he's so successful."

"Well said," the young man on her other side murmured to her. He extended his hand. "Ben Haynes," he said. "And you are?"

"Amy Monroe," she said, wondering if she would ever consider taking Justin's last name.

"You're not the usual type of woman who shows up for these things," Ben said as if it were a compliment.

"And the usual type is?"

He grinned. "Think barracuda."

Amy's stomach twisted. So her competition, if she were interested in competing for Justin's attention, which she wasn't, she assured herself, was a cunning sea animal that gnashed its prey to bits with sharp teeth. Her head started to throb. Maybe this hadn't been such a great idea after all.

At the head dinner table, Justin stifled a sigh. Despite the fact that he'd flashed his wedding ring and mentioned his *wife* several times throughout the meal, the brunette woman beside him, Gabi, whose name fit her perfectly, had hit on him so much he would need to check for bruises.

Justin wasn't chomping at the bit to step in front of this crowd. Although he knew many admired and respected him, just as many resented his success. They were professionals. He wasn't, therefore he wasn't supposed to be successful.

"Oh, Justin," Gabi continued, but he turned off his listening ear as he took a drink of water and the association's president climbed the small stairway to the platform.

"Ladies and gentlemen," the man began. "It is my privilege to introduce our guest speaker for the Spring meeting of the Virginia Stockbrokers' Association. This man started out on a shoestring budget trading low-dollar stocks, eventually building to high-dollar profits. His net worth is now well into the multiple six figures...."

Justin stifled a yawn and surreptitiously glanced at his watch. Another moment passed and the president finally said, "Ladies and gentlemen, I now present Justin Langdon." The applause seemed to fill every corner of the huge room, surprising the dickens out of Justin. He stood and climbed the stairs to the stage to stand behind the podium. The room was packed and the lighting so dark he couldn't make out many faces.

As if he were attending a twelve-step recovery meeting, he said, "Hello, my name is Justin Langdon, and I'm a—" he paused for effect "—tightwad."

In the audience, Amy's heart swelled with pride and something that felt very close to love. Justin was such an incredible man.

The crowd laughed, and Justin continued with his

speech. "I know it must irritate the dickens out of most of you to know that I built my fortune off the stock market without the assistance of a stockbroker. More importantly, no stockbroker benefited with commission. But all I've done is become my own expert. My system of trading is designed specifically with me in mind— my goals, my never-ending study of the market, knowing how much I can risk and still sleep at night, and my commitment to trade with a minimum of emotion. You have to figure this out for each of your clients, and unfortunately, your clients aren't clones."

With the exception of the tightwad remark, everything he said resonated with his actions. From the beginning, Amy had sensed he was a man who knew himself well. He had been tested and tried and had grown stronger because of it. Amy sensed many people admired him for the money he'd made. She admired him for the man he'd become.

"Most of your clients aren't like me at all," Justin said, "so parts of my plan won't work for them. But I'm going to help you with a response for the next time one of your clients says something annoying like, 'I've read about how Justin Langdon turned his portfolio from three digits to seven digits all by himself. Maybe I should try that.'

"Here is the step-by-step process for how to do what Justin has done. Number one, cheap housing. Live in a one-room efficiency in an area of town where your lullabye each and every night will be the sound of fights in the streets followed by police sirens.

"Two, eat cheap. Your regular menu should consist of cans of beans and packaged macaroni. You're allowed to splurge and go out to eat once a year. To McDonald's." The sound of the crowd's chuckles rose to the podium. They thought he was joking, Justin thought, but he knew better. He had lived it.

"Three, no car for three years. Walk or take the bus. Every penny you would have spent on payments, maintenance, gas and parking goes into your trading account.

"Four, say goodbye to your sleep. After you start making significant money on the market, get a job working the midnight shift so you can stare at your monitor all day, then work all night.

"Five, no social life for three years straight. Beer is a luxury, decent wine is a dream." Justin smiled to himself figuring he'd eliminated ninety percent of the people who wanted to "do what Justin Langdon had done."

"Six, no dating for three years straight. Dating costs money and if you want to do what Justin did, you have to put every penny into the market."

He took a drink of water and surveyed the crowd again. Light glimmered on red hair about halfway back. He paused, narrowing his eyes. *Amy?*

His heart hammered with an odd kick of joy and confusion. When had she arrived? Why hadn't she let him know she was here? She glanced from side to side, then met his gaze and smiled as if she knew he was looking at her.

He took another drink of water and noted she was dressed in a man-killer black number that faithfully followed every curve. It looked like the men on either side of her were noticing her curves, too.

He continued with his speech a bit more quickly than he'd intended. Justin wanted his questions answered. When the older guy beside Amy locked his gaze on her cleavage, Justin had to resist the urge to jump down from the stage and punch him. Justin took a slightly more civilized course, deviating from his prepared remarks.

"I'd like to take this opportunity to introduce you to my wife. She came in a little late." Justin watched her face turn the color of her hair and her eyes shoot daggers. "Amy, don't be shy. Wave to everyone."

She did reluctantly, but her expression told him there would be hell to pay. Wrapping up his talk, he nodded to acknowledge applause, shook hands with the president, then strode directly to Amy's table.

A young man beside her stood and offered his hand. "Mr. Langdon, I'm a longtime fan."

Justin shook his hand and nodded, then reached for Amy.

"I was trying to be invisible," she whispered through gritted teeth.

"Not dressed like that," he retorted in a low voice against her ear.

"Amy," the older man said with sickening familiarity that matched his lecherous smile, "now I know why you were defending him."

Justin did a double take. "You defended me?" he asked quietly.

Although it seemed impossible, Amy felt her face grow hotter. "He was—" Flustered, she broke off and shook her head. "Later."

"She's a sweet little thing," the man said with a wink. "Nice work."

Amy felt so patronized by the man's attitude she wanted to throw water in his face. She glanced at Justin and saw his jaw tighten.

Justin smiled like a shark. "If you know what's good for you," he said in a voice frighteningly gentle, "you'll pick your eyeballs up out of my wife's sweater, you old goat. Let's go," he said to Amy and tugged her toward the exit.

"Why didn't you tell me you were coming?"

Amy scrambled to keep up with his long stride. "I wanted to surprise you."

"You succeeded," he said, leading her across the marble floor. "Why didn't you come to my table?"

"It was full," she said, and couldn't resist adding, "You were already surrounded by women. Attentive women. Where are we going?" she asked when he punched the button for the elevator.

He tugged his tux tie loose. "Just as you were surrounded by attentive men," he said with an edge to his voice that surprised her. "The association gave me a parlor room for my use this evening."

"Parlor room?"

The brass elevator doors whooshed open and he pulled her inside. "This may come as a surprise to you, but some people are actually impressed by me, Amy. Some people think I'm hot stuff."

"I do, too," Amy said, feeling defensive. "I just probably think so for different reasons than many of the people in that ballroom."

"And what would your reasons be?" he asked, his green gaze glinting with challenge.

The elevator doors opened, giving Amy a moment to gather her wits. A moment didn't feel nearly adequate, she thought as he guided her around a corner and whisked her into a room.

"You were saying?" Justin prompted.

Wondering at his mood, Amy laced her fingers together and wished she hadn't felt so off balance this evening. "I admire you for giving a boy at Granger money so he could travel home to see his family." She saw a flicker of surprise cross his face and continued, "I admire you for not wigging when Nicholas got sick in your car. I admire you for being able to deal with me."

He cocked his head to one side. "What do you mean about my being able to deal with you?"

Uneasy, Amy turned away and tried to focus on the beautifully furnished parlor. "Well, you married me and I'm not really wife material," she said. "In fact, you would be safe in calling me the nonwife."

He walked up behind her. "You're going to have to explain this. I've never heard of a nonwife."

"In my case, it's a woman who didn't want to get married and has never believed she possessed an aptitude for wifely things. Add in the fact that I'm uncomfortable that I'm very attracted to you and have feelings for you, and dealing with me should be the most crazymaking thing you've ever attempted."

The silence that followed was so swollen with secret hopes and fears that Amy prayed the floor would swallow her to put her out of her misery.

"Why did you come tonight?"

"I told you," she said. "Because I wanted to surprise you and—" She broke off. Too much soul-baring.

She felt him toy with a strand of her hair that had fallen from her upsweep. "And I wanted us to have a few minutes without the kids. A few minutes of just you and me."

"Just you and me would have been okay, but you shouldn't have worn this," he said and lightly circled the back of her neck with his hand.

She stiffened. She'd felt out of place and he was confirming that fact. "Why? It's not nice enough?" she asked, turning around. "What's wrong with it? I thought

I did pretty good considering I'm usually dressed like an elementary school teacher.''

"Your outfit's nice. It fits you fine. Too damn fine. The problem is every man in the whole blazing room wanted to see you *without* your clothes," he said, hands on his narrow hips.

Amy blinked. "Oh." She felt her defiance seep out of her like air out of a popped balloon. She noticed again how attractive he looked in a tux. Curious, she met his gaze. "Well, I have a question. If every man in the room wanted to see me without my clothes, does every man include you?"

Eleven

He slowly walked toward her until he stood just a smidgeon away as he looked down at her. So much closer, but still too far away, Amy thought. Her heart beat faster at the expression on his face.

"I didn't mention any exceptions, did I, Amy of Arc?" he asked in a voice that had the potential to undo her.

"Don't call me that," she said.

"I just want my turn." He lifted his hand to her face.

She took a tiny breath. Her tight chest would allow no more. "Your turn?"

"You've been so busy saving the world. My turn," he said, lifting her hand to his shoulder. "Save me."

Her breath completely evaporated. *Save me.* It was such a ridiculous statement coming from him. He was so strong, so centered. If ever a man didn't need saving, it was Justin. "The closest I came to that was when I drove you to the hospital," she said in a voice husky to her own ears.

He shook his head. "Come closer," he said, and lowered his mouth to hers.

He took his time as if he knew she needed time and attention. She needed these moments to give without the rest of the world pressing in on them. She didn't worry that the children would burst in on them or the phone would ring or Ms. Hatcher would pay a surprise visit. It was simply Justin and her. Mouth to mouth, heart to heart.

Although she knew there was a part of her still unwilling to surrender to this marriage because self-reliance had been her salvation for too long, she also knew there was a power to her growing feelings for Justin, a power she'd never experienced before.

She couldn't find the words, or maybe she feared saying them. She had to show him. The searching, sensual open-mouth kiss went on and on, warming her, building the coil of anticipation inside her.

"Too fast," he muttered. "I always want you too fast." He rolled his tongue around the inner lips of her mouth in an erotic motion that made her weak. "I want to go slow," he said. "I want to kiss all of you."

He pulled her sweater over her head and disposed of her bra. He lowered his mouth to her swollen, aroused breasts and took first one nipple, then the other into his mouth. She went liquid and restless beneath his mouth. He moved his hands up her skirt and beneath her panties to touch her secret moistness. He slid his finger inside her and she gasped.

Unable to remain passive any longer, Amy unfastened his tux shirt and tugged it loose. Eager to feel his skin, she shoved both the shirt and jacket from him. She slowly rubbed her cheeks and mouth over his hard, warm chest, savoring the touch and taste of him, the clean masculine scent of him. The strength she felt here, she knew, permeated the entire man. The knowledge of that strength turned her on even more.

Strength deserved boldness. Her heart pounding, she lowered her hands to his waist, undid his pants, and eased the zipper down over his bulging masculinity. His quick intake of breath was a provocative invitation to go further, to give more, to take more.

Her inhibitions lowering with each beat of her heart, Amy felt the rise of feminine sensual power. It was a new heady and addictive sensation. She skimmed her mouth down the front of his chest and felt one of his hands in her hair.

"What are you doing?" he asked in a voice roughened by need.

"Getting closer," she told him and slid down his body to her knees, pulling his pants and briefs down as she went. She rubbed her cheek against his full masculinity, then kissed him. Taking him into her mouth, she savored the taste of his arousal and the sound of his pleasure. He grew harder and fuller in her mouth.

He tangled his fingers in her hair and muttered an oath. She lifted her gaze to his green eyes full of black heat.

He shuddered. "You have no idea how erotic you look between my legs with your bare breasts, sweet face and mouth on me." He groaned and tugged her to her feet. "I need to be in you."

In a blur of motion, he pushed away her skirt and panties. There was no bed in the room, only a love seat. Sitting down on it, he lifted her over him. "Hold on to my shoulders," he told her, and eased her down over him.

She sucked in a quick breath. He was so huge and so hard that for a moment Amy wasn't certain she could take him. She closed her eyes and felt herself accommodate him.

"You are almost too big," she whispered.

He gave a rough chuckle. "We just need to do this a lot so you'll get used to me."

"I'm not sure I'll ever—" She broke off when he guided her hips upward and down again. Pleasure rippled through her. He did it again, and Amy had never felt so voluptuous in her life. She began her own rhythm, riding him.

He took her breast into his mouth and the sensation zinged all the way to her core. She felt herself clench around him and he began a litany of oaths and prayers. Shuddering, she rode him until she went over the edge in a ripple of endless ecstatic spasms.

Justin thrust inside her, his face clenching from a scalding release. Aftershocks rocked through both of them.

Her knees weak, she gingerly slid to his side and wrapped her arms around him. She had never felt so powerful in a wholly feminine way, and at the same time so defenseless.

He drew her against him. "It's gonna take a long time for me to get enough of you, Amy."

Amy sighed and closed her eyes. For this moment, she would allow herself to lean on him and rely on his strength. Wouldn't it be wonderful if she could always count on him being there for her? The prospect filled her with a joy so intense it shook her. What if this truly didn't have to end?

Justin helped put her back together, making her laugh with how limp her limbs were as he dressed her. "What happened to your bones?" he asked.

"You melted them," she said, thinking he had also melted her heart.

He skimmed his hands up her bare legs to her thigh. "I like you like this. I think I'd like to keep you this way. How long did you arrange for the sitter to stay? A week?" he asked with a ridiculous mock-serious tone.

She laughed. "You're so funny. Around midnight, I turn into a pumpkin."

Glancing at the clock, he noted the late hour and groaned. "Someday I will have you for a whole night."

She shuddered with pleasure at his wickedly intent expression. "If no one is sick and we find the right sitter," she said with a smile. "And the stars are in perfect alignment."

"It will happen soon," he assured her and walked her out of the hotel to her car. He helped her into her Volkswagen and kissed her before she left, making Amy feel savored and precious in a way she couldn't remember feeling before.

On the drive home, though, other, darker realities slid into her mind. Some very important things hadn't changed. They'd agreed to try this for two years. They'd signed a prenuptial agreement that defined the terms of the end of their marriage. They'd agreed they didn't love each other.

The final thought cut like a knife.

Justin paid the sitter before Amy could open her purse. "That wasn't necessary. I could've covered it," she told him.

He waved aside her protest and studied her carefully.

She seemed uneasy with him again, and he wondered why. He wouldn't have thought it possible, but the sensual, giving woman who had taken him to the moon just hours before seemed to have erected a nearly invisible wall during the drive home.

"You're quiet," he said.

"I'm tired and I promised Emily I'd give her a kiss when I got home."

He nodded. "Okay."

She bit her lip and met his gaze. "You were wonderful during the speech and after," she said. "Wonderful. Good night."

Justin felt his mood sink. "Cold feet again?"

She paused, looking conflicted, and he had his answer. He bit back an oath of frustration.

"I think it's more because of a reality check than cold feet," she finally said in that too-quiet voice.

"Tonight wasn't real enough for you?"

She drew in a quick breath. "Our marriage doesn't feel real to me."

"Maybe if we slept together—"

"—I don't think that's the solution," she said. "It's more than that. When we made our vows, I pretended I was giving an order at Burger Doodle so I wouldn't hyperventilate. We promised to give this two years. If it were real, we would have given it forever." Her eyes filled with doubt he wanted to banish. She looked down. "We don't love each other," she said in a voice edged with pain. "And the cherry on top of the sundae is the prenup agreement."

Justin tensed. His attorney had warned him that it wasn't unusual for wives to ask for changes after the marriage. It wasn't unusual for women to use emotional or sexual blackmail to get more money. Amy wasn't that way, he told himself. He hoped she wasn't that way. "What do you mean? Do you believe the agreement was unfair?"

She shook her head. "No, but think about it. A prenup is a plan to divorce. It's an instruction booklet for how to end our marriage."

"Are you saying that if we throw out the agreement then you'll be willing to sleep with me through the night?"

Amy paled. She looked as if he'd slapped her. "No, I'm not saying that at all. You just don't get it. This is about much more than a stupid prenup agreement. Much more," she said and walked away from him.

After that, Justin felt a distance grow between them. Amy was polite and kind, but reserved. He felt he'd had something at his fingertips, something precious, and he'd lost it. They had been so close. He'd treasured her trust and generosity.

Now it was gone. Living in the same house with her was painful, much more painful than Justin had ever believed possible. He couldn't recall a time when he had felt this much pain. Not even when his mother had left him at Granger.

His frustration and dark desperation seemed to grow with each passing hour. One day he ran out to pick up some computer equipment. It took longer than he planned. When he returned, he saw a different, late-model car and pick-up truck in the driveway. Two men were unloading swings. Curious, Justin followed the path to the backyard.

Amy stood talking to the men while they put the finishing touches on a wooden swing set. Emily stood by Amy's side and the twins ran in circles. Nicholas looked up. "Justin, Justin! We're getting a swing set!" he hollered. "Right now! And I'm gonna be the first to swing on it."

"Nuh-uh," Jeremy said. "I am."

"Nuh-uh," Nicholas said. "I am."

"Nuh-uh," Jeremy said.

"Nuh-uh," Emily said. "Aunt Amy and I are gonna ride it first because we're being nice, and you're not."

Nicholas and Jeremy abruptly shut their mouths.

Amy glanced up and smiled at Justin. His heart stuttered. She looked at him with a light in her eyes as if their argument from last week was forgotten. He saw the moment she remembered. Her smile faded. "I bought a swing set."

"So I see," Justin said.

"These guys say they can have it up by the time we finish dinner."

"Woo-hoo!" Nicholas and Jeremy yelled.

"What's with the different car in the driveway?"

Amy smiled sheepishly. "Part impulse, part practicality. It's tough buckling those car seats in the Volkswageon. I stopped by an auto sales lot on the way home and voila, I have a new vehicle."

Justin felt a trickle of unease. "Why didn't you ask me? I could've helped you out with the swing set and car."

"No, the swing set's my treat. I've been planning this for weeks. And it was time to trade the Beetle." She laughed, mostly it seemed, at herself. "That's what payday is for, right?"

His gut tightened. "I guess."

"Besides, it'll all balance out with dinner tonight."

"What do you mean?"

"Cheap meal," she said. "Okay, you guys, let's go

inside and eat and give these men a chance to get their work done. It might be dark, but we might all get a chance to swing a little tonight.''

She led the kids inside and they rushed to wash up for dinner. A vague darkness hovered over him even during the kids' exuberance. He was concerned about Amy's purchases. He hadn't thought she was an impulsive buyer.

He watched her from the kitchen doorway as she chatted with Emily. ''Time to eat,'' she said and laughed at the boys. ''Are you going to be able to sit still enough to eat dinner?''

''How still do we have to sit?'' Jeremy asked.

''Just a little bit still,'' Nicholas said.

''Good, cuz I feel like jumpin'.''

''I feel like swingin','' Nicholas said.

''Me, too.''

''Sit down,'' Amy said in a sing-song voice, and the boys scurried to their seats. ''Sorry for the gourmet fare,'' she said to Justin, ''but there are times when the only appropriate choice is beanee weenees.''

Justin's stomach immediately rebelled. His brain screamed in protest. A flurry of images raced through his mind. His mother once bought him a shiny fire truck and herself a new dress and shoes. For dinner, they'd eaten beanee weenees. Another time at Christmas, his mother had bought herself a new refrigerator and television and for Justin she had bought video games. The electricity had been cut off due to lack of payment, and he remembered eating beanee weenees cooked in the fireplace. He had eaten beanee weenees himself when he'd been putting every penny into his trading account in an attempt to form the security he'd never experienced as a child.

It was just too much.

He went to Amy and spoke in a low voice for her ears only, "I'm going to my house. I'll let you know when I'll be back." He didn't wait for her response. He just walked out the door.

Hours later, Justin sat on the leather sofa in the darkness of his home pre-Amy. The silence was initially soothing, but now it felt too quiet. He'd grown accustomed to the creaks and groans of Amy's older home and the sound of children's chatter and Amy's musical voice. He'd grown accustomed to limited solitude.

Glancing at the clock, he thought he might be helping to tuck in one of the twins or reading a book with Emily. And after the kids were put to bed, Justin never stopped feeling Amy's presence. She could be at the other end of the house or asleep when he was not, but he always felt her presence.

He wondered if she ever longed for him during the long hours between darkness and morning. He wondered if he would ever stop longing for her. He felt as if he could see the missing piece to the puzzle of his life, but he couldn't hold it, and it frustrated the hell out of him.

He'd returned to his house for solitude and peace, but the solitude was suffocating and there was no peace in sight.

Later that night, the phone woke him out of a restless sleep. Justin automatically answered it.

"Hi, this is Michael. I just heard from Dylan and I thought you might want to go see him. He's at the hospital."

Alarmed, Justin sat straight up in bed. "He's hurt?"

"No. Alisa Jennings was in some kind of accident.

It's serious. She's unconscious in ICU and Dylan's determined to camp at the hospital until she wakes up."

"How did Dylan know she was hurt?"

"Apparently her mother's out of the country on an extended trip, so they couldn't reach her. They found Dylan's business card in her purse, so they gave him a call. He doesn't sound good. I'll get over there soon, but you're closer to the West County Medical Center. I tried calling you at your bride's house first," Michael said and let the question hang between them.

"I needed some time to think," Justin said.

"Hmm. Okay. Don't take too much time," Michael advised as if he'd learned something along the way about waiting too long. "I'll see you at the hospital."

Pulling on his clothes, he grabbed his car keys and left for the hospital. After getting two cups of coffee from a machine, he found Dylan in the ICU waiting room, staring unseeing through the glass door at the nurse's station. Dylan, the most outwardly carefree guy Justin had ever met, looked as if he were facing death itself.

"Hey," Justin said, offering him a cup of coffee. "What happened?"

Dylan accepted the coffee, but didn't drink it. "She was running after a neighbor's dog that got loose and a car hit her."

"Oh, God," Justin said. A picture of Alisa as a child slid through his mind. "She was such a sweet kid, and she grew up to be a beautiful lady. This is a damn shame. What's the prognosis?"

"They won't tell me much," Dylan said. "Serious head injury, internal injuries. They don't know if she's gonna wake up at all," he said, his voice desolate.

"Did they let you see her?"

Dylan hesitated. "Yeah. I told them I was her fiancé."

Justin did a double take. He'd known Dylan had carried a torch for Alisa, but he hadn't known the man was this determined.

"It was the only way I could make them talk to me. Besides, her mother is on one of those trips to Europe and Russia where they move around every two or three days. Alisa may not want me right now," he said grimly, "but she damn well needs me."

"How long have you been in love with her?"

Dylan gave a wry humorless laugh. "Forever. She's what I wished for before I knew how to wish, but I screwed up big time when we got together in college. I was so full of myself. I didn't treat her well. I'm paying now. God, if she dies, I don't know what I'll do."

"But you haven't been together," Justin said.

"You don't understand," he said looking at Justin with stark eyes. "Just knowing she exists and is alive makes the world right for me."

Justin felt an echo of recognition inside him at Dylan's words. Knowing Amy existed made the world a better place for him. He wondered what he would do if something like this happened to Amy. Just the thought scared the living daylights out of him.

What if Amy died? What if she wasn't even on the earth? What if he lost even the possibility of being with her?

Justin's stomach churned with nausea.

"When you're in love," Dylan said, raking a hand through his sun-streaked hair, "there's only two places in the world—where she is and where she's not."

Justin sat with Dylan through the long night, but in his mind, he was going home to Amy. That was exactly what he did the following morning. On the way to her house, he called his attorney and instructed him to dissolve the prenup agreement. When his attorney argued against it, Justin would have none of it. "Either you cancel it, or I'll pay somebody else to cancel it."

Pulling into the driveway at dawn, he felt a sense of resolve that went deeper than his bones. He strode into the house and headed upstairs.

Amy's voice stopped him. "How is Alisa?" she asked quietly from behind him.

He slowly turned to face her and drank in the sight of her in a nightshirt. He shook his head. "She's still unconscious, still in ICU."

She crossed her arms as if to hug herself. "It's terrible. I couldn't sleep. I tried to call you after Michael called me, but you must've already left for the hospital."

"Yeah, Michael's with him now. I needed to see you."

Amy nodded. Her nerves were shot. "You're right. I need to talk to you."

Justin held up a hand. "I have something to tell you."

Terrified he was totally giving up on their marriage, she shook her head and spoke in a rush. "No. I need to say I'm sorry. I know this has been impossible. I'm sorry I haven't been anything resembling a wife. I've just been so determined and so scared," she said, that admission costing her, "that I shouldn't rely on you. Justin, you're so strong. You're the strongest man I know, and I want to rely on you, but at the same time I'm afraid to do that. There has never been anyone I could rely on. Both my parents were alcoholics and I learned at a very early age to be self-reliant. I don't know how to be more balanced," she confessed, feeling her throat tighten with emotion. "But I'd like to learn with you."

Justin walked closer and stared at her. "I called my attorney on the way from the hospital."

Amy's stomach sank. He was already initiating a separation. She was too late.

"I told him to cancel the prenup. I want you to marry me, Amy," he said.

Her head reeled. Unable to assimilate his words, she shook her head in confusion. "I don't understand. I thought you'd had enough of our marriage and wanted out."

"I've had enough of pretending this is temporary, because it's not temporary for me," he said, slamming her heart into overdrive with his revelation. "I can't explain it, and I know it sounds weird as hell, but I think you and I were meant for each other. You are the woman I would have wished for if I'd known you existed. You make the world make sense to me. I don't—" He broke off. "Why are you crying?" he asked in horror.

Overwhelmed, Amy felt tears slide down her cheeks. "I thought you were leaving for good."

He pulled her into his arms and held tight. "No, the beanee weenees pushed a button, but—"

"Excuse me?" she said. "Beanee weenees?"

"Long story," he said. "It's one of those bad memory foods."

She winced. "They're Jeremy's favorite."

"He can have my share."

Being in his arms filled Amy with such warmth and hope. "I don't understand what you were saying about the prenup."

"Cancelled," he said. "We don't need a prenup."

"You didn't have to do that," she said, knowing it had been important to his sense of security. More than anything Amy wanted Justin to feel all the security and love he'd missed as a child. She wanted to be the woman to give it.

"Yeah, I did," he said. "I want a lifetime with you. I want a commitment with you with every possible string attached. I don't want you to get away."

Her eyes filled with tears again. "I have been so afraid of loving you, but I do. I love the child you were, the man you are and I want the chance to love the man you'll become."

He lowered his mouth to hers and kissed her with such tenderness and love that she was humbled. How, she wondered, had she gotten so lucky?

"I used to think my mission was marrying you for the sake of the kids. Now, I know my mission is loving you for the sake of me."

One week later, Amy surprised Justin when she arrived home with Chinese food and champagne, but no children in tow.

"Where are the munchkins?" he asked, giving her a welcome kiss.

"They're at a sleepover at Kate and Michael's house," she said, unable to keep a smile from her face. "We passed inspection. The kids are really ours now."

"Hallelujah," he said. "We should celebrate."

"That's my plan."

"Oh, really," he said, his voice deepening in approval. "What kind of plan?"

"I think you should take off all your clothes and go to bed immediately."

He scooped her up into his arms and strode toward

the room they'd shared as husband and wife for the last six nights. "I'm not arguing," he said. "What about the food?"

"Later," she said, and they made very good use of their time making love to each other. Justin never ceased to amaze her with how easily he read her body. With each passing day, he seemed to read her mind and heart.

Afterward, Amy slipped on a chemise and brought the boxes of Chinese food and champagne to the bedroom on a tray. They took turns feeding each other. "Did you hear about Alisa? Kate told me she woke up, but she can't remember anything."

Justin nodded. "Dylan called today. I think he's just relieved she's going to live. He said he's sticking to her like glue even though she'll probably spit in his eye when she gets her memory back."

"I feel lucky," she said.

He nodded. "I don't even want to remember what it was like before you were in my life."

Her heart filled to overflowing. "There's something I need to say to you," she told him and took his strong, gentle hands in hers. No Burger Doodle vows for her. Looking directly into the eyes of the man she adored more than anything, Amy made promises she knew she would keep. "I take you, Justin Langdon, to be my lawfully wedded husband, for richer, for poorer, in sickness and in health."

She leaned forward and kissed him with all the love in her heart. "Forever and ever and ever."

"I take you, Amy Monroe, to be my lawfully wedded wife. I will love and stand by you forever and ever," he said solemnly, then lowered his head to whisper in her ear. "Even if you serve beanee weenees."

Amy laughed at the same time a tear fell down her cheek. He had told her many secrets during the last week including the beanee weenee story. ''Now that is love.''

*   *   *   *   *

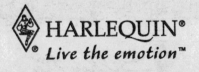

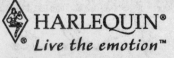